The helicopters roared over in another gun run

They circled back just short of violating U.S. airspace. If they were clever, they would just hover above Bolan and pour down fire. He was twenty yards from Texas.

A third helicopter swooped. It flew over Texas and arced around in a tight turn. The first two helicopters were Hueys wearing Mexican army olive drab. The third chopper was a massive Russian M-17. It was painted in raptor-black with the gold Aztec eagle on its nose and carried rocket pods and TOW wire guided antitank missiles beneath its stub wings.

Bolan hit his smoke dischargers, and grenades arced away from the APC in all directions. He punched a button over the transmission and fuel oil squirted into exhaust and black smoke belched up out of the twin exhaust pipes. Gray-and-black filth bloomed around the APC.

Bolan slammed his shutters shut as rocket fire blossomed beneath the chopper's wings. He was a sitting duck, dead in the water. The APC 70 just wasn't going to make it to Texas.

Neither was he.

MACK BOLAN ®
The Executioner

The Executioner

Don Pendleton's®

BORDER WAR

A GOLD EAGLE BOOK FROM

W🌐RLDWIDE®

TORONTO • NEW YORK • LONDON
AMSTERDAM • PARIS • SYDNEY • HAMBURG
STOCKHOLM • ATHENS • TOKYO • MILAN
MADRID • WARSAW • BUDAPEST • AUCKLAND

First edition June 2007

ISBN-13: 978-0-373-64343-1
ISBN-10: 0-373-64343-8

Special thanks and acknowledgment to
Chuck Rogers for his contribution to this work.

BORDER WAR

A great people may be killed, but they cannot be intimidated.

—Napoléon I, 1769–1821

Other men may be unwilling or unable to fight against evil. But no matter what the threat, I will not be intimidated.

—Mack Bolan

THE
MACK BOLAN
LEGEND

Nothing less than a war could have fashioned the destiny of the man called Mack Bolan. Bolan earned the Executioner title in the jungle hell of Vietnam.

But this soldier also wore another name—Sergeant Mercy. He was so tagged because of the compassion he showed to wounded comrades-in-arms and Vietnamese civilians.

Mack Bolan's second tour of duty ended prematurely when he was given emergency leave to return home and bury his family, victims of the Mob. Then he declared a one-man war against the Mafia.

He confronted the Families head-on from coast to coast, and soon a hope of victory began to appear. But Bolan had broken society's every rule. That same society started gunning for this elusive warrior—to no avail.

So Bolan was offered amnesty to work within the system against terrorism. This time, as an employee of Uncle Sam, Bolan became Colonel John Phoenix. With a command center at Stony Man Farm in Virginia, he and his new allies—Able Team and Phoenix Force—waged relentless war on a new adversary: the KGB.

But when his one true love, April Rose, died at the hands of the Soviet terror machine, Bolan severed all ties with Establishment authority.

Now, after a lengthy lone-wolf struggle and much soul-searching, the Executioner has agreed to enter an "arm's-length" alliance with his government once more, reserving the right to pursue personal missions in his Everlasting War.

1

It was just past four o'clock in the morning in the hard land along the Mexico-Texas border. The stars were just starting to fade. The night hunters had gone to ground and the creatures of the day had yet to emerge, but it was still too quiet.

Mack Bolan reined in his horse and loosened his Steyr Scout rifle in its scabbard. He gazed up the dry riverbed where it forked and strained to see into the gloom of a box canyon.

"Hoot." Bolan glanced back at his riding companion. "It happened in there?"

Missy "Hoot" Hootkins was one of very few women to have been accepted into the Texas Rangers. Five hundred years of Scottish ancestry had produced a six-foot-tall, second-generation Texan with the shoulders of a linebacker, an impressive chest and flaming red hair that spilled out of a Stetson with command authority.

Hoot was part of Ranger Company D. The southern border was her territory and Zapata County her home. Like all Texas Rangers, Hoot had little use for *federales*. The incident at Waco still burned in many of their minds, and the Feds' absolute refusal to do anything meaningful about the crisis situation on the border left most Rangers of the opinion that anything that came out of Washington, D.C., was about as useful as bird shit on a pump handle.

However, Hoot liked men, particularly tall dark and handsome ones with arctic blue eyes who knew how to ride a horse. She'd seen federal border probes come and go, but this was first time someone had come out of Washington who grinned, bought the first round of beers and said, "Let's go for a ride," after midnight.

"Yup," she drawled. "Happened right in there. How'd you know?"

It was an easy guess for a man with the mind of a warrior. Bolan stared into the yawning darkness of the box canyon. It was a perfect ambush site. Like the name said, the canyon was a box. A killing box. One way in and then no way out once the ambush was sprung.

Four Border Patrol agents and a federal marshal had been ritually executed. One of them had held the rank of chief patrol agent. According to the Internal Affairs Division of the Texas State BP, all four men had been under investigation on charges of bribery and illegal border trafficking. Five .38-caliber Super Automatic hollowpoint rounds to the back of their heads had ended the investigation and anywhere it might lead.

Bolan mused over the caliber. .38 Super Automatic. It had never been particularly popular in the U.S. except with competitive shooters, where its flat shooting characteristics and low recoil allowed it to clean up at shooting matches that required a full, military power pistol.

Back in the day, however, it had been every *pistolero*'s choice in Mexico. For nearly a century, the Mexican government had been afraid of a revolution. They had subsequently outlawed the civilian use of weapons chambered for military calibers, until recently even forbidding them to their police. That meant excluding 9 mm and .45-caliber weapons in particular. Thus the oddball .38 Super Automatic was the caliber of choice for policeman, citizen and felon alike south of the border.

Times had changed. Policemen could get any weapon they wanted, the criminals had automatic weapons and civilian gun ownership had seen draconian restriction.

Its appearance at the execution probably meant nothing.

A person could find .38 Supers all over Mexico, and it could have just been the random gun available for the crime. Or possibly it could mean that the shooter was old school, either a corrupt cop or criminal.

Bolan stared into the box canyon. "Who knows we're out here?"

"Jeez." Hoot shrugged. "The stable boy, the stable master, border dispatch. Why?"

That meant anybody and everybody.

"I think we're about to get hit."

"Oh, yeah?" Hoot's hand went to the butt of her .357 SIG-Sauer. "And how long have you been having these thoughts?"

Bolan's teeth flashed in the purple gloom. "Would you be mad if I said I'd suspected since we saddled up, but now I'm sure?"

Hoot chewed this over. "Probably."

"Listen, they're waiting for us to go in there and start poking around the crime scene, then they're going to catch us in a cross fire from the canyon walls."

"Good to know," Hoot conceded. "You got a plan?"

"Yeah, you're going to give me a lingering kiss, and then we're going to fade back into that arroyo fifty yards back."

This was met with a profound, lingering silence. Finally Hoot said, "And the upshot of that'll be…"

"They'll think we've gone to get romantic among the mesquite."

"Uh-huh."

"And they'll move out of their positions in the canyon and into the open to sneak up on us."

"This is the saddest, sickest pickup attempt I have ever heard in my entire life, and I've seen 'em all. While I do appreciate the effort, you…" Her voice trailed off. "You're not kidding, are you?"

"No, and we'll call for backup as soon as we're hunkered down under cover."

"Okay, so—"

"So snuggle up."

Hoot sidled her horse up to Bolan's. He reached around her head and ran his fingers through her mass of silken, scarlet tresses and planted a big one on the woman's red lips. She tasted good. Bolan took his time, putting on a good show for the gunmen way back in the bleachers.

They parted reluctantly and turned back for the arroyo.

Hoot spoke very softly. "I'm waiting for the bullet in the back of my spine."

"Won't happen. If they miss, there's the chance that one or both of us spurs on and escapes. They want an execution. They'll wait, and then catch us with our pants down."

"My pants aren't coming down, Mr. Man."

They rode slowly, knee to knee to the arroyo, leading their horses into a thicket. Hoot pulled an M1A Scout Squad rifle out of its scabbard. Bolan drew his Steyr. The little bolt-action rifle was uniquely accessorized with an M-203 grenade launcher beneath the forestock.

"You got night vision?" Bolan asked.

Hoot reached into her saddlebag for the goggles and removed her Stetson. Bolan pulled on his own goggles. His Scout was further modified by NATO standard rifle grenade launching rings around the muzzle. He pulled out a French Night-Sun illumination round and clicked it over the barrel. They put on their tactical radio and earpieces.

"Okay, so what's the plan?"

"I'm going to flank them." Bolan slung his rifle and drew his Beretta 93-R pistol. He pulled out the suppressor and threaded it onto the muzzle. "I need you to make some noise to draw them in. When I say, close your eyes keep them closed for a count of eight."

"Gotcha." Hoot threw her jacket on the ground and assumed a firing position behind a nest of tumbleweeds and a fallen cottonwood trunk. "I hope you know only the privileged few ever get to hear this performance." The safety came off her carbine with a muted click. "Say when."

Bolan pulled his goggles down over his eyes, and the border country lit up in grainy greens and grays. "When."

Hoot let out an audible sigh as Bolan moved back behind their position. He moved about twenty yards back and clambered up the lip of the arroyo. Hoot's sighs followed him, becoming louder, following a bellowslike rhythm of ragged inhale, catch and sigh.

Bolan moved forward along the lip of the arroyo, moving at a crouch among the sagebrush. Hoot's performance was growing in volume, the sighs were being broken by little cries and whimpers. Bolan moved past her position and looked down from above. Despite her mounting noise, she lay prone and motionless, sighting down the barrel of her rifle.

As Bolan moved along the high ground, he caught movement coming down from the tiny canyon. Men were spilling out into the riverbed. Others were forking out in either direction to flank the arroyo on either side. Bolan's eyebrows raised slightly under his goggles. He counted twenty. They mostly wore Western garb, denim jackets and jeans and cowboy hats, a few wearing caps.

Bolan had seen the type before. They were *coyotes*, men who ferried groups of illegals across the border. Ostensibly they acted as guides, but they were half smuggler, half slaver. The same way a pimp supposedly took care of his girls, the *coyotes* preyed upon those who made the desperate bid to cross the U.S. border in the hope of a better life. The *coyotes* were just as likely to steal whatever tiny fortune the immigrants carried with them, rape any of the women who pleased them, then leave their charges stranded in the desert and kill anyone who objected. More often than not, most of the immigrants who made it across were met by the *coyotes'* counterparts on the other side of the border. Young girls were sold into prostitution. Older women were sent to slave in sweatshops. The men were paid pennies for backbreaking jobs no U.S. citizen would take.

Coyotes were the scum of the earth, but they were small fish, and these men were flunkies being paid on a lark to perform an assassination. Nevertheless, they were flunkies who had been sent to kill him and a Texas Ranger in the course of her duty, and there were twenty of them. They came on like stalking wolves, spreading out, as silent as the shadows they slipped through. They were well accustomed to the dark, and this broken land was their hunting ground.

Hoot's rhythmic gasps were rising to a fever pitch. Three of the *coyotes* were flanking along the lip of the arroyo, coming straight at Bolan. They dropped to a crouch as they came closer. Bolan dropped to his heels among the mesquite.

Hoot was giving an award-winning performance. The *coyotes* were close enough for Bolan to hear them gleefully whispering jokes in Spanish about the condemned enjoying his last meal, and how they were all going to take a turn at making her cry out like that for them before they killed her. They crept closer, hoping to get a glimpse before their confederates down in the riverbed interrupted the action.

Bolan extended his arm, and the Beretta chuffed three times in rapid succession.

The click of the action cycling, the tinkle of the three spent shell casings hitting the dirt and even the slump of the dead men was covered by Hoot's energetic performance.

Bolan holstered his pistol, unslung his rifle and spoke quietly into his throat mike. "Close your eyes."

He raised the Steyr skyward and fired.

The French rifle grenade thudded upward, and every coyote raised his startled head. The Night-Sun round had been highly modified. Rather than a flare on a parachute, it had been constructed into four separate illumination bomblets.

Bolan flicked the bolt of his rifle to chamber a fresh round and closed his eyes. The grenade broke apart, and the four submunitions detonated like stars going supernova in the night sky with five million candlepower brilliance and cannonlike reports. They almost instantly burned out, leaving the borderland in blackness once more and the *coyotes* staggering around blind from the afterimages pulsing behind their eyes.

Bolan rose, his finger curling around the trigger of the M-203 grenade launcher slaved beneath the barrel of his rifle. He swung the muzzle over to the other side of the arroyo and the other flanking party. The M-203 thudded, and the beehive round belched out its payload of fléchettes. The 115 steel darts hissed through the air in an expanding cloud, claiming five coyotes.

Hoot was firing from cover, her rifle hammering in a steady bang-bang-bang as she acquired targets and dropped them. Bolan dropped to one knee and began firing as fast as he could work the Steyr's action. The *coyotes* were firing at everything and nothing. One hosed down two of his confederates with an Uzi before Bolan's bullet ended the felon's blind fratricide.

Hoot's voice spoke across the tactical link. "Choppers on the way."

Bolan kept his attention on his targets. Half a dozen were blindly fleeing back toward the box canyon. He let them run and bottle themselves for the incoming cavalry to deal with. Others with more of their wits about them ran south.

Bolan clicked in a fresh magazine loaded with blue-tipped bullets. A pair of coyotes ran straight down the riverbed for the Rio Grande.

The Executioner put his crosshairs on the running man and lifted them to the top of his shoulder. It was a tricky shot, but he had the angle from the lip of the arroyo. Bolan squeezed the trigger, and the little .308 kicked against his shoulder with far less recoil than usual. The runner staggered but kept up his desperate flight. Bolan flicked his bolt and gave his running buddy a bullet on the same shoulder. He, too, missed a step and nearly tripped but kept on.

Bolan clicked out the magazine of blue-tipped bullets and replaced them with a fresh one loaded with lead.

"Cease-fire."

"We've still got some runners."

"I want a few to get away."

Hoot was incredulous. "You want some of these guys to get away?"

"We have plenty for now." Bolan could hear the whomp-whomp-whomp of the Border patrol helicopters sweeping across the sky. The Executioner watched the pair of *coyotes* running for the sanctuary of the Rio Grande.

He'd be checking in with them soon.

2

Zapata County Coroner's Office

"Gulf Coast Gang." Hoot pointed at the dead perp's arm. "You can tell by the tattoos."

Bolan looked over the cadaver. Fléchettes left remarkably clean corpses. The .17-caliber steel needles had ice-picked the man to death rather than blasted him apart. The Ranger was right. Mexican criminals often literally wore their allegiance on their sleeves. The dead man had a sleeve of ink running from his shoulder to his wrist. Much of the imagery was religious. On his bicep was a prominent heart surrounded by barbed wire. Within the heart was a Gothic-lettered monogram that read GCG 100%.

"All of them like this?"

"The prisoners have clammed up, but it's a good bet that they're Gulf Coast Gang affiliates or else they pay tribute to them."

"Did we find any .38 Super Automatics?"

Hoot checked the file she held. "Naw, a few .38 Specials. They all had handguns, but mostly 9 mm and 40-calibers but, no Supers." She gave Bolan a slightly accusing look. "Of course, there were those two you let get away. Why, you think there's something to it?"

"It's probably nothing."

"Yeah, I know what you're thinking. Those five Feds got whacked with a Super, and some of these same assholes might even have been involved, but even a *coyote* is smart enough to ditch a gun he's used to pop five federal agents. The Super you're looking for is rusting away at the bottom of the Rio Grande—I guarantee it."

"Probably," Bolan conceded. "Or back in Mexico."

"What're you thinking?"

"Those agents, were any of them cooperating with the investigation?"

"Well, rumor was the chief patrol agent was asking for immunity if he turned state's evidence. But it's all hush-hush, as you can imagine. I can try and call in a favor or two I'm owed in Houston to confirm it."

"No." Bolan didn't need confirmation. Neither had the assassin. The rumor was enough to sign the agents' death warrants. They'd been snatched, taken to a desolate corner of the border—but not so desolate that they wouldn't be found—then bound and killed. The gangs and cartels used terror. They cut off hands and heads, killed entire families, did drive-bys in broad daylight.

The five federal agents hadn't been assassinated. They'd been executed. Military style. One man had walked down the line, capping each begging victim in the back of the head.

Hoot watched Bolan calculate. "Mister, this ain't my first rodeo. You got something in mind, why don't you just spit it out."

"This is bigger than the Gulf Coast Gang. These *coyotes* were cutouts, and they weren't at the execution. They were for us, they knew we were coming, and you've got traitors on your side of the border."

Ranger Hootkins's face went flat. "You know, you're gonna make yourself real popular around here talking like that. Like skunk-at-a-lawn-party popular."

"Yeah, I get that a lot," Bolan acknowledged. "But I knew instinctively you were one of the good ones."

"Well, that's sweet." Hoot smiled unwillingly. "But you did pick a Ranger. Kinda hard to go wrong."

"Yeah, but I met some of the boys at Company A on my way

down." Bolan shook his head decisively. "And I didn't want to kiss any of them."

Hoot stared at Bolan in bemused outrage. "And that's another thing you and I are gonna talk about."

"What I'd like to talk about is this. Last night I was in Houston, and I made it known in the public-safety department that I intended to examine the crime scene. Twenty-four hours later we had half a platoon of heavily armed coyotes willing to kill a Texas Ranger on U.S. soil."

"A Texas Ranger and a..." Hoot was still very curious just exactly what her partner represented. All she knew was that he was vaguely connected to the Justice Department and that she had received orders to show him every courtesy during his investigation.

Bolan smiled and avoided the question. "Someone in Houston gave us away, but it was someone a lot more local who let the bad guys know we were riding out in the moonlight last night."

"No getting around that," Hoot agreed. "So how do you want to proceed?"

Bolan checked his watch. "I've got a satellite window in about eleven hours. I was thinking about a little trip across the border tonight."

"You have a satellite window."

"Yup."

"You want to cross the border?"

"Sure."

"You know..." Hoot shook her head. Things were getting steeper and deeper by the second. "We don't have any authority across the border."

"We're dealing with *coyotes*, scumbags. We have moral authority."

"Oh, well, as long as we have that..." She followed as Bolan walked out of the morgue. "So what's the plan now?"

"Well, the bad guys know we're after them. They tried to kill us last night. They're following us. I suggest we stay alive until it's time to go on our little excursion."

"They're following us?"

Bolan stopped on the coroner's office steps and scanned the parking lot. It was a Friday morning at eight-thirty and fairly empty. All the vehicles had Texas Public Safety parking stickers. One Honda CRV with tinted windows had a visitor's ticket dimly visible on the dash. Bolan glanced at the hood and watched heat shimmers come off the hood. It wasn't that hot out yet. Someone had driven hard and fast to be here this morning. The occupants weren't visible.

"Oh, yeah. They're following us."

"How? No one knew we were going to the coroner's office. We took separate cars, and I didn't pick up on any tail."

Bolan walked over to the Ranger's beige Jeep CJ-7. The large, jacked-up off-road tires made his job easy. He swung under the Jeep, and it was a matter of seconds before he came back up with the GPS tracking system that had been attached to the frame with magnets. "They didn't tail us. They tracked you."

Hoot's eyebrows vee'd down dangerously. "Sons of bitches!"

"Don't look, but some of them are in that green Honda."

"Some of them?"

"There's more, but I haven't spotted them yet."

"So why haven't they hit us?"

"With all these cars around, we have too much cover. For that matter, we might manage to run inside and get half a dozen armed public-safety officers and security guards to back us up."

Hoot saw it. "They're waiting for us to get in our cars."

Bolan kept a casual eye on the Honda. "We'll take mine."

They piled into Bolan's truck, and the attack came right on cue. Tires screamed and smoked beneath the Honda CRV. A Toyota Land Cruiser came in from the other side near the entrance. A four-wheel-drive pickup bounced over the curb and jumped the sidewalk into the coroner's lot off the street.

It was currently the Mexican underworld's favorite form of assassination. They waited until the target left a building and got in their car. Then they pinned it in the parking lot with three or four vehicles loaded with armed men who ventilated the target with automatic weapons.

Bolan had been expecting it. His '78 Ford Bronco looked like one of the untold thousands of other aged and hard-used 4x4s that plied the Southwest. Beneath the weather-beaten workhorse exterior lay a predator. Five hundred supercharged horses ran beneath the hood, and they were shod with aggressively treaded, military, run-flat tires. More importantly the Bronco was armored up to European "extreme protection" B6 level. Its armored glass and Kevlar-backed body panels were impervious to direct hits from .30-caliber rifles. It would take a .50-caliber crew-served machine gun or a shoulder-launched rocket to penetrate the bodywork.

The Bronco roared in answering challenge and lunged from its spot. The Honda wanted to pin him in place, but Bolan wasn't playing that game. Auto aficionados considered the 70s series F-150 frame nearly indestructible, and Bolan's had been deliberately reinforced. "Hold on."

Bolan rammed the CRV head-on. The Honda's hood crumpled like an accordion, and the tinted windows filled with the dim white balloons of air bags. Bolan slammed the Bronco back six feet in reverse and shot the armored-glass sunroof open. "Drive."

"What!"

The Executioner slid out of his seat and heaved an M-60 E-4 general purpose machine gun from under a blanket in the back seat. "Drive!"

Hoot slid over as Bolan racked the action on a live round and stood up in the sunroof. The E-4 was a Navy model that had been shortened and lightened to make it easier for a single Navy SEAL to carry and operate. A 100-round belt box was clipped to the feed. The range was ten feet. Bolan cut loose.

The E-4 ripped into life. The Honda's windshield pocked with bullet strikes, the airbags explosively decompressed and the tinted windows went purple with the arterial spray erupting within the vehicle.

Hoot backed the Bronco up to the coroner building steps. "Jesus!"

"Brace for impact!" Bolan roared.

The incoming Land Cruiser T-boned the Bronco amidships. Bolan was nearly thrown out of the sunroof. The driver's-side doors of the Bronco buckled inward but stopped at the reinforced frame. The driver of the Land Cruiser had made the same mistake of ignoring his safety features, and the air bags inflated against the gunmen inside. Bolan ignored his bruised ribs and turned his smoking muzzle upon the SUV full of assassins. The M-60 hammered in his hands as he filled the Land Cruiser full of lead.

The pickup driver had been maneuvering to cut them off from the building but suddenly seemed to think better of the idea and slammed on his brakes. Men stood up in the back of the truck bed and began firing into the Bronco with rifles.

Bolan dropped down into the cab as bullets rattled off the Bronco like a hail. "Ram them."

"What—"

"Ram them!" Bolan stomped his foot across Hoot's boot, and the Bronco roared forward.

Hoot turned down the row and aimed the Bronco for a head-on collision. The driver of the pickup didn't have tinted windows. His gape of horror was quite clear as the Bronco bored down like doomsday. He slammed his truck into reverse, but the Bronco was already doing forty miles per hour. The two trucks met with a rending scream of metal on metal. Two of the four men in the truck bed went flying over the cab. Hoot made an unhappy noise as the two gunmen were ground to chowder beneath the Bronco's wheels.

Bolan stood up in the sunroof once more and leveled his weapon. Tracers streaked from the M-60, skimming scant inches over the truck's cabin, and reaped the two remaining men in the truck bed. The assassin in the passenger seat snaked his arm out the window to point a pistol. Bolan burned ten rounds and hammered away the handgun and the hand holding it. The shooter screamed and clutched his smashed stump.

Bolan put his front sight on the pickup driver's chest.

The driver quite sensibly raised his hands away from the wheel in surrender and took his foot off the gas. Bolan clicked a fresh ammo box onto his smoking weapon. Armed security guards were charging out of the coroner building.

"Secure those two," Bolan ordered. He stepped out of the sunroof and onto the hood.

Hoot slid out of the Bronco, keeping her SIG-Sauer fixed on the truck driver's forehead. Bolan jumped to the ground. A crushed gunman was bleeding out beneath the Bronco's runflat tire. The rifleman was a Latino male, not surprising given the situation. His rifle was of more interest. He was armed with a .308-caliber Israeli Galil rifle. Most Mexican criminals either bought or stole their heavy weapons from the Mexican military or police. Galil rifles in that caliber were rather rare and not standard Mexican issue.

What a Mexican gangster was doing with Hebrew steel in Texas was an interesting question.

Bolan memorized the serial number and moved on. The four men in the Land Cruiser were all dead. The "Mexican pin" was an excellent assassination technique against the defenseless, but automobiles were terrible fighting platforms unless you had a sunroof like Bolan's Bronco. It was almost impossible to maneuver one's weapon inside a vehicle, and worse, everyone inside was a sitting duck with no cover to be taken.

Bolan's fire had been lethal in the extreme. His full-metal-jacketed .308 rounds had torn through the men in the front and gone on to rip apart the men in the back. The gunmen in the Honda had fared little better.

Police cars came screaming into the parking lot, and Texas State Troopers piled out of them.

Ranger Hootkins walked up to Bolan and took a long hard look at his ordnance. "I didn't know machine guns were Justice Department issue."

"The Justice Department didn't issue me this."

"Oh?"

"Yeah. And I never said I worked for the Justice Department."

"So that would make you a…"

"Volunteer consultant?" Bolan tried.

"Volunteer consultant." Hoot wasn't buying it.

"Yeah." Bolan scanned the carnage in the parking lot and flicked on his machine gun's safety. "You know, I don't even get paid."

"Okay, Mr. Concerned Citizen, what's the plan now?"

Bolan checked his watch. "I've got a satellite window in ten and a half hours. You got anything to eat at your place?"

3

Sabinas Hildalgo, Mexico

Donato "The Butcher" Chapa was scared out of his mind. His phone was ringing. It was his current special telephone. He received them in the mail. Whenever the phone rang, he destroyed it after the conversation was through and then received another one anonymously. He had a pretty good idea why the phone was ringing now.

Things had not gone according to plan this morning.

The Commander didn't like it when things did not go according to plan. To his credit, the Butcher had never disappointed the Commander, at least not to his knowledge. Chapa was good at his job, which consisted almost entirely of collections and killing people. Barely five foot three and painfully skinny, he seemed an odd choice for such a task. The gangster was in his midthirties, but his unlined face and preternaturally youthful features had earned him the nickname *"El Nino"* among his Gulf Coast Gang confederates. "The Boy" was a nickname he had hated, but nicknames were like barnacles; once they stuck they were nearly impossible to scrape off. So Chapa had gone into his father's butcher shop, a place he had sworn never to work, and borrowed a jumbo meat cleaver. After slaughtering a Mexican judge and his entire family with it, "the Butcher" had been born and people had stopped calling him "the Boy."

At least to his face.

The Butcher answered his phone with grave reluctance. "*¿Qué, Comandante?*"

The Commander spoke in English. "Hey, Nino. How's it going?"

The Butcher squirmed. He had met his new boss only once, and that had been enough. If the Commander wanted to call him "Goat-boy" Chapa would eat it with a smile and salute.

"Uh…" The Butcher considered his options. Many men, many of them supposedly tough, had spent their last moments begging and making excuses to the Butcher. It had never impressed him. The Butcher went with the honest approach. It was the last thing anyone ever expected out of a criminal scumbag. "On my end? Not so good, boss."

There was a moment's pause. Clearly the Commander had expected some cringing, begging and excuse making. "This guy? He's a real asshole. I don't know if my boys can take him."

This was met by a disturbing silence.

Chapa began talking faster and faster. "Like, in the arroyo? He killed everybody. Then, across the border? He, like, had a machine gun, and I'm not talking about an automatic rifle, I mean a machine gun, like Rambo. And his truck? It was, like, bulletproof. This guy is a real dick, boss." The Butcher's mouth ran away from him. "He reminds me of you."

The Butcher's adolescent face suddenly paled at his own temerity.

There were a few moments of silence.

"You say he killed everyone in the arroyo?"

The Butcher bit back a sigh of relief. "No, boss. Beto and Tomas made it back across the border. I was going to cut them up, but I figured you might want to talk to them first."

The Commander favored the Butcher with a bemused grunt. "Tell me something, Nino. This dick, the one I remind you of so much?"

Chapa winced.

"And the Ranger. Where they are now?"

"I have boys watching the public-safety building, and some boys watching the Ranger's house." The Butcher checked his watch. "The boys in Laredo called in twenty minutes ago and said the two of them had left the building. I didn't think a tail would be safe. But the Ranger's place is in Zapata, and the boys said they were heading east. They must be going to her place."

The Butcher paused. He didn't like the idea of crossing the border and trying to trap this gringo terminator and a Texas Ranger in their lair. "I'm not sure if my boys can—"

"Your boys won't try to take them in Zapata."

The Butcher bit back another wave of relief. He was pretty sure he knew what the Commander was thinking. A lot could happen on the lonely, fifty-mile commute between Laredo and Zapata. "You want me to set up a little something along the road? Maybe outside of San Ygnacio?"

"I want you to call me as soon as your eyes in Zapata see them come in."

"Yes, boss."

"Then I want you to set up a little something outside of San Ygnacio."

"Yes, boss." The Butcher smiled. The boss was always thinking ahead.

"Where are Beto and Tomas now?"

"Beto and Tomas are right here, boss. You want me to start carving?" The Butcher grinned at the two men duct-taped to folding chairs in front of him. Their eyes rolled with terror over their gags.

"No, are they someplace safe?"

"They're safe here, boss. Right in my office."

"No. They're not safe there. I'm sending some people. Take Beto and Tomas to the club after hours and take care of them. We own the local police. Whoever this asshole is, he has no jurisdiction south of the border. Butcher them up there, then this is what I want you to do."

The Butcher's boyish grin was almost beatific as he listened to the Commander's plan.

The gringo was a dead man.

Falcon Lake, Zapata, Texas

BOLAN SAT in Hoot's kitchen and ate. Dusk was falling, and a cool breeze was blowing off the lake. The Ranger lived in a rustic cabin complete with rocking chair and ancient black-and-tan coonhound sprawled on the porch. Bolan wolfed down chili. Hoot was an excellent cook and a firm believer in the ancient faith that real, genuine, Texas chili did not require beans. Beans were another dish entirely and served on the side.

Bolan shoveled it down with cornbread and mashed potatoes on the side and asked for seconds. Hoot reloaded his plate. "So what's across the border?"

"The two guys we let go."

"You're tracking them? By satellite?"

"Yup."

"How…"

Bolan reached into his gear bag and pulled out a rifle cartridge. The bullet was blue. He held the bullet over a tortilla and pressed his thumb against the frangible projectile and cracked open the plastic casing. Bolan upended the cartridge, and thin, clear goo dripped onto the flour pancake and was quickly absorbed.

"So—" Hoot peered at the ruined tortilla "—that's some sort of tracking tortilla?"

"More like a marker. The technical term would be infrared luminescent material. For the next three months those two *coyotes* are going to glow at a steady 300 candle-power at a very specific frequency in the infrared spectrum. It's invisible to the naked eye but not the night-vision gear I have with me, and I have a National Security Agency satellite specifically tasked with looking for that exact frequency along this section of the border."

Hoot folded her arms across her chest. "You know, for an unpaid volunteer you sure get to play with all the cool toys."

"You have no idea." Bolan pulled out a laptop and hooked a satellite link to it. He punched a few keys, and Aaron Kurtzman's craggy face appeared in a real-time video window. "You have a fix on my position, Bear?"

Aaron Kurtzman spoke from the Computer Room at Stony

Man Farm fourteen hundred miles away in Virginia. "We have you, Striker. Patching you in."

Hoot leaned in over Bolan's shoulder as most of the thirteen-inch screen filled with a black-and-white infrared satellite image of her house by Lake Falcon.

"Okay, Bear." Bolan picked up the infrared adulterated tortilla. "Adjust infrared frequency for test."

"Frequency is calibrated, Striker. Begin test."

Hoot just stared as Bolan tossed the flour tortilla out the open kitchen window. On the computer screen, a tiny bright dot squirted out from the house, soaring a few yards before falling to the ground.

Kurtzman's brow furrowed as he watched the tortilla's flight on his end. "I have an unidentified, flying..." Instantly, multiple little heat signatures converged as the glowing object was shredded by squirrels. "Foodstuff?"

Bolan turned to Hoot. "It's nontoxic."

"Good to know."

"Tracking frequency confirmed, Striker," Kurtzman acknowledged.

"Bear, give me a sweep of the border ten miles to either side between points Zapata and Laredo."

As the satellite lens zoomed out, the U.S. and Mexican border towns formed a string of Christmas lights along the Rio Grande. Hoot chewed her lower lip meditatively. "So you can pick out a goo stain on some guy's jacket out of all that?"

Bolan smiled. "It's not a question of strength. The satellite can zero in on a cigarette lighter if it knows what it's looking for. It's a question of frequency. The material in the bullets was manufactured to emit a unique infrared signature. One that nothing on the border should have. It should stick out like a sore thumb."

"What if they saw the stuff on their jackets?"

"It's colorless, odorless and dries in seconds," Bolan countered.

"What if they aren't wearing their jackets?"

"The border's cold at night."

"Yeah, but what if yesterday was *coyote* laundry day."

"Gotta think positive."

"Yeah, but what if they're indoors?"

Bolan sighed patiently. "*Coyotes* are like their namesake. They're nocturnal predators. They do their business at night, and they have their own specific territories that they operate in and defend."

"Yeah, but you—"

Out on the porch the hound woofed.

"Your dog is barking at something," Bolan said.

"You're the one encouraging the squirrels."

Bolan glanced up as the dog suddenly went silent in mid-bark.

Hoot stepped toward the door. "That's odd. Topper usually won't shut up until I go out and—"

"Don't go out."

Kurtzman peered at Bolan from the inset in the screen. "What's going on?"

"I need satellite recon of my position, ASAP."

Kurtzman clicked keys on his end and the eye of the satellite swung back and zoomed in on the lakeside cabin. His eyes went wide. "Striker! You have multiple hostiles surrounding your position!"

Bolan could see them. In the infrared viewer the men were dark shapes among the pale trees and foliage. He watched a man work the bolt of his silenced rifle. The spent shell was a tiny burst of bright heat that swiftly cooled as it fell to the ground. The man picked the evidence and put it in his pocket.

Topper the hound had been assassinated.

Ranger Missy Hootkins's face flushed and twisted into an archetypal mask of redheaded rage. "They shot my dog."

Bolan glanced at the rifles mounted over the fireplace. Cowboy action shooting trophies were lined along the mantle. "Tell me you have ammo for those."

"Oh, I have ammo."

Bolan kept his eye on the laptop screen. "Get them, but stay clear of the windows."

Hoot moved for her weapons. Most of Bolan's heavy ordnance was in the back of his Bronco, but he took his pistols out of the gear bag by his feet and checked the loads. Hoot came back with a pair of Winchester lever-action rifles, a double barrel shotgun and four single-action Colt .45 revolvers. Bolan picked up a 30-30 carbine and began shucking shells into the loading gate.

Kurtzman's voice dropped an octave in concern. "Thirty yards and closing, Striker. I make it ten hostiles. I also see two boats beached a klick south of your position."

The Ranger stuffed rounds into her own .45 Long Colt carbine. "They came across the lake, from the Mexico side."

"Ten yards and closing, Striker."

"Roger that." Bolan shoved the two single-action revolvers into his belt. Another pistol was always faster than reloading.

Glass broke as a grenade sailed through the kitchen window. It fell to the living room floor and spun, a black cylinder the size of a beer can covered with red lettering. It was a flash-stun grenade. Bolan overturned the couch on top of the grenade as its fuse hissed. The couch rippled and spewed white light around its edges but smothered the blinding flash and deafening roar.

"Striker! You have a three-man team coming toward the door. One has a shotgun! He's going for the hinges! He—"

Bolan raised his rifle and fired. The 30-30 cracked three times in rapid succession as Bolan worked the lever. The triple report was deafening in the confines of the cabin, and three black holes appeared in the cabin door at waist height. Splinters flew inward from the door as automatic rifles buzz-sawed outside in response.

"Doorman down, Striker!"

Hoot fired her rifle out the kitchen window. A second shotgun began firing on the porch, and the black wrought-iron door hinges began warping as they were blasted with buckshot. The door kicked open, and the point man burst in. He wore a black raid suit and a black ski mask and held a green Glock automatic in both hands.

Bolan's rifle boomed twice and toppled the man backward, his Glock machine pistol spraying wildly into the ceiling. The man behind him pushed past, and Bolan flung his empty rifle like a lumberjack at an ax-throwing competition. The rifle revolved once, and the butt tomahawked between the second shooter's eyes and dropped him back out onto the porch. A grenade sailed through the open door in response. It wasn't the cylinder of a gas or stun grenade but the brutally knobbed, gray iron egg of an M-9 fragmentation grenade.

Bolan snatched up one of the Colt Peacemakers. He held the trigger down and fanned the hammer like a gunfighter of the Old West. The soft lead .45-caliber wadcutter bullet smashed and deformed around the iron grenade and slapped it across the floor. Bolan kept fanning and the Peacemaker strobed fire and spun the grenade toward the door. Bolan lowered his aim slightly, and the third bullet hit the underside of the grenade and skipped it out the door like a stone. Bolan threw himself out of the line of the doorway as the grenade detonated out on the porch. Men screamed as their flesh was shredded by jagged metal fragments moving at just under the speed of sound. A man fell forward out of the darkness against the door frame. He clutched his face and blindly waved a Glock pistol. Bolan fanned the Colt twice more, smashing apart the man's hand and ruining the face beneath it. The assassin fell bonelessly to the floor.

Bullets were hammering the house from all sides. Window glass fell in jagged shards. One of the wrought-iron chairs from the back porch had been thrown through the bedroom window. A pair of men was crawling through the bay window, preceding themselves with machine pistols. Bullets streaked down the short hallway.

The Executioner snatched up the double-barrel "stagecoach" gun. Crawling through a window left a man terribly exposed. The men were wearing body armor but not on their heads or arms. Bolan squeezed both of the shotgun's triggers. Two patterns of buckshot flew in bee swarms down the hall. In the intervening twelve yards, the patterns opened up into twin spheres the size of medicine balls. Wood stripped and splintered off the walls of the hallway. The lead clouds expanded into the bedroom to fill the shattered bedroom window. Lead balls tore and mangled the men everywhere they weren't armored. The men fell limp half in and half out of the cabin.

Bolan broke open the smoking shotgun and jacked in two more shells from the leather shell carrier stitched around the stock.

"Hoot! We have to break out of here—"

Bolan snapped the shotgun up to his shoulder like a skeet shooter as another gray lump of metal looped through the doorway. At six feet, the twin patterns of lead hit the iron grenade in a solid cloud the size of a saucer. The soft lead swatted the grenade away like a line drive back out the door. Yellow fire cracked in the darkness and a man screamed.

"We break out the back! Now!" A grenade looped in and Hoot tracked it with her carbine. Bolan roared, "No! Get down!"

Hoot was already firing. She was a crack shot and hit the grenade dead on. Had it been an iron frag, she would have knocked it behind the refrigerator. Instead, it was the gray cylinder of a white-phosphorus grenade. The bullet detonated the grenade, but its path made it detonate incorrectly. Streamers of white smoke and yellow fire ripped out of the twin holes, and it fell spinning and fountaining white-hot heat.

Hoot fell screaming as burning metal splashed across her arm.

Bolan's folding knife clacked open as he flicked his wrist and dived on top of her. He pinned her before she could destroy her left hand by bringing it to the burn. Water would not stop white phosphorus from burning. It had to be smothered with sand or dirt, and it would burn down to the bone and continue to be white-hot long after it was smothered. Hoot screamed afresh as Bolan pressed his knife down. With one precise cut Hoot's charred sleeve, the burning phosphorus and a flap of flesh the size of a playing card and half a centimeter deep flew away. Hoot's eyes flew wide with shock, but Bolan's eyes were on the wound. Blood welled up like a lake, but none of it was sizzling and he'd managed to avoid the muscle. He took her left hand and clamped it down over the wound. "Hold it until I can bind it!"

Heat and smoke rolled out of the kitchen in burning waves. The enemy had taken too many casualties and were breaking contact. Bolan reversed his knife and took the bloody blade in his hand. Not all of them were retreating. A man torn and wounded from grenade fragments leaned through the door frame and shakily tried to aim his rifle at Bolan and Hoot. The Buck tactical knife revolved through the air. It was not balanced for throwing and was a poor choice for a missile. But it still weighed a quarter of a pound, and it hit the wounded man in the face. His rifle muzzle rose as he flinched backward and bullets sprayed the scorching ceiling.

During that split second, Bolan scooped up his Desert Eagle and fired. The .44-caliber hollowpoint bullet did damage no thrown knife could dream of. The assassin dropped with the top of his skull removed.

The cabin was beginning to burn in earnest. Bolan ripped off Hoot's other sleeve and wound it around her arm. He looked into her eyes. Her face was pale and her eyes wide with shock. "You with me?"

"Yeah…" She nodded shakily but her eyes focused. "I'm with you."

Bolan shoved his Beretta into her right hand. "We're getting out of here. Follow me when I shout!"

Bolan dived through front door, expecting bullets to rip through his flesh. He came up on one knee with the Desert Eagle in both hands. He was surrounded by half a dozen bodies. Speedboat engines roared into life out on the lake. The enemy was bugging out. "Hoot! C'mon!"

Hoot came out. The Beretta shook in her hand, but her face was a mask of grim determination. Bolan glanced at their vehicles. Hoot's Jeep was shot to hell. All four tires were flat, and the hood was filled with bullet holes. The armored Bronco had fared better. The run-flat tires were chipped and cratered and the bodywork was dimpled like the surface of the moon, but the old horse was still ready and willing to run. Bolan pumped the button on his key chain twice to disarm the security suite and unlock the doors. He shoved Hoot across the seat and slid behind the wheel. Gravel flew as he threw the truck into gear. Stony Man could track the bad guys across the border. Hoot needed a hospital.

"You all right?"

Hoot's right hand was clamped over her arm in a death grip. Blood leaked out from underneath and between her fingers in a steady upwelling. She shook her head and snarled. "Well, save that you were carving goddamn lunch meat off of me, I'm tip-top."

Bolan nodded as he drove. The effect of burns on people was unpredictable. Anger and sarcasm were a good sign she wasn't spiraling into shock. "Sorry, but it beats having your arm burned off at the shoulder. Trust me. I've seen it."

Hoot had no answer for that one.

Bolan jerked his chin at the glovebox. "There are field dressings in there. Start packing them on. We're half an hour from the nearest hospital."

Hoot tore open a dressing with her teeth and took her hand off of her wound. "Jesus…" It would take a skin graft to fix the wound. Her breath came in with a hiss as she pressed the dressing against the open lake in her arms. "They were going to burn us to death."

"They used the incendiary to break contact, but yeah, that was the hoped-for secondary effect."

"Sons of bitches. I hope they—goddamn it!"

Bullets peppered the Bronco's body but didn't penetrate as rifles strobed from the trees on either side of the road. Bolan ignored them and kept his eyes on the road itself. This was the second ambush, the one the first had driven them toward. He dropped the pedal to the floor, and the Bronco lunged forward. Bolan's eyes flew wide and he stomped on the brakes. The Bronco was a big truck, and the add-on armor paneling and glass made it far heavier than the standard Ford specs. The modified engine and suspension made it far faster and more agile than the designers had ever dreamed of, but it could not stop on a dime.

It was stopped by the cable stretched across the road. For all the Bronco's might, the two oak trees on either side of the road were more than half a century old and massive with roots sunk deep into the dry Texas earth in search of water. The three-inch industrial cable was made to haul steel girders into the sky.

The jaws of the trap had slammed shut.

The Bronco did not exactly stop. Its forward momentum had to go somewhere. Its grille buckled inward, the truck whipped around to starboard and its side bounced off the cable. The Bronco was utterly out of control as it flew off the side of the road at 40 mph and slammed into a massive oak tree. The armored engine box folded like an accordion, and the Bronco stood up on its nose violently. It would have somersaulted, but the massive oak was in the way. The Bronco bounced off the eight-foot-diameter trunk and bounced three more times on its tires before it finally came to a rest.

Bolan blinked as his vision spun. His inner ears tried to regain their equilibrium. His racing harness and the all-sides air bags had saved him and Hoot from concussions and multiple bone fractures.

Bolan groaned as the air bags automatically began deflating. "Hoot…"

Hoot made a noncommital "Urk" noise and slumped against her seat belt.

Bolan unbuckled himself and hit the lever beside his seat. He reclined all the way back and crawled into the back seat. Riflefire buzz-sawed against the Bronco in long streams that indicated the enemy had general purpose .30-caliber machine guns. The Bronco rocked on its chassis as it took dozens of hits per second. The problem with most car armors was that they were not bulletproof; they were bullet resistant for a certain period of time, and the ancient oaks had had their way with the Bronco. It would not be long before bullets began penetrating to the interior. Bolan flipped the latches on an armored box bolted to the floor of the truck bed.

The enemy at the cabin had been clever. Incendiaries were one of the best ways to interrupt an ambush and break contact, and they had used it to cover their escape back to their boats. It was a tactic that had been first developed by the United States Marines during the jungle fighting in the Pacific during WWII. Bolan had come to Texas knowing that multiple ambushes were going to be a part of his immediate future, and he was well-versed in the tactic, as well.

Bolan grunted with effort as he hauled the twenty-six-pound M-202 A-1 Flame Assault Shoulder Weapon out of its molded foam packing. The FLASH was the U.S. Army's attempt to improve the flamethrower, which was short-ranged, inaccurate, difficult and time-consuming to reload. Not inconsequentially, a man wandering around on a battlefield with tanks of jellied jet fuel on his back spewing fire was a bullet magnet and inherently a danger to himself and everyone around him.

The Army had attempted to solve the problem by strapping four LAW antitank rockets together and replacing their antiarmor warheads with napalm.

Bolan flicked off the protective lids on both sides of the rocket box and yanked. The four 66 mm telescoping rocket tubes snapped out and armed the rockets, and a folding sight popped up. He reached up and shot the bolt on the armor-glass skylight and yanked it open. The machine guns and rifles were firing at them from two points on either side of the road. It concentrated their firepower and put the Bronco into an effective crossfire.

It also put the enemy into two ideal clusters for an area-effect fire weapon.

Bolan shouldered the rocket launcher and crouched up into the sunroof. Bullets shrieked across the roof, and he was hard pressed not to flinch as bullet after bullet cracked supersonically inches from his head. Bolan didn't have his night-vision goggles on, and there was no time to dig them out of his gear. He simply put the FLASH's sight squarely on the chattering flash of the nearest machine gun and fired. The 66 mm rocket sizzled out of its launch tube. The chatter of the machine gun was eclipsed in orange fire as the jellied fuel flew outward in all directions in a twenty-yard radius. The napalm illuminated the enemy as it spewed and splattered and clung to everything it touched.

The enemy was clustered around a military-style jeep hidden by brush in the trees. The machine gun was pedestal mounted, and riflemen were concealed behind the jeep body. Trees, shrubs, vehicle and men were coated with clinging fire indiscriminately. The gunfire ended abruptly from the enemy strongpoint as the jeep went up like a torch and humans flopped, fell and writhed like burning mannequins.

Bolan swung the launcher around and fired on the second strongpoint.

The rocket hit the jeep beneath its wheels, and fire blossomed out from underneath the 4x4 like the petals of an all-embracing flower consuming man and vehicle. Bolan spun the FLASH about and pumped a second rocket into his first target. He knew some gunmen had escaped, but he wanted them to keep running rather than regroup. Bolan swung around the M-202 A-1 and gave the second jeep his last rocket. He dropped the smoking rocket box and slipped back down into the Bronco.

"Hoot."

"Yeah."

"I'm going to go get us a ride. Can you back me up?"

Hoot held up Bolan's 93-R. "Oh, I got your six on these sons of bitches."

"Good enough." Bolan reached back into the same armored locker and drew out an FN Special Forces Combat Assault Rifle. He snapped out the folding stock and powered up the night-vision scope. "Unless it drops and cowers, shoot anything that isn't me." Bolan took out a pair of night-vision goggles and settled them over Hoot's eyes.

The Executioner slid out of the stricken Bronco. He fought vertigo as he stood up for the first time since the crash and jogged toward the road. He could hear an engine revving and underbrush crunching beneath wheels. Bolan strode out into the middle of the road and sighted through his night optics.

A convertible BMW 320i had pulled out onto the road a hundred yards back from the burning jeep to the left. Bolan squeezed his eyes shut as he was illuminated by the headlights. He took the opportunity to open the breech of the EGLM 40 mm grenade launcher beneath the barrel of his rifle and slammed it shut meaningfully. A fool would have charged down the 40 mm muzzle and been blown to hell. The BMW screeched to a halt.

Bolan's voice boomed out over the crackling and burning of the oaks. "Shut those lights off, or I send you to hell!"

The driver cut the lights.

Bolan roared back at Hoot, "Nuke him if he moves!"

The driver had seen the results of the nuking of the gun jeeps and had found religion. Bolan raised his night-vision optics to his eyes. There was a single man driving the BMW. Bolan walked forward, the muzzles of his rifle and his grenade launcher leveled on the Beamer. At twenty yards, the Executioner flicked on the tactical light mounted on the side of his rifle.

The driver blinked and squinted into the blinding beam. "Please…please, I'm just the driver," he pleaded in Spanish.

"You speak English?"

"*Sí!* I mean yes!"

"Shut the hell up and keep your hands on the wheel."

"*Sí* —I mean yes!"

"Hoot! C'mon!"

Hoot limped out of the darkness.

"Get in the back."

Hoot slid in without a word.

Bolan slid into the front passenger seat. "You're going to drive us to Laredo. Is there another ambush?"

"Uh…not that I know of."

"If there is, the Texas Ranger behind you is going to blow your brains out."

Hoot pressed the muzzle of the 93-R into the back of the driver's skull."

"You pull anything, and she blows your brains out. Comprende?

The man's voice was a morally devastated whisper. "*Comprende?*"

Bolan shoved the muzzles of his weapon system into the gangster's ribs. "You and I are going to talk."

The gangster yipped as the weapon was jabbed in his ribs. "Now drive," Bolan ordered.

4

Bolan gazed upon one of the most feared men in Nuevo Laredo. Donato Chapa's jewelry, tattoos, pencil-thin mustache and gangster glare only served to make him look ridiculous rather than tough. On the other hand, there was nothing funny about his rap sheet and the DEA file of crimes he was suspected of. It seemed he'd earned his nickname through good old-fashioned hard work and determination. Donato "The Butcher" Chapa was a classic case of overcompensation gone wild.

Bolan nodded at the image on the monitor. "He's our boy."

"Yeah," Kurtzman agreed. "The suspect you captured said the Butcher was behind the attack on Hoot's cabin and the ambush up the road. He's a bad boy. If there's anything major going down on the border, Chapa has a hand in it. Or at the very least, someone is giving him a taste out of respect." Kurtzman peered at Bolan narrowly across the video link. "So what are you going to do about it?"

"Find Chapa, kick his ass, compromise him and follow him to the top of the food pyramid until I find where the meat is." Bolan shrugged. "You know, the usual."

Aaron Kurtzman sighed. "The usual" was guaranteed to send the State Department into fits and much of the upper echelon of American law enforcement on a witch hunt for someone whom no one outside the Farm knew existed save for the President and a few trusted men in Washington, D.C. Long ago, Mack Bolan had declared war against human evil. It had gone from a personal war against the Italian Mafia to a War Everlasting against the goblins who preyed on their fellow humans like wolves upon sheep. As long as Mack Bolan breathed, he would stand against them. Not as their judge. Not as their jury.

He was their Executioner.

"What else to do you have on your end?" Bolan asked.

"We got your infrared signals. They went to a place called La Esencia. It's a club in downtown Nuevo Laredo."

"What happened to the signals? They went in and never went out."

Bolan suspected the two men were probably Nuevo Laredo landfill by now. He also suspected they had been brought to the club for disposal. That lead was probably dead, but he was already getting an idea to generate new ones. "What else you got?"

"Not much."

Bolan watched Kurtzman stare down at his notes with mild distress. "You have something."

"Yeah, but they're right out of a comic book."

"Lay it on me."

"You were talking about the meat at the top of the food pyramid."

"Yeah…"

"I got a whisper out of the DEA."

"Like what kind of whisper?"

"Just a name." Kurtzmann shook his head. "Not even a name. Just a rumor—Omega."

"Omega."

"Omega."

"That's it. And the DEA informant who whispered it? He's dead."

"Let me guess, he got capped through the back of the head with a .38 Super."

"You got it."

Bolan considered this tidbit. "I don't like it."

Kurtzman leaned forward. He was a certified genius. Bolan was brilliant, but more than that, he had instincts honed by waging his War Everlasting on every continent on earth. "And you don't like it because…"

"Because we're in Mexico."

"Omega?" Kurtzman's brow furrowed. "It means the same thing in English as it does in Spanish. It's a Greek root word that the Latin languages adopted. It means 'the last.'"

"Right, in English culture you would say an 'Omega bomb,' 'Omega code,' or 'Omega plan,' meaning 'last and ultimate.' We're in Mexico. 'Last' has a different meaning. 'First' is much more powerful in Spanish. A Mexican crime lord would rather call himself 'Alpha,' or in Spanish, 'Primo.'"

Kurtzman beamed. "Okay, I'm buying it. What do you want me to do with it?"

"Don't know yet. What else do you have for me?"

"Just this—La Guitarista."

Bolan perked an eyebrow. "The Guitar Player?"

"Yeah, according to Nuevo Laredan police reports, in the last two weeks someone has shot up a couple of local dive bars. The first time, killing a pair of loan-shark collection goons, and the second time, slaughtering a pretty high-profile local pimp and his bodyguard. Oh, and the goons? They worked for the pimp."

"And they call the assailant the Guitar Player?"

Aaron Kurtzman couldn't meet Mack Bolan's eyes. "He was, uh, dressed like a mariachi."

Bolan simply stared. "Bear..."

"Yeah?"

"I think I've seen this movie."

Kurtzman nodded. "According to the police report, he cut off the pimp's head with a samurai sword."

"You're kidding."

"I assure you I'm not."

"So you're saying we have *El Mariachi* slash *Desperado* slash *Samurai Jack* going on in Nuevo Laredo?"

"No, all I'm saying is you got a guy calling himself La Guitarista working himself up the criminal food chain in Nuevo Laredo."

"And a puppet master calling himself Omega."

"That's the rumor," Kurtzman concurred.

"Well, I think this has been a very productive briefing," Bolan said.

Kurtzman raised his coffee mug. "I'm here to help."

Bolan suddenly smiled.

Kurtzman recognized the look. "What?"

"I was just thinking."

"And…"

"Well, we've got Omega and La Guitarista."

Kurtzman cocked his head cautiously. "And?"

"Let's add another name to the mix."

"Like?"

Bolan leaned back in his chair. "Like El Hombre."

THE JET-BLACK EL CAMINO rumbled like thunder through the barrio streets. Heads rose. Some registered vague recognition and alarm. A year or so ago, a car just like it had moved through the city of Nuevo Laredo like a great black shark with chrome teeth. Its prey had been a splinter group of the Salvadoran gang Mara Salvatrucha that had gotten its hands dirty in international terrorism and biowarfare. The white man in the black car had followed the trail of terror, waging his own rolling war from the streets Washington, D.C., to the Central American capital of San Salvador. That war had rolled through the streets of Nuevo Laredo like a tsunami. The man behind the wheel had fallen upon the city like a sledgehammer and dismantled the local Mara Salvatrucha from top to bottom. No one knew who he was. He had been simply known as "El Hombre."

Bolan gunned the supercharged 400-horsepower engine, and the '68 Chevy bellowed like a dinosaur as he neared his destination.

El Hombre was back in town.

Bolan ended his "be seen in the barrio" tour and headed downtown. He pulled up to Club La Esencia, which was a converted warehouse and one of the hottest clubs in the city. It was half disco, and if a person knew the passwords, deeper in the bowels it was an exclusive gambling and gentlemen's club for Nuevo Laredo's gang glitterati. It was supposedly neutral territory, but gunfights erupted there on an almost weekly basis. Kurtzman's research indicated that besides the outward sporting pleasures, deals in drugs, guns and humans were held like tobacco auctions.

Rumor was the Butcher held down a permanent table at La Egencia, both in the disco and in the back. Rumor was he was one of the ringmasters. The Butcher had unknowingly become the next step in the Executioner's search-and-destroy mission.

Bolan avoided the velvet rope and ignored the valet as he parked in the back. Subarus, Hondas and Toyotas tricked out into *Too Fast, Too Furious* rice rockets lined the parking spaces among pimped-out SUVs. The warehouse loading dock doors had been bricked over and replaced with a single, steel security door. A pair of monolithic Mexican bouncers flanked the back door beneath the glare of a single bare bulb. Their casual Mexican soccer jerseys and basketball shorts were dressed up by ropes of gold chains and medallions piled around their bull necks. Both men were hovering at the three-hundred-pound mark. Both had shaved heads, religious and gang tattoos crawling down their arms to the wrists, and both men regarded Bolan with open hostility as he lit a cigar and swaggered up the slope of warehouse's loading ramp.

Bolan wore his El Hombre outfit. A pale blue guayabera shirt strained across his physique. Khaki pants and all-terrain sandals capped it off. With the Cuban cigar smoldering in one corner of his mouth, he looked like a cartoon characterization of a man who had killed people in Latin America for the CIA in the seventies. Bolan took a long pull on his cigar and blew three concentric smoke rings. He threaded the needle with a thin stream of smoke he sent directly into the starboard-side bouncer's face.

"Is the little boy in?"

Starboard waved at the smoke. Port snarled. "What?"

"The Boy. Chapa. You know, Babydick. Where is he?"

Port stared at Bolan with the grudging admiration of one confronted by a particularly spectacular form of suicide. "You know, yanqui? I don't know who you are, but you don't wanna call the Butcher that to his face, and you don't want him to find out that you said it behind his back." He loomed his sumo wrestler's bulk over Bolan. "You know? You don't even wanna think it, not until you get your skinny white ass back across the border."

Starboard leaned in and cracked his knuckles with a sound like marbles being crushed. The words Rage and Hate were tattooed on the business surfaces of his fists. "You know, Tavo? I don't think this gringo's gonna make it back across the border."

Bolan took another long pull on his cigar and contemplated all of that before grinning like a maniac and giving the portside bouncer a face full of smoke for his concern. "I'm *El Hombre,* and I'll call that needle-dick Chapa anything I want."

The starboard-side bouncer stared unblinkingly in hostile, bovine incomprehension.

Port blinked and straightened with dawning alarm. "What? Wait! You're not—"

Bolan hit him. A short, hard, right hand lead that snapped his head back like a cue ball breaking the rack. Bolan hooked his thumb into the hidden loop in his watchband, and the nylon hissed as eight inches of strap deployed from beneath the Omega Speedmaster watch. He snapped the strap behind the stunned bouncer's neck with the deftness of a Hindu strangler. He turned, knelt and heaved in one fluid motion and the defense strap's leverage sent the bouncer flying over Bolan's shoulder. The Executioner continued his turn and stood before Starboard. Behind him gravity inexorably took hold of Port, and he landed in an ugly tangle of limbs that rolled down the loading ramp and came to rest in a wheezing, half-conscious heap.

The remaining goon stared at Bolan in shock. The incident had taken less than three heartbeats, and the man stood before him grinning. He looked down at the fallen form at the foot of the ramp and bellowed. For all his bulk, he threw a credible round-kick at Bolan's head. Bolan deployed the eight-inch strap to block the kick. He cinched the unyielding nylon like a python around the bouncer's ankle and thrust both arms overhead. The bouncer yelped as his leg was shoved skyward into a tendon-tearing standing split. Bolan swung the tree-trunk-like leg back down and around as if he were swinging a golf club.

The bouncer's body torqued around in a spin that ended violently on the concrete of the loading dock. Bolan uncinched the strap. The Ultimate Defense Strap had been born out of Brazilian jujitsu and allowed their famous "sleeve strangle" to be applied by someone who didn't happen to be wearing a martial-arts uniform. As the two bouncers had learned, the leverage it gave also allowed for numerous other applications.

Bolan reeled the strap back into an extra loop beneath his watchband. Among all of the chains around the bouncer's neck hung a key card on a lanyard. Bolan snapped it off and walked back to his El Camino and scooped his "Persuader" out of the truck bed.

The Persuader was a Chinese white wax-wood staff that had been picked out, polished and custom cut for Bolan by Hermann "Gadgets" Schwarz, Stony Man Farm's resident expert in Monkey Kung Fu. It was two inches in diameter at the brass-shod butt and tapered to one inch at the naked tip like a rat's tail. The staff had been cut to just reach Bolan's eyebrow when stood on end, creating the classic Chinese eyebrow-height staff. Japanese and Okinawan martial-arts staffs were stiff, rigid, oaken rods of correction. Chinese martial artists preferred more subtlety in their sticks. The tapered wax wood was flexible. It would bend rather than break and allowed for a good deal of whip.

Bolan was a master of no martial art, but he was intimately familiar with the joy of a good piece of wood. In his last operation here, he had cleared a roadhouse aptly named The Snake Pit with Old Painless in an orgy of violence that had already assumed urban legend status in Nuevo Laredo's criminal underground. Even Tavo had heard about it, but the knowledge still hadn't saved him.

El Hombre and his "big stick" policy were back in town, and another chapter was about to be added to the legend.

Bolan took the commandeered keycard and swiped it through the lock. He held the staff semiconcealed behind his arm and leg as he walked into La Esencia. Dance mixes of Mexican rap music throbbed through the soundproofing lining the wall of the corridor. An office door opened from the side, and a skinny balding man in an electric blue silk suit gaped at Bolan. He glanced back behind him as he reached under his jacket. "Nico!"

Bolan whipped his staff up between the man's legs.

He keened like an insect as his pistol fell to the carpet. He clutched himself in agony and sagged grimacing against the door frame.

"Nico" was stamped from the same frame as the other bouncers. The three-hundred-pounder shoved the blue suit unceremoniously out of his way to get at Bolan. The distraction cost him dearly. The Executioner lunged his staff like pool cue into Nico's solar plexus. He put a good twist into the thrust, and the staff bent against Nico's massive frame. Every ounce of blood drained from the bouncer's face. His arms and legs folded tight against his body like an obese cricket. The blue suit shrieked as Nico fell on top of him in a spasming of agony.

Bolan continued down the corridor. A wall of sound hit him as he entered the disco. Nuevo Laredo's criminals, wanna-be criminals and the women who wanted to meet them writhed against one another in the cavernous enclosure. Bolan crossed the dance floor almost unnoticed save for lingering stares from more than a few of the women. He strode up to the VIP area. It was flanked by a pair of bouncers, but rather than human walls these men were built like professional wrestlers. Hours in the gym beneath heavy iron had produced their massive physiques. Skintight silk T-shirts and stretch jeans strained to contain their muscles like sausage casings. One had his black hair pulled back into a short ponytail while the other had a United States Marine-specification crew cut.

Bolan walked up smiling. "Hey, you two girls seen the Boy around?"

Buzz cut grinned with delighted, impending violence. "Chico, you must have a death wish or—"

Bolan flicked his cigar into Buzz cut's face.

Ponytail's jaw dropped and he started to raise his hands. "Hey, you can't—"

The staff blurred into motion. Ponytail wore his physique like a suit of armor, but every armor had its chinks. No matter how huge a man made his chest, no muscles covered the collarbones. The staff cracked like a gunshot across Ponytail's clavicle and snapped the slender bone like kindling. The big man's pupils screwed down to pinpricks of pain as his right arm and shoulder sagged away and unhinged at an unnatural angle. Ponytail fell to his knees while Buzz cut swatted at the smoke and ash in his eyes and lumbered forward. Bolan dropped to one knee and swung the staff like a baseball bat across Buzz cut's shins. Not a whole lot of muscle covered them, either. The muscleman's scream of agony was cut short as Bolan rose and ripped the brass-shod butt of the staff under his chin.

Bolan stepped over and past the two bouncers. Some women out on the dance floor had started screaming, but it was barely audible over the blare of the music. The soldier walked into the VIP area. On a small stage, two bottle blondes bumped and ground around a brass pole. A pair of darkened alcoves showed dimly lit figures engaged in lap dances. Off to one side, a fairly intense five-man game of Texas Hold 'Em was going on while another pair of men played pool. The room had its own bar, and waitresses in perilously low-cut outfits tottered about with trays laden with drinks.

"Hey! Any of you screw-heads seen the Boy?" Bolan boomed.

A security man moved in obliquely from Bolan's left. The soldier was aware of him, but the security guy was painfully unaware of the staff lying along the right side of Bolan's body and he made the mistake of pulling a sap rather than a gun. The staff spun in Bolan's hand and cracked across the man's mouth. The security man fell to his hands and knees mewling and spitting teeth.

A stripper screamed. A waitress dropped her tray of drinks and ran as fast as her high heels would allow. The pool players came at Bolan brandishing their cues. It was a poor choice of weapons. Bolan swung his staff like an ax. The leading gangster brought up his cue stick to block the blow, but the Chinese wax wood chopped the stick in two and split the man's forehead. He fell half conscious to the floor. His partner in crime was slightly smarter. He broke his own cue in two across his knee. Bolan dodged his head out of the way as the man threw the skinny end at his face and swung the heavy end at Bolan's head like a billy club.

Bolan swung his staff into the attack, but rather than blocking the weapon he whipped the tip of his staff across the gangster's hand. The club fell from crushed knuckles. He followed up by driving the brass butt down like a posthole digger. The thug happened to be wearing open-toed leather hurraches, and he howled as his big toe fractured. He hopped on one foot until Bolan rammed his staff into his stomach and folded him to the floor.

Bolan's voice rose to parade-ground decibels. "I said I'm looking for the Boy!"

Men were rising up from the poker table. Two were reaching under their coats. Bolan flung his staff sidearm, and it scythed through the air to clock the nearest gunman across his eyes and dropped him into his friend in a waterfall of spilled chips.

One of the poker players thrust his hand out at Bolan, and a switchblade clacked open to point accusingly. "Never shoulda thrown your stick, white boy! You're—"

Bolan had palmed a small cylindrical metal object out of his pocket immediately after the staff had left his hands. He interrupted the knifeman by baseballing it into his chest. The knifeman wheezed and sat back down in his seat. The object bounced off his sternum and fell with a clunk onto the green felt of the poker table. Everyone in the VIP area began screaming, running or hitting the floor.

The object happened to be a hand grenade.

Bolan snapped his mountaineering sunglasses out of his breast pocket and slid them on just as the grenade detonated.

The 7290M was half the size of a standard 7290 flash-bang tactical stun grenade. Nevertheless, the little grenade produced the same amount of sound and flash as its beer-can-sized brethren. Despite his shades, Bolan squinted as the grenade pushed eight million candela of light out of its twenty flash ports. Custom-fitted electronic earplugs defended Bolan from the deafening sound wave but the 175 decibels still struck his body like a blow. The thousand winking sparks of the pyrotechnic aftereffect fluttered about the poker table like someone had broken a piñata full of drunken fireflies.

Bolan dug into his pockets and began tossing out 7290Ms like party favors. Thunder and lightning rolled through the VIP area, and gangsters, gunmen, strippers and gun molls tottered and fell as they were temporarily blinded, deafened and disoriented. Bolan retrieved his stick and began delivering precision beatings to anyone who smelled like a criminal. The beatings were short, brutal and generally included the breaking of a bone or joint and the traumatic bruising of some randomly presented sensitive soft tissue of opportunity.

The door to the disco flew open, but Bolan was ready. Two men burst in with pistols drawn. They weren't disco muscle goons but genuine gang muscle. Except for the expensive cuts of their suits, they could have been accountants. They were killers, but even they stopped short and gaped in shock at the pyrotechnic sparks, the stench of high-explosives and the sea of beaten and broken Nuevo Laredo criminal royalty strewn about moaning on the carpeting.

Bolan bowled a 7290M between them like a boccie ball before they even saw him. They staggered away from the sound and light, and he disarmed each man by breaking his wrist. He then rammed each man below the belt buckle and left him fallen and urinating blood in front of the door.

Bolan's electronic earpieces filtered out traumatic noise, but at the same time on the more subtle levels they actually made his hearing far keener. Beneath the throb of the music out in the disco and the moaning and screaming of the injured and terrorized, he could hear sirens. El Nino wasn't in, and it was time to get out of town. Bolan walked up to a cringing waitress and borrowed a lipstick out of her apron. He walked to the mirror over the bar and wrote a quick message in red.

> El Nino,
> Yo, Babydick.
> When I find you,
> You're dead.
> El Hombre

Bolan pulled the adhesive strip off a pair of small radio transmitters and pressed one under the lip of the bar and another under the poker table. People out in the disco were shouting and screaming. He rolled his last grenade out into the disco, and the screaming began in earnest.

El Hombre emerged from the VIP room in a flash of thunder and lightning and strode out of the club the way he'd come.

5

"So…" There was little Kurtzman could do save shake his head. "You stomped an entire disco?"

"Only the VIP room, and I didn't stomp anyone," Bolan replied.

"You didn't stomp anybody." Kurtzman peered incredulously at the list of people admitted to the hospital the previous evening and the catalog of injuries. "So tell me, El Hombre, just because I'm the curious type. What exactly did you do?"

"I'd say I—" Bolan grinned as he searched for a word "—corporally punished a few malcontents."

"Corporally punished…" Kurtzman rolled that one around.

"In the process of intelligence gathering. Now, if I'd been in stompin-boy mode, someone might've actually gotten hurt."

Kurtzman loved his work, but he was just as glad that it was Barbara Price who wrote the after-action reports at Stony Man Farm. "So what's the plan? According to your report, Chapa wasn't there."

"No, but he'll be along soon."

Kurtzman smiled. "You bugged the club."

"I did, and three hours ago Chapa inspected the premises. He didn't sound too happy."

"Yeah, but neither he or any of his men were there."

"No, but I left him a note, and let everyone present know that I'm looking for him."

Kurtzman's smile widened. "So now Chapa's superiors will

be wondering why the mysterious El Hombre has returned and why he has a hard-on for the Butcher."

"That's about the size of it."

"You say you're expecting him presently?"

"Yeah, I parked the El Hombre-mobile outside. It's been getting a lot of attention."

Kurtzman didn't doubt it. If there were a more macho automobile south of the Rio Grande, the Stony Man computer genius would be curious to see it. "So you're just going to invite Chapa and his prom dates into the lion's den?"

"Not exactly. The safehouse the CIA was kind enough to provide is across the street."

Kurtzman rapidly checked his satellite map and imaging. "So you're…"

Bolan glanced around the room at the red velvet curtains and the round waterbed with the black satin sheets. "In the bordello across the street."

Kurtzman blinked. "And the—" he searched for the politically correct term "—employees? They're…"

"I gave the madam and the girls ten grand to close up early and go home." Bolan ran his eyes across the selection of weapons cluttering the bed. "I have the place to myself."

Kurtzman was equally thankful he had absolutely nothing to do with the accounting side of the Farm's activities. "Okay, so?"

Bolan sat up as he heard tires screeching out on the street. "Gotta go, Bear. Company's here."

"But—"

Bolan cut the connection and rose. He strode to the window and leaned out over the hollow iron pintle post he had bolted to the floor earlier in the evening and peered out the window. Two vans, two Land Rovers and a BMW had pulled up in front of the safehouse. The vans were standard Volkswagen delivery vehicles and the sliding doors slammed open to deliver the armed men within. Bolan scanned the Beamer and the two Rovers and recognized the subtle alterations of a Euro-Armor VIP kit. Euro-Armor wasn't quite as good as the protection packages that had been installed in Bolan's Bronco or the El Camino, but it would still take an RPG rocket or a .50-caliber machine gun bullet to crack their armor-glass or reinforced body-paneling.

Bolan grunted as he lifted the eighty-four-pound weight of the Browning .50-caliber machine gun off the love seat and lowered the mounting collar onto the pintle post. He clicked the ammo box onto the side, put the ammo belt into the feed and slapped down the feed cover. He then racked the action and chambered an armor-piercing incendiary round.

In the street below, men with AK-47 assault rifles were surrounding his car. Bolan picked up the two-foot-by-three-foot armor-steel gun shield and dropped it onto the mounting slots on either side of the pintle. A slot down the middle of the shield left just enough room for the barrel and the sights to look down it. Bolan grabbed the twin spade grips in his hands and put his thumbs on the trigger as he peered through the 3X optical sight.

The Butcher's back was squarely in his crosshairs. Chapa shouted out at the safehouse. "Come out, El Hombre! I know someone who wants to talk to you."

Bolan pressed the M-2's trigger, and Ma Deuce unleashed her thunder. Bullets the size of cigars slammed down into the Butcher's Beamer, shredding the armored body panels. The armor-piercing ammo drew laser lines in the night as Bolan walked them into the gas tank. The BMW's interior flashed orange as it ignited. The Executioner swung his sights onto the lead Land Rover. The SUV shuddered and buckled as Bolan stitched it from stem to stern. Gangsters scattered in all directions. A few of the crazy brave raised their rifles and fired back. Sparks shrieked off the big armor shield.

Ma Deuce thundered in response. The red lightning streaks of the tracers slanted down into Bolan's opponents. The machine-gun bullets were seven times the size of a pistol bullet and came in at Mach 3. The range was point-blank. Men came apart under the onslaught. The windows of the Beamer blew out as the gas tank detonated. The street glowed orange and red in a blood-spattered, burning approximation of hell.

Chapa took the opportunity to fall to the ground screaming and cowering.

Asphalt erupted in geysers as Bolan stitched a circle around Chapa. The soldier swung the heavy machine gun on its mount and tore the surviving vehicles to shreds. He dropped the .50 in its mount and went back to the ordnance-laden bed. Bolan selected two tear-gas grenades and a pistol. He pulled the pins and tossed the grenades out the window, then raised the pistol in both hands. It was a Beretta 92-FS Competition Model. The long, 150 mm barrel was counterweighted for perfect balance in target shooting. The glass lens of a holographic sight hung over the slide like a magnifying glass. Bolan put Chapa squarely in the screen and began methodically squeezing off shots.

Chapa flinched and coiled as Bolan shot him in both of his ostrich-skin cowboy boots. He clutched his head and howled as Bolan aerated his black ten-gallon hat. Chapa reared like a beestung horse and ran screaming down the street as Bolan shot him twice in the buttocks. The Executioner lowered his smoking pistol. The Beretta was loaded with the same infrared luminescent cartridges he had used on the U.S. side of the border.

Bolan brought a pair of infrared binoculars up to his eyes and watched Chapa disappear down the street with his hat, boots and buttocks giving off a pleasing glow.

The Butcher was a marked man.

Bolan dropped his pistol and punched a key on the laptop. "You got him, Bear?"

"That's Chapa running east?"

"Yeah."

"You marked his hat and boots?"

"Yeah, my local intel tells me that he wears them everywhere he goes. Part of his trademark. Right now he doesn't know what happened except a wholesale slaughter, and I'm betting he's not going to run his boots or his lid under an infrared scanner anytime soon."

"So why is his ass glowing?"

Bolan shrugged. "Bear, I gotta go."

"Good enough. We have satellites slaved to watch him 24/7. He moves—we can track him."

"Striker, out." Bolan cut the connection and packed his laptop and link in their case. He took a white-phosphorus grenade from the bed and pulled the pin. He walked to the door and the cotter lever pinged away as he opened his hand and dropped the grenade to the floor.

The bordello was burning out of control by the time Bolan walked out the back door. He held his breath as he walked through the tear-gas clouds and felt the sting in his eyes. Among the burning and shattered vehicles, the El Camino sat gleaming in untouched black and chrome. Bolan slid behind the wheel of his ride. Police and fire sirens howled ever nearer.

Bolan slammed the accelerator into the floor. Tires screamed and smoked on asphalt, and the El Camino's supercharged engine roared its challenge as it pulled out into the night.

Monterrey, Mexico

OMEGA WAS NOT PLEASED. He was of Latin complexion, with slightly slanted eyes and a hooked nose that betrayed Aztec origins. His black hair was pulled back into a short ponytail. A short black mustache and Vandyke beard emphasized his lantern jaw. His eyebrows were highly arched, the right more so, so that he looked like he was constantly questioning the world around him. The cruel curve of his lips told of finding the world and those in it wanting. People joked that in repose his eyebrows made him look like Spock from *Star Trek*. When his brows vee'd down in anger, he looked like Satan, himself.

Omega was angry. His right eyebrow was raised in question. Its inner edge was pulled down. His pale gray eyes stared, steel-like, out of his dark face in startling fashion. He had turned his eyes onto his right-hand man. "What the fuck is up with Chapa?"

Leland Scott steeled himself so as not to squirm under that unforgiving gaze. He was a big white man burned rust colored by the Mexican sun. "You want me to bring the Butcher in?"

"Fuck, no. The little shit is poison. I don't want him any-where near us."

Scott squirmed. Omega almost never swore, only when he was very angry and then in an almost conversational tone. It meant Omega was going to collect heads and make examples out of people. Scott was felt fairly secure in his position. He and Omega had known each other for a long time. They had put foot to ass on half the continents on Earth, and in recent years they had treated Mexico like pillaging Vikings. But at the end of the day, Scott had to admit he never truly knew what the bad man was thinking, and the look in those pale eyes still made him nervous. He drank a little too deeply from his rum and Coke. "So what do you want to do?"

"We've been played. First in Texas, and now it's come over the border." The steely eyes narrowed. "He's come over the border."

Scott scowled. "You think this observer asshole in Texas and El Hombre are one and the same?"

"How many one-man wrecking crews can there be along the border?"

Scott grinned. "Besides yourself?"

Omega gave the briefest of smiles. "Besides myself."

"Well, then, we've got this major shithead who calls him-self El Hombre, and…" Scott trailed off embarrassedly.

The right eyebrow arched. "And?"

"And…" Scott heaved a weary sigh. "The guitar player."

"You mean La Guitarista."

"Guitarista, El Mariachi, Desperado, Pancho Villa, whatever the goddamn hell he wants to call himself. He's starting to turn into a real goddamn nuisance."

"You have a line on his ass yet?"

"No, but I got feelers out. The son of a bitch can't pull this vigilante bullshit forever."

"Put a million on his head. I want a stop put to this comic-book crap. I want his Robin Hood shit over and his ass in the ground ASAP."

"A million?" Scott snorted. "You're gonna get the head of every mariachi from here to El Paso blown clean off."

"Good, I hate that shit anyway. It's about time the primates around here discovered Zeppelin."

Scott laughed. "So what about El Hombre wanting to kill Chapa?"

"If El Hombre wanted Chapa dead, he'd have been dead a long time ago. He had a .50-caliber and complete surprise. El Hombre's fucking with him and following him."

"They swept Chapa for bugs at the warehouse on the river." Scott shrugged. "He's clean."

"I don't give a shit. This Hombre freak is following him. Following him up the food chain. I know it in my bones."

"Yeah, but how's he doing it?"

"I don't know how, and right now I don't care. I want the scumbag dead."

"Who do you want to put on it?"

Omega's lips curved up into a wolflike smile. "The three of us."

Scott's brow furrowed. "The three of us?"

"That's right. You, me—" Omega looked meaningfully at the weapon leaning against Scott's chair "—and Old Bess."

Scott grinned from ear to ear. Old Bess was his personal preferred device for problem solving. It was a Remington 870 magnum shotgun that had been customized into a door-breaching device. The most glaring modification hung at the end of the brutally shortened eleven-inch barrel. A four-inch muzzle brake flared outward to terminate in a jagged crown of teeth-like spikes designed to bite into obstacles like door hinges and rip off doorknobs.

Scott generally used his Remington to rip open heads. Even Omega had admit his amusement as he looked at the weapon. Scott had painted the steel crown of thorns around the muzzle white like shark's teeth with red gums and put a pair of glaring eyes behind the compensator. The shotgun was painted like a WWII fighter plane, and the glaring eyes and the gaping 12-gauge maw surrounded by teeth was the last thing most people saw before Scott rammed their eyebrows into the middle of their brain and pulled the trigger.

"Okay, but how do we get him in skull-crushing range?"

"You know—" Omega steepled his hands before him in thought "—we're going to have to break some eggs on this one, and the general is turning into a pain in my ass. El Hombre wants to work his way up the chain? Fine. We'll give him a good five-step jump up the ladder, some bait he really can't refuse and then…"

"And then?" Scott prompted.

Omega stood. "Then he gets to meet the chairman of the board."

6

The El Camino rumbled through the streets like a chrome-plated predator. Bolan glanced over at the laptop mounted onto his dash and rechecked the file Kurtzman had sent him. The Butcher had gone to ground, so his prey this night was Ernesto Anila, Chapa's right-hand man. Anila's stats had him two inches shorter than Bolan, but his shoulders were ax-handle wide. He had been a *luchador*, one of Mexico's masked professional wrestlers. His wrestling name had been El Corbeta Plata, "The Silver Corvette." He had driven a silver Corvette Stingray to every auditorium he wrestled in, and his silver mask had been sewn into a convincing effigy of the sharklike front profile of the famed sports car. Drugs and multiple charges of sexual assault had finally gotten him thrown off the circuit. In the file photo he wasn't wearing his mask. His nose had been broken so many times it was like a flattened squid tacked to his face. Both his ears were deformed cauliflowers. He grinned into the police camera, exposing missing teeth and not a care in the world. His black hair was cropped short on top and then splayed across his shoulders in a spectacular mullet.

Bolan read Anila's stats again. His stock-in-trade had been launching off the top rope and doing spectacular aerial acrobatics. His exposed neck and shoulders were packed with muscle. Bolan had been on the wrong end of wrestlers before. They were about the most dangerous opponent one could ask for in a physical confrontation. Years of wrestling six nights a week made them incredibly tough and inured to pain. Even the smallest ones had the sinewy strength of orangutans. Though almost all their moves in the ring were fake, they could become deadly earnest in a real confrontation.

Donato Chapa had given Ernesto Anila a new lease on life. Mexico revered its wrestlers. A wrestler gone bad was just the sort of star-power muscle Chapa required to enhance his reputation and awe his competition, and the diminutive Butcher enjoyed basking in the wrestler's machismo. Rumor was Anila was Chapa's personal trainer in the gym, his right-hand man and personal bodyguard. Rumor was, when the Butcher went to work with his knives, it was Corbeta Plata who held the victims down.

Rumor was he took an unhealthy enjoyment in his job.

The black El Camino rumbled toward the east side of town. Kurtzman had tracked Chapa from the battle at the bordello to Anila's estate in the suburbs. A few hours later, Chapa had gone back downtown. Kurtzman still had his satellite eye watching Chapa's penthouse, but he hadn't moved. Bolan needed the Butcher moving. He figured an interview with Chapa's right-hand man might send Chapa running in more interesting directions.

Bolan rolled past Anila's house. It was a pastel stucco, glass-brick monstrosity of modest proportions for a criminal. With his window cracked, he could hear angry Spanish rap music blaring at deafening decibels. "What have you got for me, Bear?"

"I have four vehicles up in the drive circle. A silver Corvette and a yellow Hummer, both belong to Anila. There's also an unidentifed '68 Cadillac and a '73 Firebird Trans Am. The angle of the drive is preventing the satellite from getting license plates, but I'm betting Anila has company."

"Anything else?"

"Yeah, I have three randomly moving heat sources. They're dogs of some kind. No handler present. By their patterns, I don't think they're guard trained."

Bolan frowned. Ernesto Anila was just the sort of guy to let untrained animals out at night. The animals' only training or socialization would have been in fight pits. They wouldn't bark to warn, hold an intruder at bay or try to immobilize. They would simply maul and kill any man, woman, child or beast that came into their territory until Anila chained them again at dawn.

"Roger that, Bear."

Bolan pulled over, reached into his gear bag and scooped his stick out of the back seat. Anila's security suite was predictable in its barbarism. Besides the vicious dogs, he'd cemented bottles all along the top of his adobe perimeter wall and then broken them to make jagged shards to discourage anyone climbing over. Bolan flopped his shooting mat over the top of the wall. The padded mat was Kevlar on the bottom, and there was no chance the glass would penetrate. Bolan tossed his stick over the wall, took two running steps and heaved himself up and over.

He landed on his feet in a crouch. The dogs were already burning toward him. They were pit bulls, and they didn't even bother to bark. They were little more than muscle, fangs and aggression. Drool flew from their jaws as they arrowed toward him in wedge formation, snarling with bloodlust for the mauling.

Bolan drew a black cylinder the size of a security flashlight out his bag and closed his eyes as he pressed the trigger. Twin strobes pulsed out a one-second flash of six-million-candela power. At the same time, a ten-foot fan of pressurized industrial-strength citronella-oil compound sprayed the oncoming wedge of canine violence. The light temporarily blinded them, but the spray was the deal breaker. The average dog had twenty-five times the number of olfactory receptors in its nasal cavities compared to humans, and citronella was one of dogdom's absolute least favorite smells. The citronella spray was the equivalent of pouring a rotten-egg smoothie down both a human's nostrils. Bolan reversed the cylinder in his hand to expose the prongs of the stun gun, but there was no need. Between the blinding flash and the olfactory overload, the dogs tumbled over their front paws and fell squirming, sneezing and wretching to the lawn.

Bolan had no desire to harm the dogs. They couldn't help

the fact that their master was a criminal. They had scented Bolan as they came in, and for the rest of their lives they would associate his smell with the onset of the olfactory overload that was citronella.

Bolan scooped up his stick and walked through the shuddering pack of sensory-devastated dogs. He went along the side of the house and came to the back patio. The sliding glass door was vibrating with the sound of the music inside. Bolan grabbed the handle and gave the door a slight push.

Anila was either too dumb or too macho to lock his doors. Bolan took a moment to pull on a pair of well-worn brown leather work gloves from his bag and then slid the door open and stepped inside. A cold smile crossed his lips as he walked into the living room.

Maybe Anila was just too tweaked to care.

Anila was the smallest of the three men seated around a black glass coffee table shaped like an amoeba. One man had a shaved head and was built like a bodybuilder. The other was as fat as a sumo wrestler, and even though he was Hispanic he had his hair done up in a samurai topknot. The Silver Corvette's face was planted nearly on the top of the table, and his mullet hung down around his face like a shroud as he snorted a line of crystal meth without the benefit of a straw. A pair of women of apparent loose moral virtue hung on his cantaloupe-sized shoulders, but they seemed much more intent on getting some of the meth themselves than having any real affection for Anila.

The sea of beer bottles and shot glasses implied the party had been going on for a while. In Bolan's experience, when big men went bad, alcohol and speed were the drugs of choice. Ernesto Anila sat back, rubbing his nose and sniffing. Crystals glittered like fairy dust in the fringe ends of his mullet. He tugged at his mustache and peered at Bolan with pupils the size of pinpricks.

Bolan smiled in a friendly fashion. "Yo, ape-drape."

Anila blinked.

"Yeah, you." Bolan sighed. "Yeah, I'm talking to you."

Anila tried to make sense of the apparition that had materialized in his living room.

Bolan took in Anila's pupils, his bleary gaze and the circles under his eyes. He was pretty gone. He might very well have been tweaking for the past two days, and that might explain why he wasn't with Chapa. Bolan stabbed his staff into the CD player, and the sudden silence was deafening.

Bolan tried again. "You know who I am?"

Anila got it. His eyes narrowed and his lips peeled back to reveal brown teeth rotted by smoking amphetamines. The women screamed as he lunged up and overturned the table in a crash of bottles. "You're El Hombre!"

"That's me." Bolan tapped his staff into his left hand with the patient rhythm of a metronome. "Now you're going to tell me where Chapa is, or I'm going to beat you like a rug." Bolan nodded toward the other men. "You and your little mook amigos."

The mooks rose up in anger and stepped into a V formation beside Anila who twitched his head toward the four-hundred-pounder. "You know something, you skinny yanqui fuck? Sumo is gonna shove that stick up your ass and hand you to me like a Popsicle." He snapped his chin at Bolan. "Get him, Sumo!"

Sumo barreled forward. He was surprisingly light on his feet for all his bulk, and beneath the rolls of fat he clearly had the power to break a moose across his knee. The bodybuilder didn't wait for orders. He charged in right behind his obese buddy. Bolan laced his fingers together and cracked his knuckles in preparation. However, he wasn't loosening up for a brawl.

Bolan was activating his gloves.

The interior mitten was insulating Kevlar. Careful examination of the open palm and fingers would reveal metal disks—each about half the size of a camera battery—embedded in the leather in rows of three between each knuckle. They were skillfully camouflaged with conducting metallic paint. The battery packs were hidden in elastic wrist gathers.

Sumo came on like a freight train, his hands held defensively before him, clearly willing to take any blow Bolan might deliver just to get in range and then crush him like a bug. Bolan's right hand seized Sumo's outstretched wrist and sent 750,000 volts through his blubbery body. Sumo lost control of his limbs, but his momentum kept him moving forward. Bolan took the opportunity to torque Sumo's arm around in a short, hard circle and send his whalelike mass hurtling on into the fireplace. Sumo shrieked as he was singed and rolled back onto the bearskin rug, blistered and shuddering.

The bodybuilder came on. He lurched forward awkwardly without the grace or speed of a wrestler. However, he was high on meth and could probably bench press five hundred pounds, and Bolan wasn't in the mood to trade blows with him. The Executioner flicked his staff into his right hand and dropped to one knee beneath the muscleman's pawing hands. Bolan's left hand shot up between his adversary's legs and made a fist. The bodybuilder screamed as Bolan sent 750,000 volts through his steroid-shriveled sack. Bolan flipped him over his shoulder and on top of Sumo.

Bolan stood up without missing a beat and smiled at Anila as he resumed tapping his staff into his palm. "You gonna sing for me, or do you want a piece of the action, too?"

Anila's lower lip quivered in shock.

"Oh, I'm sorry." Bolan quirked a sympathetic eyebrow and held up his staff. "Is this what's bothering you? Here." Bolan dropped the staff to the floor and beckoned Anila in. "Is that better?"

Anila's fists creaked. His knuckles went white. Veins stood out in his neck and arms as his entire body purpled and clenched like a fist. Bolan stood relaxed and ready and smiled at Anila in infuriating fashion. The stun-gun functions were one-trick wonders, but they weren't the only trick Bolan had up his gloves.

Spittle flew from Anila's lips as he screamed in berserk fury. He charged forward with his pupils blown and his hands curled into animal claws.

Bolan's foot flicked out and raked the top of his staff. It rolled back toward him like a cue ball with a lot of English. It rolled on top of Bolan's toes, and he snapped his foot to pop the staff back up into his hands. He didn't want Anila dead, and no normal beating would stop him.

Bolan flung the staff outward with both hands as if he were passing a basketball. Anila swatted the staff aside like a toothpick, but the action made him drop his left hand. Bolan hit Anila in the jaw with a right-hand lead that had every ounce of his two hundred pounds behind it. The second trick up Bolan's gloves was that the knuckles were loaded with lead.

Anila's jaw shattered.

The Executioner's left hand flew forward in a bolo punch that shattered Anila's cheekbone. The flesh and bones of his face sagged into a nonhuman configuration as he reeled stupidly. Bolan grabbed his opponent's right arm and yanked it straight. His fist rose in a hammer fist and fell to snap the ex-wrestler's collarbone. He turned the unhinged arm over and shattered the elbow. Bolan took Anila's wrist in both hands and shattered it. Anila fell to his knees in shock.

Ernesto Anila's days as a leg breaker for Chapa were over.

Bolan dropped him and turned to Sumo and the Muscleman. The two men were beginning to stir. He methodically hammered them unconscious. Their was no vindictiveness in it. They were scumbags. They would be another chapter in the myth of El Hombre, and they were going to motivate Chapa to scurry for his life toward his superiors.

The reward for their suffering was their lives.

Bolan pulled off his gloves and stuffed them into his back pocket and stepped over Sumo. Bolan took out a thick-point, blue permanent marker and wrote on the mirror over the mantel:

> Yo, Needle-dick.
> Don't make me chase you.
> You run?
> You'll just die tired.
> El Hombre

He peeled the adhesive strip off the back of an electronic bug and pushed it underneath the mirror frame. There were bound to be some interesting conversations between the people who read the message in the next twenty-four hours.

7

"You gotta bring me in!" The Butcher's already high voice was rising toward a shriek.

Omega sat watching Chapa across a secure satellite link. Chapa sat in Ernesto Anila's house. He was being babysat by an acerbic, balding man in an exquisitely tailored English-cut suit. Juliano Mondragon looked like a London banker, but he was in actuality one of the highest profile criminal-defense lawyers in Mexico City. He had no idea who Omega was. Omega was just a voice on the phone that caused suitcases of money to appear. Mondragon was a famous and powerful jurist and had the ear of the president. He was a perfect cutout. A man like Chapa would have every reason to seek his services, and anyone going after Mondragon was going to start an international incident. Mondragon smoked French cigarettes and watched Chapa squirm with detached interest.

Across the video link Omega could see Chapa staring into a blank screen and listening to his words through a voice scrambler. Omega had read the writing on the mirror over the mantel, and he had a copy of the medical reports in his hand. He'd also read a police report from a detective who did not know that Omega owned him. Of the three victims, Juanito "Sumo" Suarez was the only one with his jaw still firmly attached to his head. According to Sumo, El Hombre had simply walked into Anila's house and beaten the three of them half to death.

Omega scowled at the blood workups in the medical reports. All three men tested positive for high levels of alcohol and methamphetamines in their bloodstreams. Still, between the three of them, they should have stomped a mud hole in this El Hombre and taken turns walking it dry. If Omega himself had to take out any of these men, he would do it with a head shot at six hundred yards or a .44 Magnum at point-blank range. El Hombre had done it in hand-to-hand combat, against all three of them, at the same time.

Apparently, he hadn't even bothered to use his stick.

"You gotta bring me in!" Chapa whined.

Chapa wasn't coming in anywhere. Anyone near him got shot, blown up or badly beaten. "Nino?"

Chapa flinched at the hated nickname but cringed obsequiously. "Yeah, boss?"

"Who is this guy and what did you do to piss him off?"

"Boss! I swear! I—"

"I mean besides being a sick little fuck. Just what did you do?"

The Butcher's voice rose to a panicked squeak. "I don't know!"

Omega leafed through another file. El Hombre had apparently rolled through Nuevo Laredo before. It appeared he'd been after Mara Salvatrucha, and he'd shagged them rotten. In a way, Omega almost owed El Hombre. By smashing Mara Salvatrucha, he'd created a power vacuum in Nuevo Laredo—a situation that Omega had exploited to his immense profit. But El Hombre was now sticking his nose in Omega's business and was officially a pain in the ass.

Omega turned off the voice scrambler. "Doni?"

Chapa started in surprise at the solicitous tone and the use of his name. "Yeah, boss?"

"You're a valuable business asset to me."

Chapa swallowed with difficulty. If he'd been a puppy, his tail would have been wagging. Hope smeared across his face. "Thanks, boss."

"So I'm going to take care of this El Hombre personally."

Chapa wrung his hands. "Thanks, boss!"

"Nuevo Laredo is too hot for you right now, and I'm not disrespecting you, you understand, but I can't bring you in. This yanqui asshole is trailing you."

Chapa's face fell. "I...understand."

"So I'm going to send you to the general."

Chapa sat up straighter. "The general?"

"If you aren't safe surrounded by a hundred of his men, then you sure as hell won't be safe with me. Let me kill this asshole, and then we go back to business as usual."

Chapa beamed like a kid at Christmas.

Omega smiled like a hunter in the Amazon gentling a goat he'd staked out to bring the jaguars out of the jungle. "You okay with that plan, Doni?"

"Yes, yes! Thank you, boss! Thanks for looking out for me!"

"I'll contact the general. Stick with Mondragon until I call you," Omega directed.

"You got it, boss! I'll—"

Omega cut the link.

Scott looked on with disgusted awe. "Boss, you are one sick fuck."

Omega shrugged modestly. "Scotty, drop a line to the general. Tell him he's going to have a guest, but stroke him and tell him no one will dare do anything."

"You got it, boss." Scott's brutal face was smug. "Then you want me to get a bunch of the boys waiting in the wings?"

"You got it, Scotty." Omega considered his immediately available assets. "Platoon strength. Let's finish this shit."

"GENERAL MARIA SIMON Bolivar del Vincente-Lopez Lothario." Aaron Kurtzman shook his head. It was quite a mouthful. If General Lothario hadn't been such an utterly unrepentant scumbag and betrayed Mexico and the United States, he would have been quite a character. If someone in the U.S. had done a simple pencil drawing of him, most people would have considered it an ethnically insensitive cartoon. He was short, fat, bald headed, sleepy-eyed with a handle-bar mustache Pancho Villa would have envied and wore his trademark Ray-Ban

sunglasses indoors and outdoors, morning, noon and night. He
wore an incredible mass of service ribbons and decorations on
his uniform, and a very surprising number of them had been
earned the hard way.

Bolan read Lothario's file. Despite appearances, he was a
very powerful and dangerous man. He was on the Pentagon's
watch list, but there was nothing to be done about it. Lothario
was a fixture in Mexican crime and Mexican politics. Politically, he was a chameleon, able to shift sides with apparent ef-
fortlessness. If General Lothario met an opponent he could not
easily cow or kill, he made remarkably reasonable and mutu-
ally profitable deals with them, making them rich beyond their
dreams as he slowly took over the operations for himself. Rumors about him abounded, but he shed scandal and inquiry like
Teflon. In the military hierarchy, he had let other generals become commanders of the regular army, fat, dumb and happy
with the usual perks and graft.

Lothario didn't make waves as long as his special forces
were left alone. In the 1990s, the United States had devoted
huge sums of money to train, equip and back Lothario's new
Aztec Raptor Company to become the tip of the spear in the
War on Drugs in Mexico. Once trained, the Raptors had gone
to work for the crime cartels they had been sworn to fight,
bringing Special Forces doctrine, weapons and tactics into the
internecine warfare between the Mexican crime lords. They had
done so to their immense profit, and according to rumor, they
had done so with General Lothario's blessing and always sent
him his cut up the line if they didn't outright take over a criminal operation and put it under his jurisdiction.

Bolan punched up another file. It showed a platoon of men
lined up for a photo. The front row had taken a knee. The men
wore plain black battle-dress uniforms. Their only adornments
were gold shoulder patches featuring the stylized head of a
golden eagle. The eagle held a snake in its beak. Bolan recognized the scenery behind the men posing. The picture had been
taken in the United States at Fort Benning. Crouching among
the Aztec Raptors were U.S. Army Ranger training instructors

in green fatigues. Everyone was grinning into the camera. The Raptors had been trained by the U.S. Rangers. They were Special Forces qualified, and rumor was they acted as General Lothario's personal death squad.

Bolan considered the latest satellite intelligence. "Chapa ran to Lothario?"

"He's at his hacienda. Why? You don't buy it?"

"Lothario isn't Chapa's boss. Street crime in Nuevo Laredo isn't the general's style. Someone else sent him there."

"So you think he's just a babysitter, an outsider doing a favor for somebody?"

Bolan's instincts spoke to him. "I wouldn't say he's an outsider. He's definitely part of the chain, but he's quite a few steps up the ladder from the Butcher."

"Well…" Kurtzman pondered. "Maybe they think no one would dare go after Chapa if he's under the general's wing."

"Maybe." Bolan smelled a trap.

"You think it's a trap?"

"I'm going to have to recon the situation. I'm going in soft. Contact the CIA. This is what I'm going to need."

THE AZTEC RAPTOR SERGEANT drove up to the gate of General Lothario's hilltop compound. The military-style jeep lurched to a halt, and the sergeant jumped out wearing his dress uniform, with a dispatch bag beneath his arm. The Aztec Raptor Company private at the gate instantly snapped to attention and saluted. The sergeant snapped his hand up in a sharp return salute and then slashed his hand around in a knife-hand strike to the side of the private's neck. The blow buckled the private to his knees. The second knife-hand strike left him lying senseless on the gravel.

Bolan swiftly gagged and hog-tied the soldier and then rolled him down the hill into the drainage ditch paralleling the road.

His cover was very slim. He wore the formal dress uniform and shoulder badge of the Aztec Raptors, and a Heckler & Koch P-7 M-13 pistol was holstered on his belt. Blue-mirrored aviator glasses hid his eyes, and a sergeant's dress cap was pulled down low over his head. Spray-on tanning solution had stained the skin of his hands and face to a deep mahogany, and a black mustache adorned his upper lip. Bolan moved with command presence and looked every inch like a battle-hardened Mexican special-forces sergeant on official business.

The problem was that the special forces of all countries were small, tight-knit and clannish. The Aztec Raptors were built on the U.S. Special Forces model of a strong company. At full strength, they would have 190 men. The good news was that special-forces groups around the world were sergeant heavy, usually with a sergeant leading each squad. However, that still meant that there were only nineteen or twenty of them, and most of the men would know most of the sergeants by sight. Bolan could only pass the briefest of scrutiny by the enlisted men and none at all by the officers.

He strode purposefully into the compound. A limousine, several sports cars, and a Mexican Marine APC 70 wheeled light-armored vehicle were parked in the drive. Bolan walked straight to the front door of the three-story hacienda. A couple of civilians in suits were standing in the vast foyer. One he recognized from Stony Man files. He was the lawyer who had been accompanying Chapa for the past forty-eight hours, Juliano Mondragon. Bolan's instincts told him the other man was a legal assistant or aide in Mondragon's employ. They lawyers looked up as Bolan walked in and gave him the briefest of nods before they resumed smoking cigarettes and talking. Bolan followed his nose to the scent of air freshener and popped into a hallway bathroom.

Bolan stripped off the dress uniform. Beneath it he wore a French-cut, French-blue tropical-weight suit that even Mondragon's tailor would have approved of. Bolan emptied the contents of the courier pouch and turned it inside out to reveal the reversible dark suede exterior. Some of the contents he put back. Bolan threaded the stubby tube of a sound suppressor onto the muzzle of the P-7 M-13 and tucked it away into a shoulder holster. He applied a short beard that met his false mustache in a Vandyke and slicked his hair back with gel.

Bolan had gone from special-forces sergeant to gangster lawyer in five minutes.

It was time to do a little fishing.

OMEGA PICKED UP HIS PHONE on the first ring. "This is Omega. Report."

"Omega, this is Raptor Vision 2. We have a situation at the general's compound." Raptor Vision 1-6 were the Aztec Raptor's sniper section. RV 1-4 were currently watching General Lothario's compound through some very high-power optics in rotating six hours shifts 24/7.

"What kind of a situation?"

"A man in a sergeant's uniform drove up to the compound, assaulted and subdued the gate guard and entered the compound."

"What kind of vehicle?"

"A jeep. I ran the markings through the database. It doesn't belong to you, the general, nor is it part of Raptor battalion inventory."

"Could you identify the sergeant?"

"No, the Raptor badge on his shoulder was identifiable, but his back was turned most of the time. My first instinct is that he is not one of us."

"Have you informed the general?"

"No, sir. I thought it best to inform you first."

"Excellent, Raptor Vision 2. What kind of reaction has there been on the compound?"

"No alarms. No movement. At this point, I believe the infiltration has been completely successful."

"Very good, Raptor Vision 2. Keep me informed of any change in situation status. If the target attempts to leave the compound, you have the green light."

"Green light confirmed. Target to be terminated upon leaving compound. Raptor Vision 2, out."

Omega clicked his satellite phone shut. Scott looked up curiously from running a rag over his shotgun. "And?"

"And by the pricking of my thumbs, El Hombre has successfully penetrated the good General's security."

"He attacked Lothario?"

"He went in soft, dressed as an Aztec Raptor."

Scott snorted. "They didn't recognize him? And they let him in?"

"He's good, and he got in."

"You gonna tell the general?"

Omega checked his watch. "In a minute or two." He walked out of his personal tent and went to the large assembly tent. Forty men in the black battle-dress uniforms of the Aztec Raptor company lounged, smoking, drinking coffee and cleaning weapons. They shot to attention as Omega entered the room. Omega lazily lit a cigar and blew a stream of smoke up toward the ceiling of the circus-sized tent. *"Che amigos!"*

Forty very dangerous men nodded and grinned expectantly.

"Any of you boys heard of this El Hombre asshole?"

Every man in the tent had heard of El Hombre. As they had waited in the assembly tent and cleaned their already gleaming weapons and sharpened their already razor-honed knives, the topic of El Hombre and what each man in Omega's special cadre would do to the yanqui son of a bitch when he got his hands or his sights on him was a popular topic of conversation.

"Well…" Omega examined his cigar and spoke distractedly. "I just happen to know where the yanqui bastard is."

The Raptors leaned forward eagerly like the predators they were.

"Can you believe the asshole is in the general's compound?"

This was met with open shock.

"He took out Private Gonzalez at the gate. He's dressed like a Raptor company sergeant."

Dangerous, angry muttering moved through the tent like a gathering storm.

"This son of a bitch thinks he's the Man," Omega continued. "He's like every other yanqui jackass. He thinks he came come to our country and do anything he wants to anybody he wants, and there won't be any consequences. I think he's wrong—" Omega shrugged modestly "—but I don't think he will listen to me."

The men laughed.

"But I think he will listen to you."

Cheers rang out.

Omega's voice boomed. "I want this son of a bitch! Alive or dead, but I want him! I'm tired of these goddamn Americans coming here and acting like they can do anything they want! I want him shipped back across the border in a box! In a lot of little boxes! El Hombre? He's dead! Dead! Dead!" Omega pumped his fist into the sky. *"¡Viva la Raptors!"*

The tent thundered with the response. *"¡Viva la Raptors!"*

Omega shoved both fists into the sky. *"¡Arriba, Raptors! Arriba!"*

The Aztec Raptors scooped up their weapons and deployed by squads. Engines roared into life and the rotors of helicopters began to beat the sky.

Scott grinned, his shotgun lazily tilted across his shoulders. "Nice."

"Thanks." Omega blew a smoke ring. "You lead them, and please ensure that the general dies tragically."

"You got it, boss."

"And Scotty?"

Scott turned back. "Yeah, boss."

Omega dropped his cigar and crushed it beneath his heel. "Bring me the asshole's head."

8

Bolan walked into the foyer, sat down at a little computer table and plugged in a laptop from his diplomatic pouch. The attorney Juliano Mondragon and his aide were still there. They peered at him narrowly as he put on a pair of rimless reading glasses. Bolan looked up distractedly. "Excuse me. This is very important."

Mondragon grunted condescendingly and deigned to accept Bolan's existence. The General was a man with a lot going on, and Mondragon was not privy to all of it. He had no idea who Bolan was, but he might be an important flunky.

Bolan plugged in his earpiece and adjusted the hidden camera. "Bear, I got Juliano Mondragon here in the house. You got a read on the second guy?"

"Checking, Striker." Back in Virginia, Kurtzman ran his Mondragon file. "Affirmative. Louis Arguello. Junior partner in Mondragon's firm and his right-hand man. Particularly in shady situations."

Bolan had enough Spanish to get around though his accent was far from perfect. But he could overhear enough of the lawyers' conversation to understand that Chapa was their chief concern.

As the two men rose to walk away, Bolan typed, "Gotta go." He planted a bug under the edge of the little table and put his laptop in his bag. Bolan took out his cell phone and listened and nodded thoughtfully at nothing as he walked upstairs. He peered out a window and saw a small helicopter parked out on the back lawn. Down the hall, a pair of soldiers stood guard outside a bedroom door. Bolan walked toward them still nodding and grunting into his phone.

"Goddamn it!" General Lothario burst out a room halfway down the hall. He was flanked by a phalanx of men in Raptor black. The guards outside the door snapped to attention. Lothario whirled on them. "El Hombre is here! He's dressed like a Raptor sergeant! I am sealing the compound! You two, don't let Chapa out of your sight. The son of a bitch will be coming for him!" The two men saluted and cradled their G-36 rifles.

Bolan didn't have the time to wonder how he'd been discovered. Lothario turned and gave Bolan a sudden scowl. "Who the fuck are you?"

Bolan hunched his shoulders and let his jaw wobble once or twice. "Señor Mondragon, he—"

Bolan shrank against the wall as the general stormed past. "Get in there with Chapa! Keep him calm!"

Bolan went to the bedroom and one of the guards assisted him with a shove. "Keep the little son of a bitch quiet!" The door slammed behind him.

Donato "The Butcher" Chapa glanced up blearily from his chair. A soccer game was blaring on a plasma screen TV that nearly took up an entire wall. A nickel-plated Colt .45 and a half-empty bottle of whiskey lay on a little table next to him. "What's going on?"

Bolan shrugged. "El Hombre is here."

"Here!" Chapa spilled his drink as he lunged to his feet. "Where?"

"Right here."

"Where?" Chapa's head snapped around in panic. "And who the hell are you?"

Bolan switched to English. "Look real close, needle-dick." The Executioner's blue eyes blazed into Chapa's. His lips skinned back from his teeth like a wolf. "Are you sure you don't know who I am?"

In a single, lightning-bolt instant of horrifying clarity, the

Butcher knew exactly who the stranger was and all that his presence implied. Bolan had never seen a conniption before, but Chapa gave it a run for his money. The blood drained from his face and at the same time his eyes flew wide and bulged right out of his head. The Butcher's limbs attempted to flee in four separate directions at the same time. Spit flew from his lips as he made a sound like a teakettle.

Bolan was already in motion as dim thoughts of the .45 occurred to Chapa.

The Executioner's left hand pistoned into three, hard, quick jabs. Chapa's head rubbernecked as the blows connected with his chin. He dropped like a man whose legs had been magically removed.

Bolan spent a couple of heartbeats considering his options. He had smelled a trap of some kind, but he had not thought the enemy was playing for these kind of stakes. Sacrificing Chapa was a no-brainer, but they also seemed ready to sacrifice both the general and Mondragon. Whoever had spotted him had done it from the outside. Bolan suspected there was an observation post and at least one very powerful rifle on one of the surrounding hillsides. Guards would be coming upstairs any second.

Bolan stuck his head out the door. "Hey, Chapa's fainted," he called in Spanish.

The two guards pushed their way into the room. The one who had shoved Bolan pushed him aside and again snarled, "Goddamn it!" He slung his rifle and bent over Chapa. The Butcher lay on the carpet with his eyes rolling.

"Help me."

Bolan's knife hand chopped down into the back of his neck like an ax. The guards were Aztec Raptors and highly trained. The second guard recovered from his surprise in an eye blink and started to bring his rifle to bear, but Bolan had already closed the distance. Bolan's elbow rammed between the sentry's eyebrows like the pneumatic gun at the end of a slaughter chute. The rifle fell from his hands as his head snapped back. Bolan's second elbow broke his jaw, and the third took the Raptor in the temple as he fell to make sure he stayed down.

The big American slung their short assault rifles across his back and stuffed spare magazines into his jacket and pouch. He opened the bedroom window and then went over to the TV table and picked up Chapa's .45. Bolan popped the magazine and racked the action to eject the round in the chamber. Chapa sat up and rubbed his jaw. He shrieked as Bolan walked over to him holding his own gun.

"Shut up."

Chapa clamped his mouth shut.

"Listen, there's a helicopter outside. You and me are going to walk out to it, natural as can be, and go for a little ride. You keep it together and don't screw this up, I'm going to let you live."

Chapa looked close to tears. "What did I ever do to you?"

Bolan tossed Chapa his empty pistol. "Don't screw this up."

Chapa jerked away from the gun.

"Pick it up."

The Butcher grabbed the .45 and shoved it at Bolan with a scream. "Die!"

The hammer fell upon an empty chamber with a sad, impotent click.

Bolan's eyes narrowed as he laced his fingers together and cracked his knuckles. His hands dropped into loosely curled fists as he loomed over Chapa. "What did I say about not screwing this up?"

Chapa dropped the pistol like a dead rat. "You'll let me live!"

"I said pick it up."

Chapa grabbed the pistol.

"Stand up." Bolan yanked him to his feet by his shirtfront. Chapa looked at Bolan and at the pistol. The Executioner read his mind. "Chapa, you try and hit me with that and it's going to take a proctologist to remove it." Bolan thrust his face into Chapa's. "And you're still going to have to walk out of here with me. Like a man, or mincing sidesaddle. Choice is yours."

"Like a man!" Chapa squeaked.

Bolan clamped a hand on Chapa's shoulder and spun him

to face the door. He pressed the silenced muzzle of the P-7 M-13 pressed into his lower spine. "Let's go for a walk."

Cold sweat squeezed out of every pore in the Butcher's body in a wave of sick, watery fear. Bolan opened the door and shoved the man forward. Four Raptors stood at the end of the hall in sentry position. Half the doors in the hall were open. Raptors were moving in pairs sweeping the house room by room. A man with sergeant's stripes stood among the men at the landing talking into a radio.

A man shouted from an open room three doors down. "Guest bedroom! Clear!"

Another shout came from directly opposite. "Hall bath! Clear!"

The sergeant took one look at Chapa and Bolan and purpled with rage. "What the fuck do you think you're doing? You want to get shot! Get the f—"

Bolan snaked his silenced pistol over Chapa's shoulder and shot the sergeant in the face. The pistol stuttered in whispering hiccups as he double-tapped the three sentries around him. Chapa ruined the silent kills by screaming as hot brass from the pistol ejected into his face. Bolan propelled the Butcher forward. A Raptor burst out of the bathroom, and Bolan hammered him back. Glass shattered as the dead Raptor fell through the shower stall with three bullets in his chest.

Raptors came out of the spare bedroom. A point man armed with a pistol and two men with shotguns spread out on either side. Bolan kept his pistol out of sight behind Chapa and yelled and pointed down the hall. "The bedroom! The bedroom!"

The Aztec Raptors loped down the hall like wolves.

Bolan reaped them like wheat. He ejected his spent magazine and slammed in his spare. Bolan pressed the smoking muzzle against the back of the Butcher's head. "Chapa, I need you to start screaming '*He's upstairs.*'"

Chapa gibbered.

Bolan screwed the muzzle painfully into the back of the Butcher's skull. "Don't screw this up."

"He's upstairs!" Chapa shrieked loud enough to wake the dead. "He's upstairs!"

Boots hammered the stairs at the end of the hallway. Bolan and Chapa moved to meet them. "In the bedroom," Bolan barked. "Where you and I first met."

The Raptors hit the second floor in squad strength. A corporal led them, and his face went cold at the sight of the carnage in the hallway.

"The bedroom! The bedroom!"

The Raptors moved toward the master bedroom, two by two. Two point men lunged in with pistols leveled in both hands. They shouted back as Bolan pulled Chapa toward the stairs. "Bedroom clear! Two men down! The window! He went out the window!" Bolan could hear someone shouting into a radio in response downstairs.

"Negative! Back windows are being watched! Sweep again!" Bolan propelled Chapa to the landing.

Over a dozen rifles were pointed up at them. Even the general, Mondragon and Arguello were pointing pistols. Mondragon shook his head. "No, he doesn't work for me."

The general grinned. "El Hombre, I presume."

Bolan leaped back and dragged Chapa back with him. Riflefire erupted in response downstairs.

The general roared out, "Raptors! He's behind you! Behind you!"

Chapa howled as Bolan grabbed him by his belt and collar. "You said you'd let me live! You said you'd—" Chapa's voice broke into a keening scream as Bolan gave him the diminutive gangster a bartender's heave-ho. The Butcher was flung out into space arms outstretched and screaming. Bolan heard the shouts, snarls and thuds as Chapa hit the oncoming Raptors and tumbled them down like bowling pins. The Executioner spun with his pistol spitting in his hand.

Upstairs, there was confusion, and Bolan took it for all it was worth. The Raptors lining the hall turned from covering the bedroom entry team to find the American striding down among them. Bolan fired his pistol dry and spun one of his two purloined rifles on its sling. The entry team burst back out from the bedroom, and Bolan burned them down. He dropped his spent rifle and unslung the second. He spun and burned the entire magazine back at the landing to keep the Raptors down, then tore a pair of grenades from the belt of a dead Raptor. Bolan did a moment of math with his memory of the satellite photos of the compound and chose the guest bedroom to his left. Raptors erupted onto the landing.

Bolan pulled the pin on the fragger and tossed the bomb out into the hallway.

"Grenade! Gren—"

Bolan reloaded and slung his rifle as the grenade exploded. He tore his laptop out of his diplomatic bag and flipped it open. Keys clicked as Bolan touched the destruct sequence. He strode to the double glass doors that led to the balcony. As he opened them, he could hear men shouting below. Behind him the laptop snapped and hissed as the twin one-ounce charges of thermite ignited. Bolan pulled the pin on a second grenade and tossed the lethal egg to the patio below. He took two running steps, jumped to get his foot on the low stone rail and soared out into space. Men roared below. Several guns fired, and Bolan heard the supersonic crack as bullets ripped by him.

The big American tucked into a ball as he hit the kidney-shaped pool in a cannonball. Water closed over him, and he blew out his air and sank like stone. The detonation of the grenade on the tile was a muffled crack. The screams that answered the whistling shrapnel were equally muted. Bolan's heels hit the black lava pool bottom hard. He instantly stood up and began shooting. The grenade had done its work. There was little cover on the pool deck save for folding deck furniture. Bullets geysered the water to Bolan's left, and he turned and shot down the two wounded Raptors who were still standing.

Bolan heaved himself up out of the pool. Men were already racing for the helicopter on the pad. It was fifty yards across the open lawn, and he would be cut down by riflefire from the house before he could reach the aircraft. Bolan ran dripping around the side of the house and doubled back toward the front. A dozen men were guarding the front perimeter, but they were all looking at the house. Bolan came on firing, and half a dozen men were down before they'd located the threat.

"Out front!" Everyone was shouting, screaming and shooting. "He's out front."

Bolan dived behind the APC 70 as rifles from inside and outside the house sought him. The Mexican armored vehicle was basically a Russian army BTR-60BP. It was essentially a vaguely boat-shaped welded iron box that rode on eight enormous wheels. This particular model seemed to be set up for command, control and communication. Half a dozen antennas for radio, video and satellite feeds stuck up from the top of the hull. A brief scan told Bolan this rig had been set up to control weapons fire, as well as troop and vehicle movement. For self-defense, a Mk 19 40 mm grenade launcher was mounted over the commander's hatch. Bolan slid around the vehicle as bullets hammered and sparked off of it. He grinned as he came to the back.

The twin troop hatches were wide open.

Bolan jumped in and slammed the two hatches shut. Bullets rattled like rain against the hull, but small-arms fire was exactly what the welded iron hull was meant to repel. The cabin had three workstations loaded with computers, radios and video monitors. Bolan moved to the front and took the driver's seat. He flipped the twin ignition switches, and the twin eight-cylinder gasoline engines stuttered and then spit blue smoke with a roar. Bolan checked his rearview mirror through the armor glass.

Mondragon and Arguello had jumped into the parked Ferrari. They glanced in horror at the armored vehicle come to life. Bolan slammed the APC 70 into reverse. The armored personnel carrier's massive road wheels crunched across the hood of the Ferrari, and both of its front tires blew as the nose crumpled. Bolan took a little tour around the circular drive. He ran over a jeep and two motorcycles with Mexican army markings and mortally wounded a Hummer by staving in its in the side and pushing it partway through the wall of the mansion.

Bolan felt a brief twinge of regret as he crushed a cherry-red 1965 Mustang. He felt no remorse at all as the shovel nose of the APC went skyward as he clambered over the armored limousine. It had been armored up to resist small-arms fire for VIP ambush situations. The Bavarian designers had never considered being run over by a ten-ton armored personnel carrier. The BMW limousine folded in the middle as the APC 70 rolled across it amidships.

Bolan put the engine in neutral and popped the commander's hatch. The Mk 19 conveniently had a 48-round belt in the feed box and the good taste to have a curved armor "chicken plate" to defend the gunner. Bolan racked the action and cut loose with a burst of 40 mm fragmentation grenades that swept the drive and front patio clean of gunmen. Bolan put a burst of grenades into any window where he saw a muzzle-flash.

Grenades detonated like whips cracking as he sent a stream of munitions through the front door into the foyer and in an arc through the front windows of the ground floor. Bolan checked his belt. He had about seven grenades left. Guestimating the range to the helicopter pad on the back lawn at 150 yards, Bolan yanked his muzzle skyward and began slowly arcing grenades over the house.

9

Raptor Vision 2 watched the battle going on in the compound in awe as he keyed his satellite link. "Omega, this is Raptor Vision 2, please respond. We have a situation developing at the general's compound."

Omega answered instantly. "This is Omega. Describe."

RV 2 shook his head as he watched. He didn't need his binoculars or his scope to take in the carnage. "I have over two dozen men down outside the house both front and back. Number of dead inside unknown. Status of the general and Chapa unknown."

"What about Mondragon and Arguello?"

RV 2 brought his scope to his eye. The two lawyers sat in their half-crushed Ferrari screaming and hugging each other as the APC's 40 mm automatic grenade launcher swept the mansion like a broom. "Currently alive and pinned down."

"What else?"

"All vehicles other than the general's APC have been destroyed." RV 2 swept his scope to the back lawn. "The general's personal helicopter is burning on the pad." He shook his head as he checked the sea of bodies on the back patio by the pool and the flame and smoke sheeting up out of the balcony above. "The second floor appears to be on fire. Source unknown."

"Where is El Hombre?"

"He is in the general's APC."

There was a moment of silence as Omega contemplated this. "Have you engaged?"

"No, sir. My orders were to observe and engage only if target tried to escape. He is currently still on the grounds, engaging the general's men." RV 2 shook his head again. "And he's winning, commander. He's winning big."

"Raptor Vision 2, do you have the shot?"

RV 2 put the crosshairs of his 10x telescopic sight directly between El Hombre's shoulder blades. The Barrett Model 82 A-1 .50-caliber antimateriel rifle had an effective range of well over a thousand meters. He had El Hombre, standing up in a hatch and dead to rights at 375. "Affirmative, Omega. I have the shot."

A second passed. RV 2 knew that Omega wanted a capture rather than a kill. Both men knew that El Hombre in an armored vehicle changed the entire equation.

"Take the shot, Raptor Vision 2. Terminate the target."

"Affirmative, Omega. Taking the shot." RV 2 peered through his optic. He let out half a breath and his right fingertip began taking up slack on the custom-tuned trigger. The rifleman's mantra played unconsciously in his mind. Don't pull the trigger. The gun going off should be a surprise. Squeeze…squeeze…squeeze…

BOLAN HEAVED his weapon around on its ring mount as a shotgun blasted from an upstairs window. Lead spalled off the gunner's shield and the Mk 19 hammered a fragger into the window. The assassin was eclipsed by the crack of yellow fire. The window glass shattered, and the curtains pulsed as razor-sharp bits of metal tore them and the man behind them to rags.

Bolan's head snapped around as a hole the size of a quarter magically appeared in the chicken plate beside his shoulder. No shotgun had pierced the curved steel of the chicken plate. The punched-in hole told him the bullet had come from behind him rather than the front.

There was a sniper in the hills, and he had a really big rifle.

The assessment took Bolan approximately half a heartbeat. He dropped down the hatch like a genie going back in his bottle as the second .50-caliber bullet smashed sparks from the Mk 19 and slammed it pinwheeling around on its mount.

Bolan yanked the hatch closed and slid down into the driver's seat. The APC 70 had been designed to resist riflefire and metal fragments from air-bursting artillery. Its frontal armor was 10 mm's of welded iron, with 7 mm's on the sides and top. The ugly hole in the chicken plate upstairs told Bolan the bad guy on the hill was packing a .50-caliber at least, and it could reach into the APC and touch him from any angle. As if in answer, a bullet punched through the hatch Bolan had just closed and down through the passenger's seat.

He rammed the APC 70 into drive. The sniper should've been going for the engine, but he'd probably figure that out in a minute. The APC rumbled forward and smashed the corner of the gate off of the perimeter wall in passing. The driver's window exploded. Bolan snarled and his eyes went to slits as glass fragments peppered his face. The big bullet cracked by his head at supersonic speed to smash a hole through the driver's-side troop hatch in the back. Bolan slammed the armored shutter over the driver's window, though he doubted it would do much good.

He had to get out of range.

Mobility he had going for him. The twin eight-cylinder engines each had 120 horsepower and delivered power to all eight wheels. In the world of light armored vehicles, speed was life, and the APC could do a decent 50 mph on road and 30 mph off. Bolan cleared the compound and went off-road down the hillside. A bouncing, bucking vehicle made for hard precision shooting, and Bolan wanted trees between him and the shooter ASAP.

The shooter knew what Bolan was up to, and the hull of the APC rang like bell seven times in rapid succession. Shafts of sunlight skewered the dim interior of the APC like lasers as the hull was perforated. Ten shots, and the last seven rapid. That told Bolan the bad guy had a Barrett .50 or the equivalent. It would take him a couple of seconds to reload. Bolan took the APC 70 jolting and bucking like a bronco down the hillside.

He hunched as a bullet tore through the top of the hull and ripped through his armored shutter. The shooter was now behind him. Bolan scanned his controls. The Russian markings had been painted over in Spanish. He saw three switches with a little plate marked HUMO. The hull thrumbed as the four triple-smoke-grenade dischargers fired and sent smoke grenades arcing off in all directions. Two more bullets pierced the hull and then stopped.

Bolan rolled down the hill through blooming clouds of gray smoke. No more bullets hit the APC. He was rolling into his own smoke and effectively obscured. Bolan opened his armored shutter and squinted against his smoke screen. He found a stand of poplars by ramming into them. Bolan backed the vehicle up and began creeping through the trees. After a minute, he was out of his smoke screen and out of sight of the compound.

The Executioner stopped and dug around in the arms lockers. There were two G-36 rifles racked. After opening a couple of storage lockers, Bolan found a spare belt of grenades for the Mk 19 and reloads for the smoke dischargers. He had about two dozen holes in his hull, but it appeared nothing critical had been hit. Bolan reloaded his rather limited arsenal. The Mk 19 wasn't in good shape. The .50-caliber bullet had put a dent in it, but it racked in a fresh round. Bolan dropped down the hatch and got rolling again. He flicked switches on the radio rig and put on the headset. Lights pulsed like a Christmas tree across the police band radio.

It was blowing up.

Calls were screaming back and forth in Spanish almost faster than Bolan could follow, but he could capture the gist of it. El Hombre had attacked General Lothario's compound. The entire state of Nuevo Leon knew about it and was about to fall on him. Local and state police had been dispatched. The *federales* and the armed forces wouldn't be far behind. Bolan checked the compass in his watch to the one bouncing crazily on the APC's dash. They were comfortingly in tune with each other. Bolan straddled a small creek with his wheels and took advantage of the flat gravel to put his accelerator down. He was only a few miles from the Rio Grande. He was in an armored amphibious vehicle.

Bolan ran for the border.

Bullets rattled against the starboard side of the APC. Bolan shot the shutter on his side window. A Hummer was tearing precipitously along parallel to him on a hillside one hundred yards away. The Hummer was black with the gold Aztec Raptor emblem emblazoned on the hood. A soldier in black BDUs was standing up in the commander's cupola and blazing away at the vehicle with an M-60. Bolan halted the APC and crouched behind his weapon. Sparks shrieked off the gunner's shield. The Hummer had come to the gunfight without one.

Bolan fired.

The Mk 19 cycled once and jammed. Bolan's grenade flew across the Hummer's bow and detonated against a rock. The gunner in the Hummer fired his M-60 like a fire hose. Bolan racked the action on his weapon. Something was wrong with the cycling. He now had a manually operated grenade machine gun. Bolan peererd down his sights. Grenade launchers were not particularly accurate. They were area-effect weapons.

A man stood up in the back hatch of the Hummer and snapped open the telescoping tube of a LAW antitank rocket.

Bolan fired.

The grenade hit the Hummer in the front passenger-side wheel well. Bolan had been aiming for the passenger compartment amidships but the damage was done. The HEAT grenade detonated into the tire, spewing its jet of superheated gas and molten metal designed to pierce armored vehicles. The jet melted the tire in two like a knife through butter and sheared the wheel off the axle.

The Hummer slid two feet down the hillside and tipped. The men standing in the hatches screamed and abandoned their weapons a second too late. The Hummer rolled, and the rocky scree of the hillside scraped the men away from the waist up. Bolan racked a fresh round and dropped back down into his vehicle. The Hummer rolled six times and came to rest at the bottom of the hill and lay on its back like a stricken turtle.

Bolan gunned his twin straight-eight engines and ran for the river.

The creek squirted out between a pair of hills and a tiny, one-lane bridge spanned it. Bolan crunched up the creekside and slammed down onto the dirt road. He put the pedal down again to make time.

He cocked his head as he caught motion out of the corner of his eye. A motorcyle was paralleling him. The man riding it was wearing a black suit and white shirt that flapped in the wind. His head was obscured by a silver-and-black helmet with a visor. His most interesting features were the guitar case across his back and silver spurs on his boots.

He was waving enthusiastically.

Bolan didn't have the time. He caught sight of the Rio Grande running wide and brown between the low hills, and put his foot to the floor. The APC red-lined for the river under emergency war power. Bolan shook his head wearily and glanced upward as hail rattled on the roof of the APC. He couldn't hear rotors above the sound of his twin engines, but the sound smacking along the roof told him he had a helicopter making a gun run.

A second hailstorm hit the APC. Bolan cocked a concerned eyebrow as the welded-steel roof dimpled under another onslaught and bits of paint spalled into the cabin.

There were two helicopters.

Bolan shot a quick glance out of his side window. The motorcycle rider had disappeared. The Rio Grande loomed before him. He had no time to stop and erect the trim vane or prep the APC 70's water jet propulsion system. It was a tin can that would float, and the forward movement of the road wheels would limp the vehicle across the river. Bullets hammered the top of the hull, and flakes of paint stung Bolan's cheek.

It was going to be a long, exposed limp across the Rio Grande.

The APC 70 hit the water. Brown water sprayed up in geysers. The giant wheels bit into the river bottom and shoved the APC forward. There were parts of the Rio Grande where a person could ride a horse across. This wasn't one of them. The APC slewed as it went buoyant and its wheels left the riverbed.

Each of the eight wheels was five feet tall with massive, aggressive treads to cross battlefields. Each one had power, and they bit into the water like eight paddle wheels. The current still took the bobbing box iron, and Bolan made more progress sideways than forward. He grimaced through his steel shutter.

Texas loomed thirty yards away.

Bolan crept toward the United States at five miles per hour.

The helicopters roared over in another gun run. The top hull began dimpling dangerously. Like all APCs, the armor was thin on top, designed to repel shell splinters rather than direct hits. Sooner or later, some dimples were going to buckle. Bolan watched the helicopters roar past. They circled back just short of violating U.S. airspace. If they were clever, they would just hover above him and pour down fire. But they were used to making runs on insurgents who were firing back, and past experience told in Bolan's favor.

And he was twenty yards from Texas.

A third helicopter swooped. It flew over Texas and arced around in a tight turn. The first two helicopters were Hueys wearing Mexican army olive drab. The third chopper was a massive, Russian Mi-17. It was painted in Raptor black with the gold Aztec Raptor eagle on its nose and carried rocket pods and TOW wire guided antitank missiles beneath its stub wings.

Bolan hit his smoke dischargers, and grenades arced away from the APC in all directions. He punched a button over the transmission, and fuel oil squirted into the exhaust and black smoke belched up out of the twin exhaust pipes. Gray-and-black filth bloomed around the APC.

Bolan slammed his shutters shut as rocket fire blossomed beneath the chopper's wings. He was a sitting duck, dead in the water. The APC 70 just wasn't going to make it to Texas.

Neither was he.

"I HAVE MISSILE LOCK—goddamn it!" Leland Scott snarled as the APC disappeared in clouds of gray smoke and burning fuel oil.

Omega spoke in Scott's headset. "Sitrep."

"The asshole's thrown up a smoke screen. I can't get a lock with the TOW."

"Scotty?"

"Yeah, boss?"

"This asshole doesn't make it back to Texas."

"No way, boss. Ain't happening today." Scott flipped a switch on his weapons display board. On a schematic of the Mi-17, the green light on his starboard TOW launchers went red, and the lights on the port and starboard rocket pods went green.

"Switching to rockets." Scott thumbed his trigger and 2.75-inch Hydra rockets rippled out of the twin twenty-four-tube pods, hissing into the smoke cloud. Most hit water, but at Mach 2 they still detonated in bursts of orange fire. The Rio Grande erupted in geysers, and the water and the multiple blast waves shredded the smoke screen.

Scott caught sight of the APC 70. The rear top hatch was mangled, and smoke was pouring out that had nothing to do with the smoke screen oil injectors. The nose was blackened, and three of its eight wheels were floating away downriver in shredded ruin. The starboard side of the APC was torn open amidships and rapidly taking on water.

Scott flipped the switch back on his weapons control panel. "Going to missiles."

The sight on the TOW screen showed the crosshairs directly on the stricken APC. No tatters of smoke were going to save it. Scott squeezed his trigger with a savage grin. The Mi-17 vibrated as the TOW antitank missile screamed off of its launch rail.

"Missile away."

The TOW accelerated toward the APC trailing its guide wires. Obscuring smoke drifted across the APC like a sheet, but Scott had the APC's position firmly fixed in his mind and he kept his sight squarely where he'd last seen the APC 70. Only one thing on earth looked like a shaped-charge warhead striking an armored vehicle, and Scott was rewarded by the sight of orange fire, yellow streaks and violent black smoke pulsing outward as the missile struck its target and detonated.

"Drop her down, Jose!" Scott flipped the switch on the weapons panel for the 7.62 mm minigun. "Right on top of the son of a bitch!"

The pilot dropped the Mi-17 downward, and its rotors beat the smoke out in all directions. The APC was a blackened hulk, open to the sky and taking on water. Its shattered nose stuck straight up as it sank like the *Titanic*. The spare belt of 40 mm grenades suddenly began cooking off like a string of firecrackers, and every hole in the APC strobed fire and molten metal. The APC 70's prow dropped into the water as the crippled armored personnel carrier snapped in two. The two parts sank below the brown water bubbling and hissing.

"Omega, this is Raptor Bird 1." Scott grinned into his mike. "We have a confirmed kill."

10

Bolan awoke in a cave. His ears were ringing, but it was a rhythmic thudding noise that had awoken him. He didn't open his eyes right away. Instead, he maintained the slow, steady breathing of a sleeper and let his other senses roam. He could tell by the odor of wet earth and rock he was underground. There was also the smell of stale pizza, flat orange-flavored soda pop and the scent of fresh gun oil. Beneath it all was a faint, underlying stench of ammonia. That meant bats had roosted here but not recently.

Bolan's body instantly knew he was lying on a well-used army cot beneath one of the polyester Mexican blankets mass produced for sale to American tourists. His head and right hand were bandaged, and someone had applied iodine to his cuts. On top of the thudding noise he could not identify, he heard the distant sound of a generator. The back of his eyelids told him that wherever he was there was illumination.

Bolan remembered the death of the APC. He remembered the wash of blistering heat as the hull of the personnel carrier had buckled and water rushed into the troop compartment. He remembered diving for the floor as both the driver and passenger shutters had blown inward. At the time, Bolan had been lucky enough to remember that second-generation Soviet armored vehicles had escape hatches in the floor. Bolan was able to squirm down the narrow hatch and into the nearly opaque water with ten tons of armored vehicle sinking above him. He remembered the world ending in an orange flare of light.

He didn't remember much after that.

Bolan eyes flicked open as he rolled to his feet.

His Mexican army P-7 M-13 pistol lay on a breakfast tray beside the cot. The sound suppressor was still in place, and the weapon appeared to have been cleaned and oiled. Bolan scooped up the 9 mm gun, and the red loaded chamber indicator told him the pistol was locked and loaded on a live round. He didn't remember having reloaded it.

Bolan glanced around at his surroundings. He'd been mistaken. He wasn't in a cave. He was in a mine shaft. The rock of the ceiling brushed his hair. The dim light of the naked bulbs every ten yards had been supplemented with strings of Christmas lights. Bolan was interested to notice a later-model El Camino in fire-engine-red was parked behind him, as was a Honda CX 500 motorcycle, which Bolan remembered from his escape run. Downslope there was a minifridge, a small desk with a laptop and a couch facing a flat-screen TV that had been bolted into the wall. A guitar in a guitar stand stood beneath the TV. Beyond that a young man stood in a circle of light beating the bejesus out of a telephone pole. Bolan's eyes narrowed. It wasn't actually a telephone pole.

It was a *mook jong*.

The kung fu wooden dummy was a five-foot-tall post with three protruding wooden arms and a bent arm at the bottom representing a human leg. The man beating on the *mook jong* appeared to be in his twenties, but his head was shaved so it was hard to tell. Bolan noted the raised white scars on his skull. He had stripped down to a sleeveless T-shirt and embroidered black mariachi pants. His body was sheened in sweat. His hands blurred between the three wooden arms, and his palms and fists slammed against the post in rapid blocks and strikes. His legs alternately lashed out at the lower limb of the *mook jong* in kicks and leg sweeps.

The young man suddenly stopped and turned toward Bolan. His shoulders hunched in shyness but his face split into a guileless smile. He didn't seem to register the gun in Bolan's hand. "El Hombre!"

There was something wrong with the man. Bolan cocked his head and grinned back. "La Guitarista, I presume?"

"Yes!" The young man looked as if he might burst into flames.

"You saved my life."

The man stared down at his boots sheepishly. They had silver spurs. He was so giddy he couldn't meet Bolan's eyes. "I heard of the attack on the general's compound. They said it was you. It is not far from here. I went to help. You seemed to be okay. Until the helicopters came. I watched from the trees. I thought you were dead. Smoke was everywhere. I was about to leave, but then, through the smoke, I saw you washed up on the shore. So I brought you here." He seemed to run out of things to say and stared at Bolan with a vaguely disturbing blankness.

Bolan put his pistol under his belt and stuck out his hand. "My enemies call me El Hombre. My friends call me Matt."

"Matt!" La Guitarista eagerly pumped Bolan's hand. "Esteban! Esteban Buriche!"

Bolan retrieved his hand. "You cleaned my gun?"

The man kicked the floor in embarrassment and jerked his head at his laptop. "I did not know how to fieldstrip it. So I went online."

"Thanks."

"It was nothing!" His head snapped up eagerly. "Would you like to see my guns?"

"More than anything." The young man appeared Caucasian, but his English was thick with the Mexican border accent. He practically ran over to an ancient wooden wardrobe that squeaked as he opened the double doors. Bolan had a sneaking suspicion he knew what they would be. He was right as the young man produced a pair of stainless-steel KP-45 Rugers. La Guitarista presented them butt first to Bolan, unable to meet his eyes.

Bolan took the pistols. They were typical 1990s Ruger pistols. Adequate in the accuracy department with crunchy, gritty trigger pulls, but on the plus side they were built like bricks.

Bolan blurred both pistols into road-agent spins. The gleaming stainless steel flashed as he whirled the pistols forward and back in .45-caliber pinwheels. The young man stared on rapturously as Bolan performed the gunslinger spins. The pistols snapped to a halt and Bolan held them back out butt first.

"Nice."

The young man beamed.

"You got anything to eat?"

The man nodded and went to his fridge. He came back with a breakfast tray laden with a six-pack of Corona beer and a box of blueberry breakfast pastries. He shrugged sheepishly. "I was not expecting company."

"No problem. Mind if I use your computer?"

La Guitarista grinned. "Mi computer, su computer, El Hombre! I must finish my workout."

"Thanks." Bolan took the tray over to the little computer desk. He ate the modest meal while he waited for the outdated notebook to connect. The young man went back to pounding on the *mook jong* as if it owed him money. The laptop had instant messaging but only barely.

Bolan logged in and looked for Aaron Kurtzman. Somewhere in Virginia, cybernetic alarms were going off all over the Computer Room as an ancient and very unsecure network contacted it. Bolan typed in his latest security codes.

Kurtzman came online. "Striker?"

"Yes."

"We thought you'd been blown up."

"I was blown up."

"This line is not secure."

"No."

"So…"

"I'm all right." The line wasn't secure, but Bolan considered the risk pretty low. "La Guitarista saved me."

"Really?"

"Yeah. I need a line on a young man named Esteban Buriche. Assume he is a Mexican citizen born in Nuevo Laredo, age approximately twenty to twenty-five."

"Okay, but Mexican public records and data bases aren't—"

"I'll wait."

Kurtzman messaged back in seconds. "I've got thirty-seven matches."

"Give me the most interesting."

"Okay, Esteban Buriche, age twenty-one, son of Police Inspector Lorenzo Buriche."

"Give me the info on the inspector."

"Seven years ago Inspector Buriche was murdered in his home by unknown assailants. Wife raped and murdered. Survived by son, Esteban, and daughter, Griffin."

"Where was Esteban?"

"According to the police report, Esteban and his sister, Griffin, were staying at the grandparents in Mexico City at the time of the attack."

Bolan watched the young man's moves. He was blindingly fast. "Then what happened?"

"Another police report. Three days later Esteban Buriche was found in an alley behind a bordello horribly beaten and left for dead. Trauma consistent with pistol-whipping. Assailants unknown. Two nights later his sister, Griffin, was admitted to the hospital. She'd been assaulted."

Bolan sighed. It was a scenario as old as civilization. Inspector Lorenzo Buriche was an honest cop, or at least one who wouldn't be pushed or intimidated. It had cost him and his wife their lives. His young son had gone out for vengeance. At fourteen, he had stood no chance at all. They had beaten him, left him for dead and gone after his sister. When he had lived and they found out he was brain-damaged, they had left him and the shattered remnants of his family as a warning to others.

But whoever had gone after the Buriche family had made a terrible error. They had left an enemy behind. They had beaten any normal, human fear of consequence and remorse out of him. They had filled the dead areas of the brain of that enemy with the terrible, unswerving resolve of a child who knew what he wanted.

Esteban Buriche wanted revenge.

Bolan felt the woman's presence before he heard her. He looked up from the computer and smiled. "Griffin?"

The woman was tall. A six-footer with cascades of brown hair falling down her shoulders and the rail-thin body of a runway model. Like her brother, she looked Caucasian but had the Latin vibe. She carried a plate of steaming tamales. She took in Bolan with grave trepidation. "El Hombre."

"Griffin!" Esteban called out happily without missing a blow. "Call him Matt!"

Griffin rolled her eyes defeatedly. "Would you care for a tamale, Matt?"

Bolan smiled. "I'd kill for one."

Griffin loaded Bolan's plate with tamales wrapped in cornhusks. "Out on the street they say El Hombre is dead."

"That's to my advantage. I'd like him to stay dead. For a while at least."

Griffin glanced toward her brother. "I see you have met Esteban."

Bolan wolfed chicken and pork tamales with the gusto of a man who never knew which meal was his last. "He saved my life."

Griffin's brown eyes went huge and stared into Bolan's unblinkingly. Her voice was the barest whisper. "Then save his."

Bolan considered that and all that it implied. The look in her eyes told him she would do anything if he agreed. There was a final thud like a Japanese wooden gong being struck.

"I'm done with my workout!" Esteban called. Sweat steamed off him in the cold and damp of the mine shaft.

Griffin loaded another plate. "Come have some dinner, brother."

Esteban spun his chair backward, sat down and began to chow down.

Bolan chose his words carefully. "Hey, Esteban. You mind if I take a ride in your car?"

Esteban bolted upright proudly in his chair. "My car is your car, Matt!"

Bolan shot Griffin a quick glance. She picked up the ball without missing a beat. "Can I go?"

Bolan smiled. "Can I take her? I promise I'll have her back early."

He shrugged as he took a long drink of beer. "Griffin's a big girl. She can do what she wants." Esteban suddenly smiled ingenuously. "But thank you for asking. That was very respectful."

"So, Griffin, you want to go for a ride?"

Esteban beamed and shook his head delightedly. "He called you Griffin."

Griffin looked back and forth between the two men and nodded at Bolan. "I would love to go for a ride."

THE RED EL CAMINO RUMBLED down the country lane. Griffin looked out the window as the moon shone down on the slow-moving waters of the Rio Salado. Bolan broke the silence. "Blunt trauma."

"Yes." Griffin kept her eyes out upon the river. Her voice was cold. "After our parents were killed, Esteban took our father's pistol and went after them. He was only thirteen. He had never fired a gun. He didn't know the safety was on. They took the gun away from him and beat him with it. I think they meant for him to die, but he lived."

"He's lucky."

"Yes, very lucky." Griffin's voice turned bitter. "They beat his brains out and left him little more than a child."

"I meant he's lucky to have a sister like you."

Griffin was quiet for long moments.

Bolan changed the subject. "Tell me about the kung fu."

Griff snorted. "Well, even as a little boy, *Enter the Dragon* was his favorite movie. He started disappearing early in the morning and in the evening after dinner. I followed him. In the morning he was going to the Nuevo Laredo Martial Arts Association and in the evening to a man teaching at the YMCA. At first, I was not concerned. The doctors said he needed to exercise, and it stopped him from just sitting and watching TV all day."

"And the guitar?"

Griffin shook her head. "Can you guess?"

"He saw *El Mariachi*."

"Yes…he did. And *Desperado*." Griffin rolled her eyes skyward. "He watched them many, many times. Then he asked me to buy him a guitar. There is a line in the movie, when the mariachi is talking to a child with a guitar on the curb. He said, 'Practice all day, practice every day.' That is what Esteban did. He taught himself. He would play all day. He would play sitting on the toilet until his feet went numb. He never stopped except to eat and sleep. A year later he was playing in cantinas and getting paid."

Bolan could see unspilt tears brimming in Griffin's brown eyes. "Esteban's kung fu teacher called him a prodigy, or natural. You would weep to hear him play the guitar."

"And when he found they'd turned you out, he took up the gun."

Griffin flinched and the tears spilled. She leaned her head against the window. Her voice was emotionless. "I wanted those men dead. Guns are highly illegal in Mexico, so gunrunning is a very common crime. I was a whore. I knew where to go. I bought Esteban his guns."

"And he started practicing, all day, every day."

"Yes, and after six months of practice he killed my pimp."

Bolan glanced back the way they had come toward the abandoned mine. "And the bat cave?"

"I think he discovered this place on a hiking trip as a boy." She turned to face him. "Can you help him?"

"I've looked in your brother's eyes, and you know him better than I do. He won't ever stop. The only way to stop him would be to kill him or incarcerate him. His skills might allow him survive the first few attacks in prison, but particularly when they found out who he was, they'd come at him in ways he couldn't fight with his fists. For that matter, when they find out who he is, and that's only a matter of time, they're going to go after him through you."

Fresh tears spilled down Griffin's face. She stared at Bolan hopelessly. "So he dies in jail or on the streets."

"Or I can help him. There's a chance that if he thinks he's avenged you and your family, that his enemies are dead, that he'll stop."

"That's right. You have a mission here in Mexico, don't you?" Griffin's face turned cold. "So you'll use my brother. You'll point him like a weapon."

Bolan knew how ugly it sounded. It didn't just sound ugly. It was, but there was no other choice. "No, I'm going to take him all the way, and maybe he comes out the other side."

Something resembling hope moved behind Griffin's eyes. "You can't promise that."

Bolan shook his head. "I can't promise any of us is going to live to see sunrise."

They finished their loop through the hills and came back to the mine entrance. Bolan reversed the car down into the shaft and pulled the screen of brush back over the entrance. Once he cut the rumbling engine, he could hear the sound of Spanish guitar. Griffin was right. Esteban was a prodigy. His martial arts had given him incredibly strong fingers, and it showed in his incredibly clean and precise finger picking.

Esteban suddenly looked up shyly. "Did you like my car?"

"Very much. Griffin and I had a long talk."

Esteban cocked his head and his expression went blank. "Oh?"

Bolan knew the young man would explode into violence if he said the wrong thing. "Yeah, El Hombre is dead."

Esteban nodded slowly. "Yes?"

"So now is the time for La Guitarista."

Esteban looked as if he might burst into flames again.

"Tomorrow, you and me? We go to war."

"Tomorrow we go to war." Esteban suddenly frowned. "So what do we do tonight?" His eyes slid to the gun cabinet. "I was going to go out tonight."

"Tonight?" Bolan shrugged. "I got blown up yesterday. I need some rest. Maybe we should stay in and watch a movie."

Esteban began popping up and down on his toes. "We could watch *Desperado!* Have you seen *Desperado? Desperado* is my favorite movie! Is *Desperado* your favorite movie?"

"*Desperado*'s not bad." Bolan scratched his chin thoughtfully. "But favorite? I'd have to say that would be *Enter the Dragon*."

Esteban's face became gravely serious. "That's good, too."

11

Bolan had La Guitarista in his crosshairs. The weapon was an exact replica of a Delisle commando carbine. It was an old WWII Lee-Enfield rifle cut down and rechambered for the .45ACP pistol bullet. The shortened barrel was enshrouded from receiver to muzzle with the thick black tube of a sound suppressor. The .45 was fat, slow and subsonic, so there was no supersonic crack as it passed its target. Its low chamber pressure made for ease of silencing at the muzzle. The suppressor tube technology was more than fifty years old, and yet many experts considered the Delisle the world's only truly silent weapon and the finest of its kind ever built.

The technology on top of the weapon was more recent. A Burris 2.5x scout scope was mounted ahead of the receiver. With the scope mounted forward, the operator could keep both eyes open. The scout system was arguably the fastest optic for engaging multiple targets, and the Enfield action was the fastest manual bolt ever built. The carbine was not effective out past three hundred yards. It was not a precision sniper rifle.

The Delisle carbine was made for rapid, silent, multiple kills.

It also had the advantage of being chambered for the same cartridge as Esteban's pistols, and that figured heavily into Bolan's plans. He watched through his optics as La Guitarista walked down the dusty road to the cantina.

Bolan spoke into his throat mike. "Desperado, this is Striker. Do you copy?"

"This is Desperado!" Esteban was giddy about his call sign. "I copy."

"Don't start shooting until I tell you."

"I will wait for your word, Striker."

The cantina was a hollow square of connected buildings surrounding a vast patio. The Gulf Coast Gang owned it, and they controlled it and the surrounding ranch lands like a feudal estate. Members came here if they needed get out of Nuevo Laredo and let things cool off after a particularly heinous crime. It was a secure place where gang members came to talk territory and mediate inner disputes. They also came here to let off steam. Cockfights, dogfights, orgies and executions were the usual entertainments. It was also a favorite place of theirs for weddings and christenings. It was a place where the Gulf Coast Gang boys felt secure. Bolan shook his head as he scanned the area.

Someone should have told security about how to clear a kill zone around an encampment.

Bolan had dropped to one knee thirty feet up in the fork of a spreading cypress. He was a little over one hundred yards away, and he and his carbine owned every living that moved in or out of the hacienda. Griffin had done some legwork for them out on the streets of Nuevo Laredo for the past few days. She had heard there was something going on at the hacienda today. A lot of the working girls had been told their presence would be required tonight for after-event activities.

Things were already bustling.

A lot of bad guys were having breakfast, and more kept arriving. The patio was full of men in silk suits and gang muscle openly wearing guns over T-shirts several sizes too small. There were also a disturbing number of men in military uniforms. Bolan adjusted his scope to maximum power. It wasn't a high-power optic, but he could make out the insignias on the shoulders. Every shoulder bore the stylized, golden Aztec eagle and jump wings of the former general's Aztec Raptor company.

Esteban strode up toward the front gate, guitar case in hand

and spurs jingling. A pair of guards with M-16 rifles stood outside leaning against a rust-colored Jeep, smoking cigarettes and apparently bored out of their minds. Word of the La Guitarista had not made it out into the rural areas, and on the street many people still thought it was hoax. The two gunmen watched the approach of the lone mariachi on foot with vaguely interested contempt. One man had his rifle slung. The other sat on the Jeep's fender with his rifle held loosely across his knees.

Bolan put his sights on the chest of the man holding his rifle and fired.

The carbine made the barest of whispers. The muted click as Bolan instantly worked the bolt was louder. The Delisle was all wood and steel, and it soaked up the soft, fat recoil of the .45 as if it didn't exist. A round, red spot erupted between the seated guard's clavicles. His cigarette popped out of his mouth, and he slid off the fender. The second gunman turned, clearly wondering why his partner had spit out his cigarette and fallen down. Bolan's second shot took him in the temple.

Esteban walked up and nodded approvingly as he glanced at the two fallen men. "*Bueno,* Striker."

"You see the gas can on the side of the Jeep?"

Esteban stared at the side-mounted jerrican. "Yes?"

Bolan's next bullet traversed the aluminum can, and gas began leaking down the side of the Jeep and filling the back bed. "So light her up."

"Ah!" Esteban struck a match off his heel and tossed it into the back of the Jeep. Red-and-orange fire whooshed in the back of the vehicle. "And now?"

"Go on in, but remember, I can't see the very front of the patio or the left side of the cantina under the eaves." Bolan clicked in a fresh 7-round magazine. "Those are my blind spots. You have to keep your eye on them."

"Yes, Striker. I will keep my eye on them."

"The servants? The help? They're just trying to earn a living. You don't throw down on them unless they throw down first."

"Not unless they throw down first," Esteban repeated.

"Good, then go on in. Be yourself. I got your six."

Esteban savored the English phrase. "I will be myself."

Esteban strode forward and put his spurs into the double doors. Bolan rolled his eyes as the doors flung open with a crash he could hear from his perch.

People on the patio looked up from their platefuls of eggs and chorizo and stared at the mariachi in confusion and irritation. Their eyes went wide with horror as La Guitarista drew his two Rugers and began to fire.

The .45s boomed into rapid life in Esteban's hands. Bolan methodically began picking targets and firing. He left the sitting ones and went for the muscle wearing the guns. Bodyguards began falling. Renegade soldiers stood clawing for the pistols on their belts. Seated in circles around the breakfast tables, the bad guys were lined up like ducks in a shooting gallery. The range was point-blank for the carbine, and there was no cover. Bolan shot seven men, slapped in a fresh magazine and shot seven more.

Esteban's speed and accuracy were impressive. He put down a dozen men and then rolled behind the bar. He ejected his empties, reloaded and came up blazing away without missing a beat. There were forty men out on the patio, and they began firing back. Pistols of every size and description began popping off at Esteban from all directions. Bolan couldn't pick them off fast enough, and neither could Esteban. Bullets ripped across the top of the bar. Esteban flinched and took hits, but he paid them no heed. He stood and shot.

Esteban's advantage was that he was wearing armor beneath his mariachi jacket. The Pinnacle Threat Level III concealed armor vest would stop anything up to a .44 Magnum round. The thick wood of the bar was defending the rest of him, but there was nothing to stop a bullet from ripping off one of his arms or punching a hole between his eyes. Bolan grimaced as Esteban dropped, but he had only taken cover to reload.

Bolan dropped his spent magazine and reloaded. The Delisle's bolt slammed home on a fresh round. A man in a military uniform ran out of one of the buildings spraying at the bar with an M-16. Lieutenant's bars gleamed on the collar of his uniform. He was a member of Aztec Raptor company, and it showed in his courage and his tactics. Bolan could hear him shouting at parade-ground decibels.

"Charge him! Charge the son of the bitch! Swarm him! He can't get all of—"

Bolan put a bullet through the lieutenant's face and one through the throat of the man running up behind him. The men who had started to charge looked around in confusion as their leader fell almost as quickly as he had appeared. Bolan used their confusion to reap them like wheat.

Esteban rose up. The gangsters overturned tables in a desperate attempt to take cover. The thick wood was dubious cover against Esteban's full-metal-jacket .45s. They were no cover at all as Bolan reached down from his height and shot down into the crouching killers. Esteban unloaded on anyone who shot at him as if he were some terrible B-movie character come to life. He shot with a gun in each hand with speed and accuracy that Bolan would have been hardpressed to match.

Men ran out of the outbuildings, some half-dressed, some loading weapons as they came.

Bolan shot and shot. The air shimmered over the black barrel of the suppressor tube, and inside he could hear the wire baffles ticking and hissing as they heated up. The Delisle was a weapon had been designed for a few quick, quiet kills, not slaughter at video-game speeds.

Bolan shot until no man was standing. He flicked his bolt and chambered a fresh round. A sea of spent brass shells littered the ground below his perch. Bolan had checked the range of his ejection. His empties had all landed on a six-foot-by-six-foot plastic tarp he had laid down for the purpose. The cacophony of gunfire had ended as quickly as it had begun. The patio was a sea of blood. The carnage was terrible. Bolan had been going for head shots, and so had Esteban. The only sound was the muffled screaming of the hired help inside and the moans of the wounded littering the patio tiles.

Bolan's eyes narrowed. There had to be more men inside.

The Mexican mobs had a culture of machismo, but the men who reached the top were cunning if not bright. Survivor types didn't run toward the sound of gunfire.

"Desperado, this is Striker. Take cover. Let me take a recon."

"Yes, Striker." Esteban dropped down behind the bar once more and reloaded his smoking pistols.

Bolan noted Esteban's torn right jacket sleeve and the bloody tuft of white shirt beneath it. "You're hit."

Esteban glanced down at his arm. "Yes!"

The young man was grinning proudly. It didn't seem to affect his ability to reload his guns. Bolan swung his rifle's sight around the perimeter. Back and side doors were flying open, and men and women were running for the trees. Most were help, but Bolan discerned gunmen and gangsters among them. Bolan let them run.

He wanted them to live to tell the tale.

"Desperado, this is Striker. Give them the good news. Keep your eyes under the eaves on your left."

"Yes, Striker. I copy." Esteban's voice rose up into a clear, cold Spanish tenor. "I'm La Guitarista! I want the Boy! The Butcher? He's mine! I'm going to kill you all until I get him! I'll kill you in your kitchens in front of your families and burn down your houses! I want the Boy!"

Bolan nodded. Nothing was moving. "Good. Do it quick, and bug out."

Esteban strode to his guitar case and flicked it open, keeping an eye to his left. The case was full of tequila bottles filled with gasoline and detergent with oily rags stuffed down the neck. Esteban took a lighter from the string compartment and began lighting Molotov cocktails.

Bolan caught motion in a shattered window. A rifle barrel slid over the sill. The Delisle hissed once and the rifle fell with a clatter.

Esteban ignored the altercation and began throwing bottles. Some through windows, some onto the roof. He ran out and closed his case.

"Desperado, bug out. Bug out now."

"Yes, Striker." Esteban closed his guitar case and picked it up with his wounded arm. He kept his pistol in his left and backed out the way he came. The moment he was clear he turned and ran, grinning like a little boy racing with the wind. Bolan waited a few moments to discourage any pursuit. There wasn't any. Black smoke began to rise into the sky.

Bolan slung his carbine and descended the cypress. He hit the ground and did a quick scan for errant empties. He plucked up the few flyers and then rolled up his tarp around his spent brass and shoved it in his pack. Esteban's motorcycle was about five klicks away in an arroyo. Bolan himself had a five-mile run back to his car and then two hours of back-road driving to get back to the mine. The operation had gone off better than Bolan had given himself any right to expect. Esteban's previous activities had been a prologue. Bolan faded back through the trees.

The first chapter of the saga of La Guitarista had been written.

12

"Forty men?" Omega was appalled. "This guitar player? Single-handed?" Omega's eyes went to slits. "You're telling me you buy that, Scotty?"

"Yeah, well…it's looking that way." Scott swallowed nervously. "I checked the scene. There was a sea of .45-caliber brass by the gate and the landing and a shitload more behind the bar. That's where he took cover to reload. I pulled a few bullets and checked a few bodies. The Raptor company boys? The Gulf Coasters? The hired guns? Two of them were our guys, boss, and they all had .45ACP bullets in them, and one whole hell of a lot of them were head shots." Scott shook his head wonderingly as he recalled the scene at the killing ground. "I'm telling you, this Guitarista? His shit is goddamn surgical."

Omega contemplated this. "And then?"

"Then?" Scott snorted. "Then he demanded the Butcher and burned the place to the ground."

"You talk to witnesses?"

"Yeah. Some of the hired help and a few of the assholes who beat it for the trees." Scott sagged back into his chair and scratched his chin. "They all say the same thing. A guy dressed like a mariachi and carrying a guitar case kicked in the door and shot everybody on the patio. He blazed away with a gun in each hand and the bastards just kept falling like bowling pins. Just like the goddamn movie."

Omega didn't like movies. However, he had ordered the movie trilogy on pay-per-view and watched what he considered the relevant parts while he had waited for Scott to return from his recon of the cantina massacre. He didn't like what he was hearing. He didn't like it at all.

There was something very, very wrong.

"This Guitarista, you get a description?"

"I sent two idiots into Nuevo Laredo to talk with a police sketch artist, but I haven't heard back yet. I'm waiting for the fax on my laptop."

"This Guitarista asshole." Omega steepled his fingers in thought. "He couldn't be El Hombre?"

Scott frowned. "El Hombre's dead, boss. We fragged his ass."

"I never saw a body."

"Well, that would be pretty goddamn hard, considering."

Omega stared unblinkingly. "I said, 'Could this guitar player be El Hombre?'"

"Well, I haven't gotten the police sketch yet, but I talked to some of the survivors and got a general description. This guitar player was about middle height, young guy, shaved head, kind of Caucasian-looking but spoke Spanish. Nobody there doubted he was a Mexican, though, and he doesn't match El Hombre's description at all. By all accounts, El Hombre was big, scary guy who beat people with sticks, was definitely a gringo and loved to blow shit up."

"I want a list of every mariachi in Nuevo Laredo. There have to be Internet listings, and the bars and restaurants have to have phone lists of guys they'd call. I want a list going back five years."

"Well, that assumes this guy really is a mariachi and not just some psycho—"

Omega's smile chilled Scott's bones. "Oh, this guy is psycho, all right. Only a total nut job would take on forty armed men, and only a psycho could win. But psychos make mistakes. I want him found."

"Okay, so he's psycho, but just because he dresses like a mariachi doesn't mean he—"

"No stone unturned, Scotty." Omega smiled in a friendly fashion. "Don't fuck this up."

Scott's blood turned to ice water in his veins. "You got it, boss."

"El Hombre wanted the Butcher. Now this Guitarista son of a bitch wants him, too."

"Yeah, that's kind of odd." Scott was glad of the change of subject. "Why do you think they both want him? I mean the Butcher is a sick little monkey but—"

Omega smiled again. "They don't want the Butcher."

"They don't?"

"No." The smile reached Omega's eyes. And that was frightening, too. "They want us."

"Us?"

"Somewhere, someone has figured out there's someone pulling the strings, and they really don't want the Butcher, the general or anyone else with more than two squares in the food pyramid." Omega held up a huge, scarred hand and wiggled his fingers. "They're looking for the old black magic, and the men making it happen."

"You're right." Scott nodded as the situation began to dawn on him. "They want us."

"Oh, they want us, Scotty. But we're on the wrong side of the Rio Grande, and they don't know who we are. So who's coming after us? A deranged yanqui in an El Camino? A psycho guitar player who stepped out of a bad B-movie? These guys are implausible and totally deniable. Nut jobs, psychos."

Scott nodded as he put the pieces together. "You know, they're remarkably effective for rubber-room assholes."

"Oh, yeah." Omega sniffed the air. "You smell that?"

"Oh, yeah." Scott grinned ugly. "It stinks. It stinks like black ops."

Omega smiled. "Scotty?"

Scotty recognized the look on Omega's face and it warmed his heart. "Yeah, boss?"

"Someone's running an operation against us."

"You're never wrong, boss."

"Thank you, Scott. And these assholes? They're way out on a limb. I think they're deniable, and, sad as it is, expendable."

"And we know all about that, boss."

"Oh, we know all about that, all right. I think this operation is the kind of shit only the President and couple of his closest advisers get to know about, and frankly they sleep better at night if they don't know about it."

"So we kill them, and it ends."

"Scott."

"Yeah, boss?"

"Find me the mariachi. He stinks like an asset, and if he's a psycho bent on revenge, then he's the weak link."

BLOOD LEAKED as Bolan teased the bullet out of Esteban's bicep. Esteban was grinning from ear to ear. He didn't even flinch as Bolan extracted the bullet. Bolan turned to Griffin. "Can you sew? It's not my strong point."

Griffin nodded without a word and bent over her brother and began stitching his wound. Esteban was happy. He'd been shot in the shoulder and he was being stitched up without the benefit of Novocain. It was just like the movie. Griffin began stitching with the precision of a woman who had grown up doing it.

Esteban sighed. "We got them, Griffin." He suddenly looked quizzically at Bolan. "How many did we get, Matt?"

Bolan began cleaning his carbine. "I counted forty."

Esteban nodded with immense satisfaction. "We got forty."

"And you're proud?" Griffin trembled and she made a visible effort to calm herself. "You're proud you killed forty men?"

Esteban sat up straight. "You are right." He walked over to his gun closet and knelt before the silver crucifix hanging between his pistols. He crossed himself and murmured solemnly. "Bless me, Father, for I have just killed quite a few men."

Griffin bit her lip and murmured under her breath, "It's a line. It's a line from that movie."

Bolan nodded. "I know."

"Did he really kill forty men?"

"I'd say he killed about fifteen, but it was enough." Bolan

replayed the action in his mind with the attention to detail of a trained sniper. He had watched through his optics as Esteban had killed relentlessly and without remorse. The young man had been given the gift of emptiness. Once he was in motion, only death would stop him. It occurred to Bolan that before this was over he might have to take the young man down. "Your brother is a very dangerous man."

Griffin clutched Bolan's arm desperately. "You're going to help him, yes?"

"I'm doing what I can." He hoped he wasn't making things worse.

Esteban rose from his act of contrition and came back over. "I'm hungry."

Griffin went to the hot plate and began rummaging through grocery bags. Her desperate eyes never left Bolan. Esteban looked at Bolan expectantly. "So, what next, Matt?"

Bolan set down his rifle and rag. "Well, I've been thinking about that."

"Me, too!" Esteban was popping up and down on his heels again. "There is a drug dealer, Ernesto Anila, who lives in a mansion just outside of the city. He is a very bad man. I think we could do to him just what we did today."

Bolan shook his head. "No."

"No?" Esteban's face went blank.

Bolan could smell danger. Esteban was set on his course. Derailing him and setting him on a different one was going to take the finesse of defusing a bomb. "They'll be expecting it."

Esteban blinked once as he processed this. "I don't care."

"I care." Bolan smiled. "I care about you and your sister. We have to plan our next move carefully." Bolan read Esteban's body language and grinned again. "We need to hit them where it hurts."

"Hit them where it hurts." Esteban nodded instantly, liking the sound of it. "Where is that, Matt?"

"From the inside."

Esteban cocked his head. "How do we do that?"

"Tell me something." Bolan kept grinning conspiratorially. "Where is El Hombre?"

Esteban peered at Bolan askance. "You are right here."

Bolan nodded patiently. "Yeah, but where do the bad guys think El Hombre is?"

"They…think you are dead."

"That's right." Bolan encouraged. "And where is La Guitarista?"

Esteban's brow furrowed mightily as he contemplated the question like a Zen koan. He finally gave up and shrugged. "I do not know. I am right here, but where is La Guitarista?"

Bolan met the young man's gaze and held it. "He's on the warpath."

"On the warpath…" Esteban savored the words.

"And the bad guys? They've been taking a lot of hits recently, and they've got you on their trail."

Esteban strove to grasp the riddle. "And…"

"And they think I'm dead, and they're going to be looking for a few good men."

Esteban's face shone like a light. "You are going to infiltrate them!"

"Oh, yeah." Bolan nodded. "And then I'm going to hand them to you, from the inside, on a platter."

Esteban glowed. "And what shall I do until then?"

Bolan folded his arms across his chest. "Train. Train all day. Train every day. Wait for my call. Then we drop the hammer, again and again, until they all go down and vengeance is satisfied."

Esteban began jumping up and down and clapping his hands.

A VERY DANGEROUS LOOKING MAN sat at the bar. His black hair was pulled back into an inconclusive ponytail that left dark locks falling across his face. His faded jeans had holes in the knees. His cheap Hawaiian shirt looked as if he'd bought it the day before and slept in it. He was in desperate need of a shave. His pale skin was burned red by the Mexican sun except for the pink patches where it had peeled. He'd been holding down the corner stool of the Perro Bar for the past three days, refusing the advances of the girls and had beaten the holy hell out of three of the local street toughs who'd tried to shake him down. His scary blue eyes seemed to burn holes into the mirror behind the bar. But he was polite and tipped for every drink. He seemed bored, desperate and beyond caring all at the same time.

He said he was looking for work.

The bartender had a pretty good idea of what kind of work he might be looking for. There was a lot of call for that kind of work in Mexico. He'd seen the type before, but things had been very hectic in Nuevo Laredo lately and no one was cozying up to strange white men these days. Fifteen minutes ago, the man had sighed, dug into his pockets and paid for his last beer in quarters. At that point, the bartender had poured him a beer for free and made a phone call.

Bolan had seen the bartender make the call and noticed the sidelong glance he'd been shot. He wasn't surprised at all when a big white man who looked like a hard case walked into the Dog Bar. He was tall, running around six-two, and probably ten pounds heavier than Bolan. The man wore jeans, cowboy boots and a black leather vest. He was accompanied by the biggest Mexican Bolan had ever seen, and he'd been seeing some big ones lately. The man wasn't a bodybuilder, or a wrestler. He topped six foot nine, was muscular but stripped lean. Massive cheekbones and a jaw like a steam shovel were crowned by the flat features of a Mayan. His black hair fell to his shoulders. He'd paid someone a fair piece of change to tailor gray tropical silk into a suit to fit his frame. He looked as if he should be playing in the NBA except that he walked with the loose-boned saunter and assurance that screamed special forces. The white guy had it, too, and he was clearly in command. He walked up and sat down next to Bolan. The giant loomed over Bolan's shoulder.

Bolan smiled, his blue eyes watching the mirror over the bar. "You'd better get your geek the hell away from behind me."

"Oh, I'm sorry." The white man smiled. "How rude of me. Chavo? Why don't you take a seat."

The bar stool on the other side of Bolan creaked ominously beneath the big man's weight as he sat down and stared at Bolan, looking for any sign of weakness or fear. The other guy looked the big American up and down with sleepy eyes and a lazy grin that never wavered, measuring, calculating. He rested an elbow on the bar and his chin in his palm. "You ain't from around here."

Bolan sipped his beer. "No shit."

"So, uh—" the dangerous white dude waggled his scarred eyebrows "—where you from, sailor?"

"Canada."

The man's eyes narrowed. "No shit."

"No shit."

"Whereabouts in Canada you from?"

Bolan finally deigned to turn his gaze on the man and spoke in veiled challenge. "Moose Factory."

The man blinked. "Moose Factory?"

"Yeah." Bolan's blue eyes went arctic. Looking for any insult real or imagined. "Moose Factory, Ontario."

"Moose Factory, Ontario!" The man grinned delightedly over at the giant. "Chavo! This fucker is from Moose Factory, Ontario! You believe that shit?"

"No." Chavo shook his massive head. "I don't believe it."

The American shook his head sadly. "Chavo doesn't believe you."

"Chavo can go play hide-and-go-fuck-himself."

The white guy shook his head again, clearly bemused. "Chavo? Did you hear what he just said?"

Chavo grinned delightedly. He was seconds from slipping his leash and breaking bones. "Oh, I heard him all right."

The white guy leaned in close. Beneath the sleepy cant of his eyebrows his eyes became like two pieces of flint as he lowered his voice. "You know something, Canada? You're a long way from home. I don't know you. I don't know anyone who knows you. You look like shit, and you stink. So why don't you just 'take off' back to the Great White North, see if your mom will give you back your old bedroom back in Moose Factory and go manufacture some—" the man searched for a plural "—meese? Before you get yourself hurt."

Bolan finished his beer, sighed and set the empty bottle down on the bar. "Why don't you and Chavo go play hide-and-go-fuck-each-other."

"Well, fuck me blind!" The man slapped the table gleefully. "I don't know, Chavo! I like him! You like him?"

"Dunno." Chavo's head slowly cocked back and forth at Bolan. Reading the warrior beneath the shabby exterior. "You got bona fides?"

"I was in the army."

The man cleared his throat in mock politeness. "The... Canadian...army?"

"Yeah."

"Oh, yeah?" The white guy was still grinning insultingly, but he snapped his fingers at the bartender to bring Bolan another beer. "And what exactly did you do up there in Christmas-tree country?"

Bolan acknowledged the beer with a nod and resumed staring into the mirror. "Sergeant, Fifth Field Artillery Regiment."

"Oh, well, it's your ship just came in, sailor!" The white guy leaned back and snapped his fingers for a beer. "We get a lot of call for...cannonading...here in Nuevo Laredo."

"I was a forward observer."

Shadows fell across Chavo's eyes as he lowered his craggy brows. "You know, I was a forward observer. Mexican Third Artillery Battalion."

"We did some cross-training with the Second Battalion." Bolan gazed on the giant Mexican noncommittally. "I don't remember you."

"I'm not surprised." The giant leaned in and looked Bolan up and down derisively. "Old-timer."

Bolan glared into his empty mug and said nothing.

"So why'd you leave Canada?"

Bolan shrugged. "The pay sucked, my stint was up, we mostly did United Nations missions. Kosovo, Cyprus. All real politically correct, stand-around-in-blue-helmets-and-get-shot-at shit."

"And so…" The man milled his hands encouragingly.

"So I joined the Legion."

That caught the man flat. "Really."

Bolan took a pull on his beer. "Yeah."

The man was clearly impressed. "The French Foreign Legion?"

"Yeah, Second Reconnaissance Battalion."

"Mmm." The man sipped his beer meditatively. In the shadowy world of mercenaries the French Foreign Legion still rang of romance, heroics and exotic locales. "How'd that work out for you?"

"The pay sucked, my stint was up and there was nothing politically correct about the shit we were pulling in Africa."

"I think I may have heard a little something about that." He motioned for another beer. "So what brings you to our little neck of the woods?"

"My U.S. visa expired. I heard there might be work here."

The man looked Bolan up and down speculatively. "You couldn't get work in the States?"

"I tried. Black Water, Knight Securities, Aegis…" Bolan trailed off and resumed burning blue holes into the mirror.

"I did a stint with Aegis. I made some coin. Why wouldn't they hire a nice man like you?"

Bolan shrugged and sank his beer. The man motioned the bartender for another. Bolan peered off into the middle distance. "Black Water? Aegis? Shit, man, they got Navy SEALs, Rangers, SAS, you name it, all waiting in line. They got Delta Force commandos taking early retirement just to get those fat VIP and executive protection jobs in Iraq and Afghanistan and then come home to even fatter consultant jobs."

"Yeah." The man nodded thoughtfully. "And you?"

"And I'm Canadian artillery." Bolan finished his beer in a single, bitter pull. "And the nation of France will neither confirm nor deny my activities in Africa."

"Man." The giant scowled and drank off his mug. "That sucks."

"Yeah."

"So what now?"

"So I need a job." Bolan turned his gaze on the bartender. "All I got is ten euros in my pocket, and this asshole ain't accepting them."

The bartender flinched in alarm.

"Ah, man, don't worry about that. I got your bar tab."

"Thanks."

"So what kind of work you looking for? Ain't no war going on around here."

Bolan let a smile crawl across his unshaven face. "I hear this whole fucking state is at war."

"Yeah, well, one hears all kinds of crazy things once you get across the border."

"I hear there's some asshole named El Hombre raising all kinds of hell."

The man exposed his teeth. "I ended his career."

"Yeah?" Bolan shrugged. "What about this guitar-player guy? Someone needs to put a bullet in him."

"You want to take on La Guitarista?" The man looked Bolan up and down and grinned. "Well, listen, slick. He gunned down around forty guys three days ago. Single-handed."

Bolan shook his head. "Bullshit."

"Yeah, that's what I said. Until I saw it. It was goddamn Armageddon. And nearly every body had taken a head shot, and every single one had taken it from a .45-caliber Ruger."

"Sounds like a sniper."

"Naw, he walked in like it was the OK Corral and killed everybody. We got witnesses."

"I ain't saying he didn't come in and shoot a shitload of scumbags—" Bolan smiled and examined his beer "—but it sounds like he had a sniper backing him up."

"And I just told you everyone had taken it from a .45-caliber Ruger. The asshole had one in each hand."

"Yeah, and Ruger makes .45-caliber carbines, or at least they used to. I know. I had one. You can put a scope on them." Bolan motioned the bartender for another beer. "Did you check the ballistics on the bullets? All the bullets? You sure they all match?"

The man peered at Bolan for long moments. "You know, you're a real smart fella."

"Canadian public education." Bolan nodded. "The first one's free, for the beers." Bolan polished off the drink in front of him and motioned the bartender for another. "The next one's going to cost you cash money."

"You know?" Chavo was smiling. "I like him."

13

"What have you got?" Omega sat back in his chair. Leland Scott slapped a file down on his desk.

"Three guns between two shooters at the hacienda."

"Really."

"Cooper, the new guy, figured it out. At first I didn't buy it, but I dropped a dime on Dr. Lupino up in Mexico City CSI and reminded him he owed me a favor. There was like an entire file cabinet full of bullets from that fight, but I had him run every .45ACP through ballistics."

"Tell me about this Cooper."

"I got a phone call from Eduardo at the Perro Bar. Saying some gringo who looked military was asking for work. Bodyguarding, consulting, anything. So I showed up with Chavo, and this guy? He didn't even blink."

Omega raised one vaguely satanic eyebrow. "A tough guy, huh?"

"No, just real capable." Scott put down a second file. "Here's the background I could get on him."

Omega flipped it open and his eyebrow rose again. "Canadian Artillery?"

"Yeah, yeah, I know. But check it. He wasn't punching buttons on a fire control computer or counting cannon shells. He was a forward observer. We're talking sneak-and-peek skills. Now, check out page two."

Omega raised both eyebrows. "He was French Foreign Legion?"

"Yeah, the Canadian stuff checked out. But unless you got contacts I don't know about, things get weird in France. All I could dig up was what it says in the file. He 'honorably discharged his duties to France.' That stinks of ugly ass shit, and in the Legion? He was a para commando, recon battalion, the Legion's best of the best. The guys France sends to do the ugly stuff in the dead of night when they don't want French citizens dirtying their hands. He said he was in Africa, and man, the look on his face? That said it all."

Omega had been to Africa, and the kinds of atrocities spawned in African conflicts made Central American civil wars look like church socials. "What else?"

"Well…" Scott grinned in memory. "He told Chavo to go play hide-and-go-fuck-himself."

Omega snorted despite himself. "And?"

"And now Chavo's in love with the guy, and I trust Chavo's instincts, boss. I got him babysitting Cooper now."

Omega trusted Chavo's instincts, too. The giant had what Omega would describe, and with admiration, as low animal cunning. "Tell me more about what Dr. Lupino and Mexico City forensics came up with."

"I told Dr. Lupino to run every .45 bullet recovered from the scene. Well, one hell of a lot of the bullets came from two separate Ruger KP-45s. That's our guitar player son of a bitch."

"And the rest were with a Ruger rifle?"

"No, no match. I also had Lupino check for Marlin camp carbines. No match there, either. But Cooper was still spot-on. Dr. Lupino's definite. The nonmatching .45ACPs all came from some sort of long gun. Maybe a Heckler & Koch with a scope and a suppressor. Hell, maybe a Thompson with the same rig. I've been looking up .45ACP long guns on the Internet and having Lupino check them, but he says the ballistics definitely say something with a long barrel. I did a perimeter check. I couldn't find any trace of a second gunman, but there's a stand of cypresses out front that own that patio. We could give Chavo a couple of MAC-10s and pull the same stunt ourselves. La Guitarista? He ain't no action hero. He had serious backup."

"This Cooper, was he packing?"

"He had a Browning Hi-Power and a Canadian army knife."

"You let him keep them?"

"Chavo and four of the boys are with him."

"You said Cooper wasn't scared of Chavo."

"I said the Canadian wasn't intimidated, but if Chavo doesn't scare him, then he's as nuts as the guitar freak."

Omega conceded the point. "So you put him on the payroll?"

"I told Chavo to give him five hundred bucks, pay his beer tab and to keep an eye on him." Scott warmed to the subject. "I was also thinking, Chavo's been doing collections downtown since we've been keeping the Butcher under raps. And Chavo, when he ain't sneaking around out in the cactus, is one huge target. I figured the big man could use an extra gun around him if the guitar player comes looking for him."

"Tell you what. Have Chavo lean on a few people. Some poor saps that would arouse public sympathy. Have him do it in public, and tell him to hold down the Perro for the next three days. Let's see if we can entice this Guitarista asshole to come out and do his mariachi avenger routine at a time and place of our choosing."

"You got it, boss."

"Oh, and Scotty?"

"Yeah, boss?"

"I liked your earlier idea. Issue Chavo and the boys the MAC-10s. Let's see just how fast this Guitarista gunfighter really is."

BOLAN SAT WITH THE BOYS at the Perro Bar. "Barril," "The Barrel," was shaped like his namesake and liked really young girls. Raul was skinny, ugly and really liked knives. Armando dressed like a pimp and really liked West Coast rap. Carlos was barely out of his teens and liked fast cars.

Bolan could tell that Chavo would have really liked to put them all under the ground, but apparently good help was hard to find. Chavo was Aztec Raptor company. His men were punks and street thugs. They'd earned themselves a position of vague trust because each had murdered someone in cold blood for the organization. All of them were to various degrees failing to conceal .45-caliber MAC-10 submachine guns under their jackets.

They were cannon fodder.

Bolan idly wondered what that made him.

However, the giant actually addressed him in a cordial fashion rather than with the glares and grunts he directed at his men, and as the two soldiers traded war stories the punks gazed on in fascinated rapture.

Chavo wasn't a very nice man.

He'd spent time down south, suppressing the Zapatista rebels in Chiapas. Mexico was a macho culture, and Chavo had the size and personal machismo of a mountain. When the Mexican government wanted "rebel autonomous Zapatista municipalities" in their separatist, southernmost state terrorized, they sent Sergeant Chavo Inarritu.

General Lothario had asked for the giant by name when forming his Aztec Raptor company.

Bolan listened to the giant's stories with some interest, gauging Chavo as an opponent. Besides his sheer physical power, he was also utterly ruthless, without conscience and U.S. Special Forces trained. He would also have a line on who was at the top of this phantom crime empire operating behind the scenes along the border. Bolan needed him alive and in his pocket.

Bolan feigned interest at the wretched stories the gangsters told of predations they'd committed in their barrios against their own people to impress him and the giant. Every big city on Earth had just such scum telling the same stories.

Bolan's real attention was on his watch.

He wore the battered, military-issue Timex on the inside of his left wrist. Unnoticed in the dim bar, he was pressing the bezel in short, delineated sequences. Esteban was in an alley two blocks away. Esteban was able to grasp Morse code quickly. Bolan dotted and dashed and Esteban sat out in the darkness on his motorcycle watching a little black box with a green LED blink at him.

"Do you read?"

Bolan felt the buzzer against his wrist silently pulse in response.

"Affirmative."

Bolan gave Esteban the sit-rep. "Six of us. Targets heavily armed. Don't shoot giant unless necessary. Wait for my signal."

Esteban came back almost instantly.

"Affirmative. Holding position. Awaiting your signal."

Bolan had respectfully declined a MAC-10 and instead wore a well-worn but perfectly tuned Browning Hi-Power in a crossdraw holster beneath the new shirt he'd bought with Chavo's money. The four-inch blade of a Canadian army russell belt knife hung horizontally sheathed to the back of his belt.

Chavo had unleashed his four malcontents like Huns on the barrio surrounding the Perro Bar. He hadn't let them rape or burn, but they had smashed up shops, beaten down the owners and threatened their families. Most of the victims were already paid up or at least paying the interest on what they owed the protection rackets. The giant had come demanding a special cut of his own just to go away. It was a crushing burden and calculated to bring La Guitarista to the killing ground.

Bolan had watched as Chavo's men had circled, snarled and savaged like a pack of hyenas. Bolan hadn't participated. He wasn't a leg breaker. He behaved like the hired gun he was. Bolan had glowered at their prey, and the baleful glare of the blue-eyed gringo had its effect, but for the most part he'd kept his eyes on the street and on every door and window, his hand never far from his concealed pistol while Chavo let his dogs off leash. He knew Chavo was watching him, measuring him, and Bolan had simply stepped into formation and let Chavo know without words that he had his six.

Bolan had felt the giant's unspoken approval.

The Barrel looked at his watch. "It's 2:00 a.m. That guitar player isn't coming."

Bolan pressed the bezel of his watch. "Begin approach."

He made a show of checking his watch. "It's 2:02, the streets are empty, no one's in the bar except us…now's the exact time he should come."

The buzzer pulsed out code against Bolan's wrist.

"Affirmative," Esteban acknowledged. "Making approach."

Raul was nervously opening and closing his switchblade. He'd been eyeballing Bolan all day with a bad case of little man's disease. Bolan was pretty sure that the last time Raul had hit the head he had gotten high on some kind of stimulant. He pointed the switchblade with a sneer. "You know something, white boy, I—"

Bolan grabbed Raul's wrist and yanked him halfway across the table. His thumb compressed Raul's ulnar nerve.

"Aaa!" Raul groaned as his hand popped open like a puppet Bolan controlled and the switchblade fell from his nerveless fingers to the table. "Shit! You—" Raul's eyes flew wide as Bolan's four inches of shaving-sharp Canadian steel lashed beneath his chin.

"You point that knife at me again, and I'll open you like a letter." Bolan put his knuckles against Raul's collarbones and shoved him back in his seat.

Raul rubbed his wrist and stared in shock. He started to reach for his switchblade, flinched as he looked in Bolan's eyes and left it where it lay.

Chavo grinned. "Smart boy."

Bolan's watch pulsed.

"Outside Perro," Esteban communicated. "Awaiting signal."

Chavo glanced at his watch and around the bar. "Cooper."

"Yeah?"

"La Guitarista." Chavo's almond-shaped eyes narrowed to slits as he ran his gaze around the Perro again. "You think he's coming for me tonight?"

Bolan shrugged. "Pushing around those peons this morning in the farmer's market? That's gotta be like waving a red flag at a bull."

"Yeah." Chavo locked his gaze with Bolan. "And?"

Bolan took a long breath and let it out. "And I got a bad feeling."

Chavo nodded very slowly. "Yeah, I got one, too."

They were both Special Forces. They had both seen the elephant. They trusted their gut feelings implicitly.

Chavo leaned back in his chair. "Barrel, get behind the bar. Armando…"

Bolan signaled to Esteban, "Go."

"Armando, I want you at the table by the door. Try not to shoot each other. Raul, get your skinny ass—"

Bolan roared. "Down!"

La Guitarista came through the door of the Perro with both guns blazing. Raul was the first to get hit. Bolan shoved Chavo as hard as he could. The big man's chair was already creaking dangerously beneath his bulk, and as it went up on two legs it snapped underneath him and dumped him to the floor.

Esteban put a pair of bullets into the wall where Chavo's head had been. Bolan's Browning was already in his hand and it spit fire at Esteban.

Esteban ignored him as he took off the top of Barrel's head and swung his guns onto Armando. Armando had gotten his weapon out, but too late. Esteban's pistols rolled in continuous fire, hammering Armando back against the wall. The thing burned his entire clip straight into the ceiling and was dead before he hit the floor.

Chavo bounced to his feet like a 310-pound jumping jack. Carlos was spraying the landscape with his MAC-10 and killing ceiling fixtures.

Bolan's Browning barked in his hand.

Chavo thrust out a Russian P-9 Gurza pistol. The Gurza, or "Viper," was a huge pistol, but it looked like a toy in the giant's hand. It threw out a special tungsten-core, armor-piercing 9 mm bullet at nearly 1600 feet per second.

It would cut through Esteban's armor like tissue.

Esteban put four bullets into Carlos and sent him crumpling and still firing to the floor. Chavo thrust his pistol out at arm's length. Bolan pointed his Browning at the side of Chavo's skull and fired. Chavo's pistol barked once and sent a round into the door frame by Esteban's head. The pistol dropped from the giant's hand, and he toppled over like a tree. Bolan nodded at Esteban as he fired off the last five rounds in his clip.

Esteban put his hand in his pocket and it came out dripping red. He smeared his hand on the Perro Bar's doorframe and ran back out into the night for his motorcycle.

Bolan reloaded and fired off a few more rounds before kneeling beside Chavo to access the damage. His Hi-Power held fourteen rounds. The first nine had been blanks to fire at Esteban. The last five had been for the boys around the table in case things had gone wrong. Bolan had shot Chavo in the side of the head with a blank.

A blank cartridge contained very fast burning powder so that it would develop enough force to cycle the gun. A blank powder load with a real bullet would blow up most guns it was loaded into. A blank cartridge had no bullet, but it did have a wad that sealed the casing and held in the gunpowder. The wad was usually made of plastic or in this case hardened waxed paper. The jet of gas and unburned powder had torn a furrow along the side of Chavo's head, and the wad had dealt him a horrific blow to the skull. Blood was everywhere, and bone gleamed through the torn flesh.

Chavo looked as if he'd been shot in the head. The burns might be hard to explain, but Bolan would just have to hope that the doctor who treated him wouldn't know any better. The giant was pushing himself up to his hands and knees. Bolan heaved him up to his feet. Chavo swayed and blinked groggily.

Bolan held up two fingers. "How many fingers?"

Chavo lost his English. *"Dos."*

"Where are you?"

"Perro…"

Bolan scooped up Chavo's Gurza pistol and shoved it into his hands. "You gotta walk. You hear me? You gotta walk out of here."

Chavo put a massive hand against the wall to steady himself. He blinked as he took in the four dead street soldiers and spoke in English. "What happened?"

"La Guitarista happened." Bolan draped a massive arm across his shoulder and began dragging Chavo out of the bar. "He killed Carlos, Raul, Armando and Barrel. He took a real good stab at blowing your head off."

"Where?" Chavo brought his hand to his head. He was bleeding a river all over Bolan. "Where is he?"

"He ran."

"He ran?" Chavo pulled up short and stared at Bolan.

Bolan nodded at the doorframe and the smear of blood. "All three of us were exchanging fire. I don't know if it was you or me, but one of us got a piece of him."

"Why didn't you go after him?"

Bolan shrugged beneath Chavo's gorillalike arm. "I stayed with you. I didn't know how bad you were wounded."

Chavo accepted that with a grunt and stared at the bloodstain. There was a decent amount of it dripping down. "Well, I hope he dies." Chavo grinned, and the effort seemed to cause him immense pain. "I hope he dies in a gutter with dogs pissing on him. He'd better hope he does, too, because if he doesn't, then God help him when I get my hands on him."

"Hey."

Chavo sighed heavily. "What?"

"You're bleeding on me."

Chavo dug into his pocket and dug out the keys to his Cadillac. "You drive. I'll tell you where."

14

"How's Chavo?"

Scott cracked himself a beer and flopped down in one of the overstuffed chairs in Omega's den. "Well, for a guy who took one in the melon, he's tip-top."

"Where is he now?"

"He's outside. You wanna see him?"

Omega pressed a button on his desk. "Send in Sergeant Inarritu."

Omega's adjutant answered over the intercom. "Immediately, Commander."

Chavo limped into the den. The entire left side of his head was swaddled in bandages, and his eyes were splotched red with broken blood vessels. He walked over to Omega's bar and poured himself a shot of tequila, shook two painkillers out of an amber medication bottle and chased them down his throat with the liquor. He twisted the cap off a beer.

He grimaced as he took the chair next to Scott.

Omega smiled sympathetically. "How you doing, big man?"

Chavo stared at Omega flatly. "I have a headache."

"I can imagine. You want to tell me what happened?"

Chavo's voice rumbled like a distant storm. "Those clowns you sent me were worthless. You should have sent Raptors to do the job."

Aztec Raptor company officers and men had been dropping like flies recently, but Omega kept that observation to himself. "Cooper seems to have acquitted himself with distinction."

Chavo sat up straight and grimaced as the effort sent an ice pick of pain through his left eyebrow. "Cooper fucking rocks."

Omega leaned back. "Tell me about that."

"First off, like I said, those guys you sent me sucked. They were okay for putting the fear of God into the locals, but I could have done that by myself." Chavo raised a finger as thick as a sausage. "Now, Cooper on the other hand, he went into body-guard mode. My bodyguard. Now I ain't the kind who needs a babysitter, but his shit was tight. Kept his eye on every window and door. Always scanning the street."

"You don't think he's a cop?"

"No way he's a cop. I let the scum off the leash. I didn't let them rip anyone a new rectum or violate anyone's wife or daughter's holiest of holies, but those pukes you sent me? Even for Nuevo Laredo they pushed the envelope for public misbehavior. And Cooper didn't blink. He didn't give a good goddamn. Scott told me to give him a job. I gave him five hundred bucks and paid his beer tab and he had my back. That was his mission, and he made it his mantra."

"So what happened at the Perro?"

An animal snarl rumbled low in Chavo's throat. "La Guitarista happened. That little shitter is insane."

"And?"

Chavo lowered his voice. "And so I started to get a bad feeling. At first, I thought it was Cooper. Maybe he stunk like something was wrong. But then, I looked at him, and I knew he knew something was wrong, too. He told me he had a bad feeling. And right then? I knew we were going to get hit. I told Armando and Barrel to put the door in a cross fire, and before they could even get up there was that Guitar Player son of a bitch. Dressed like a mariachi, gun in each hand."

"So what happened?"

"That Guitarista son of a bitch is fast. The son of a bitch couldn't miss."

"He missed you."

Chavo brought a finger to his bandages. "That ain't a miss. That was a question of bullet placement, and if hadn't been for

Cooper, Guitarista's first two shots would have opened up my head like a melon."

"Really."

"Yeah, well, you wanted me to be the big target. So the little shit came straight for me. But Cooper shoves me out of the line of fire and engages the little puke."

Omega already knew the story, but he wanted to hear it from Chavo. "So why didn't La Guitarista finish you two off?"

Chavo smiled an ugly smile. "Because we got a piece of him. There was blood on the door. Nice big swath of it. Cooper and I ain't sure which of us hit him. He thinks it was probably me because I was loaded with armor-piercing, but one of us tagged him. There was blood out on the street, too."

"Why didn't Cooper pursue?"

"Cooper stayed with his commanding officer and made sure his brains stayed in his head and then extracted." Chavo's brows bunched dangerously. "I'm standing by his decision."

Omega nodded thoughtfully. "Scotty, what do we have from ballistics?"

"Same two Ruger KP-45 pistols as the hacienda massacre. Perfect match. Bunch more .45s from the MACs, one Gurza shell from Chavo's gun, bullet not found, and a bunch of 9 mm shells from Cooper's Browning."

Omega ran the story and the strands of evidence in his mind. "Anything else?"

"Yeah, I had the paramedics take a blood sample off the door. Interesting piece of trivia. La Guitarista? His blood type is O-negative."

Omega lifted his chin. "Universal donor."

"That's right. O-negatives can give blood to anybody else, but not only that, they can only accept blood from another O-negative. It's a rare blood type. The blood banks are always trying to find them as donors."

"You didn't happen to find out how rare."

"Yeah, I chatted up the lab guy." Scotty was pleased with himself. "Only four percent of Hispanics in Latin America are O-negative."

"So we're looking for a mariachi with O-negative blood."

"Yeah, with luck that might narrow it down a bit."

"Scotty, I want you to check the records of all the hospitals in the city. I don't care who you have to bribe or how much, but I want every record checked. I want a list of every O-negative male between the ages of twenty and thirty who's had anything so much as a hangnail in the past ten years."

"Figured you'd say that boss. I got Carvalo and Balbi on it. They're making nice with the good hospital administrators even as we speak."

Omega nodded. "Good."

The Aztec Raptors had been designed to go after the drug dealers, both out in the field and in the urban environment. Carvalo and Balbi and their three-man teams were the Raptors' urban-recon detail. They were former Mexican military police investigators. Their main mission was the aggressive collection of sensitive intelligence on the enemy. Kicking doors, kidnapping, intimidation, blackmail and "aggressive interrogation" were their stock-in-trade.

"Tell them to drop everything else. This one is ASAP."

"You got it, boss."

"So." Omega looked at the file in front of him. "Cooper."

Scott shrugged. "I like him. We need some replacements, and we have big things coming up."

Omega nodded. "Chavo?"

"Well, I ain't about to spend the night on Brokeback Mountain with him in a pup tent—" the giant flicked the cap off another beer with his thumb and waggled his eyebrows "—but man I love that guy!"

"Okay." Omega closed the file. "Let's give the man a job and see what he can do."

Coahuila

SCOTT WAS LEADING. "Okay, Coop. It's gonna be you and me, sex machine, and I'm wearing you like a thong, you got me?"

"I got ya." Bolan was dressed in the black battle fatigues of

Aztec Raptor company. He wore a black do-rag on his head.
Gray, green and black greasepaint was painted in disruptive patterns so that his face was nothing but blue eyes and white teeth
staring out of a hostile collage. He had been issued a
G-36 C short assault rifle and given a box of 9 mm ammunition
for his pistol. Scott had asked Bolan if he wanted anything else.

Bolan had requested a tomahawk.

Scott had raised eyebrows at the request and started referring to Bolan as "sex machine."

But Bolan had gotten his tomahawk within the hour. He'd
been hoping for one of the titanium hawks the Army Rangers
had been adopting as unofficial issue in Afghanistan or a Cold
Steel reproduction of the infamous Vietnam hawk. What he'd
gotten was Native American–style Missouri war hatchet that
had been manufactured in India and was realistic down to the
tribal heart and star shaped cutouts in the blade. That didn't
bother Bolan. The cutouts made the blade lighter and faster, and
Indian bladesmiths didn't mess around. Even if the blade
wasn't titanium, the boys from back in the Old West would
have killed for steel this good.

Bolan had dipped the mirror-bright head in black paint and
then honed the five-inch edge shaving sharp. They were rumbling across the Coahuilan badlands in blacked out Hummers.
The drivers were operating from night-vision telescopes
mounted on the roof. The interiors of the Hummers were dim
and lurid in the red glow of the emergency running lights. Scott
glanced at the blackened weapon thrust under Bolan's web belt.

"How's that working out for you there, sex machine?"

"It'll do."

Six men were crowded into the Hummer troop compartment. They all wore subdued Aztec Raptor uniforms and
badges, but Bolan had become aware that not all of the men in
three Mexican army vehicles were Mexican. The man next to
Scott was a German named Heinricht.

Dundee, a wiry man with an Australian accent, sat opposite
Bolan. He looked at the tomahawk and then grinned to show
his missing front teeth.

"Hey, Hiawatha. You gonna scalp anyone, tonight, then?"

"Dunno." Bolan glanced at Scott. "You paying a bounty?"

Scott laughed. "How much you charging?"

"A hundred?"

Scott blinked.

"Crikey!" Dundee sat up in alarm. "He's bloody serious!"

"Coop…" Scott's smile disappeared behind his greasepaint. "You aren't serious, are you?"

Bolan shrugged. "Back in Africa they offered us 150 francs per rebel head."

"Bloody hell!"

Bolan's blue eyes burned into the middle distance in memory. "That was about twenty-five bucks American back then." Bolan glanced at Scott. "I think it was one of you Yanks in the unit who figured that scalps would be easier to carry."

The men in the Hummer stared, slack-jawed.

Dundee was appalled. "Ya fucking savages!"

The driver, Juanito, interrupted. "Scott, we're five klicks from deployment. ETA fifteen minutes."

"Roger that." Scott leaned forward. "All right, settle your asses down. We're going after Juan Hidalgo tonight."

Bolan had heard the name before. Hidalgo was the heir apparent to the throne of the Charros gangs. *Charros* were the horsemen in traditional Mexican rodeos and came from the ranches in the Mexican countryside.

Mexicos's rural poor had always been the traditional prey of the city gangs. Their women were rounded up and sold into prostitution. Their men used as slave labor in drug factories. If they came to town, they had to pay tithes on their crops or goods to the gangsters and protection money for their stalls in the marketplace.

The Charros gangs had changed all that.

They had formed themselves into gangs for self-protection and then realized their own profit potential. Northern Mexico was vast, and nearly all commerce was done by trucks. They had gone into business as hijackers, then demanded protection from anyone sending trucks through their territory. The enraged urban crime lords had used their connections to get the government to send troops to stamp out these "revolutionaries" in the hinterlands.

Few of the Charros were actually cowboys, but they knew their mountains and their deserts from childhood. Several Mexican army patrols had gone into the mountains and never come back. The Charros could hide in the hinterlands or just melt back into the population. They were horsemen, people of the land. They made up for their lack of criminal sophistication with machismo and daring. They would fight anyone at anytime, no matter what the cost.

One of the Aztec Raptor company's founding missions had been to seek out and destroy the Charro gangs in their own unforgiving territory.

Bolan and his teammates were deep in that territory tonight.

"Listen, this Hidalgo is supposed to be a tough son of a bitch, and he's given us insult, but this isn't an Old Testament situation. Hidalgo's a dead man. But his machine? We want it intact. His guys? Within the year we want them working for us. You guys got that?"

The men in the Hummer all nodded.

"You see money? Take it. Gold or silver? Take it. Drugs? Take it, but we don't rape and we don't burn. You leave the hired help alone, and besides Hidalgo and his closest asshole buddies? We don't kill anyone who doesn't ask for it. We want this surgical."

Scott checked his watch. "Juanito, get us moving. The rest of you guys pipe down and get frosty! We got shit to do."

The column of Hummer began grinding forward again.

Scott pulled out a map and leaned forward. "We're going to make our approach and then deploy by foot five klicks out." Scott clicked his throat mike. "Hummer 3, break off and make your approach on the ridge."

"Affirmative, Hummer 1."

Hummer 1 and 2 were in troop carrier configuration, each carrying an eight-man section. Scott was in command of 1, and Chavo in number 2. Hummer 3 was configured for fire support and had a TOW wire-guided antitank missile launcher mounted over the cabin. It was a very interesting strategy. There was no way the government could launch any traditional kind of military or law-enforcement attack on the Charro gangs without them knowing it long before it happened. They would simply melt away or set up ambushes depending on the size and strength of the raid. A helicopter assault was probably what the Charros most feared, but their scouts would hear the rotors from miles away. Paid informers would probably leak the airborne assault before it was even launched, and the Charros would either put up suicidal resistance or again simply melt away into the countryside. The Charros owned the local police from top to bottom, and they acted as their scouts both in town and by setting up checkpoints out on the desert roads and mountain passes.

The Raptors had circumvented all of that.

A Mexican army C-130 had been requisitioned and taken the three palletted Hummers into its belly in the dead of night. They had flown over the desert of Coahuila and dropped the vehicles out the loading ramp, and the soldiers and vehicle crewmen had jumped out after them. The drop had been perfect. Someone had done their homework. Men and vehicles had landed without a hitch on a soft pan of sand that was a desert lake every twenty years when the rains came. The men were equipped to move light and fast. but the vehicles were laden with food, water, fuel and spare weapons and equipment for a week. If things went south, Aztec Raptor company was prepared to fight their way back to civilization.

The mission had been well thought out from top to bottom, and the wherewithal to organize, requisition, and keep the mission secret smacked of someone higher up the food chain than Scott or Chavo. That someone had to be Omega, and this night Bolan had to prove himself to the man he intended to bring down.

Scott went over the particulars.

Hidalgo was holed up in one of his favorite resting spots, the town of Cabra Diablo. White adobe buildings lumped up against one another in a pile like a medieval castle that had melted and spread out in the sun. A single dusty dirt road cut the pueblo in two.

They would move in on foot, and once the attack started Hummers 1 and 2 would come in with their machine guns and hold down both ends of town. Hummer 3 would hold back and blow away any unexpected strongpoint or any vehicle that broke the cordon.

The Raptors crawled out of the desert.

Juanito checked his GPS and brought Hummer 1 to a halt. "We're at minimum deployment distance."

Scott checked his shotgun. Bolan had noted the brutal weapon and its shark maw. "All right! We walk it from here! Check your weapons and gear. We got five klicks to hump, and I want absolute silence. Four-man fire teams! Heinricht, Cooper, Dundee, you're with me."

The Raptors spilled out of their vehicles into the desert night.

15

Cabra Diablo

"Omega, this is Scott. We are in position. Operation Strongarm is a go."

Bolan listened across the radio web, but Omega's response was for Scott's ears only.

Scott nodded at what only he could hear and clicked his radio. "Heinricht, you in position?"

The German came back across the radio web immediately. "ETA one minute, Scott."

They were fifty yards outside the pueblo. The Mexican desert was bright with tens of thousands of stars. Bolan crouched beside Scott, scanning the pueblo through the sights of his rifle. The mountains rose like a black wall behind the town. It was built where two creeks came down out of the mountains and met. Goatherds had been bringing their flocks down from the mountain pastures since Aztec times. The town was buttoned up for the night, though lights were visible through the heavy wooden shutters in the largest cluster of adobes. Intel said that was where Hidalgo kept house when he was in this area of the desert.

Bolan could see four sentries on the roof. The men had AK-74 rifles, but they lounged about smoking cigarettes. One man squatted next to the satellite dish and was fiddling with his MP-3 player. None of them had night-vision equipment. They were watching the town rather than the perimeter. It was clear that Hidalgo felt he was untouchable here.

Hidalgo was wrong.

"So who's Omega?"

Scott turned and his teeth flashed white out of his camouflage paint. "Why, he's the jealous, angry, Old Testament, desert God of your forefathers with no sense of humor. He's Santa Claus, keeping a list of who's naughty and nice. But you, Coop—" Scott shrugged "—you just think of old Uncle Omega as your invisible friend."

"I'll keep that in mind."

"You do that."

They waited in the darkness while Heinricht crept toward his target. The town of Cabra Diablo had gotten electricity only in the 1960s and was still dependent on the same power line that had been stretched across the desert more than half a century earlier. Six dim streetlights hung suspended by wires across the single road through town.

Heinricht spoke over the radio. "In position, charge in place, awaiting your signal."

Scott thumbed his mike. "Hummer 2, status?"

"In position."

"Hummer 3?"

"In position. We are within maximum range and have a clear arc of fire. We are locked and loaded, awaiting firing orders."

Scott pulled his goggles down over his eyes. "All units, check night-vision."

The Raptors powered up their night-vision goggles, and all units checked in in the affirmative. Scott rose up. "All units, move in."

Bolan flicked the safety off of his weapon and followed Scott's lead. The Raptors descended on the Cobra Diablo. Behind them, the Hummer's diesels rumbled into life. Ahead, the pueblo plunged into darkness as the streetlights and the light spilling from the few open windows blinked out. Heinricht jogged out of the darkness and fell into the Raptors' advancing arrow formation.

The single road into town had a gate and checkpoint, but it

was not manned at that time of night. The Raptors spilled past it, splitting into four-man groups paralleling one another on either side of the street. Chavo and his team from Hummer 2 would be doing the same thing on the other side of the pueblo. The vehicles and their roof-mounted machine guns were roaring up to put the cork in the bottle.

Hummer 3 reported from its firing position on the ridge overlooking town. "The sentries on the roof are starting to look alert. They're starting to figure something's wrong."

"Roger that." Scott held up his fist and the two fire teams halted. "Dundee, frag the sons of bitches."

"Affirmative." The Australian raised his rifle and the attached AG-36 40 mm grenade launcher. The weapon thudded and belched a puff of yellow smoke. On top of Hidalgo's roof, one of the sentries pointed and shouted in alarm.

Heinricht raised his rifle, and a single shot cracked out to knock the sentry back out of sight. A second later, Dundee's grenade detonated, and men screamed.

Scott's voice rose to a roar. "All units! Go! Go! Go!"

The Raptors charged down the dusty street for the main villa. The wooden shutters of a second-story adobe flew open, and a man with an AK-74 and a flashlight was scanning and screaming in something that was half Spanish and half indigenous dialect.

Bolan stopped and fired three quick rounds from his G-36. The AK and the flashlight fell to the street, and a second later the body of the man followed.

Windows and door began flying open all over the pueblo. Hidalgo's people had been trained by hard experience as ambushers. They, themselves, were always expecting it, but the Charros had been caught flat-footed. Many were half-dressed and blinking away sleep. They had no night-vision equipment, and the Raptors were little more than shadows in the gloom of the narrow street. The pueblo became a shooting gallery. Any Charro who popped up in a window or door got knocked down.

Bolan's ears pricked up at a muffled sound beneath the hammering of gunfire. "Generators! They have generators!" Bolan shoved his goggles up on his forehead. "Take cover!"

The six streetlights clicked on one at a time, and just as fast Bolan's rifle cracked and shattered them in showers of sparks.

Scott waved at Bolan. "Good work! You and Dundee! Go around the back of the main villa. Anyone who—"

The hard glare of floodlights was something that satellite recon had not prepared them for.

Heinricht squinted up the street and pointed and shouted, "Down! Everyone dow—"

A sound like tearing canvas bounced off the foot of the mountains as hell erupted from the bell tower of the pueblo church. The green laser lines of tracers from a Russian KPV 14.5 mm heavy machine gun streaked through the night straight at the big German. Heinricht was splattered across an adobe like a water balloon full of red paint. What was left of him flopped down to the dust, leaving half a dozen fist-sized holes behind him.

Bolan brought up his rifle and fired off three rounds. Sparks flew in the bell tower, and the giant machine gun began jackhammering just for him. The Russian KPV had been designed immediately after the WWII. It had been built around the 14.5 mm high-velocity antitank rifle round. Bolan threw himself down out of the line of sight, but brittle clay was no defense against the massive bullets screaming in at 600 rounds per minute. Bolan rolled into the gutter as a clay wall shattered and fell around him in showers.

Hummer 1 rolled up, nearly filling the narrow street. The gunner, Roldan, was manning the MAG machine gun.

Bolan shouted to wave them off. "Get back! Get back! Get back!"

Roldan swung his machine gun up and sent a stream of bullets into the bell tower. Sparks shrieked against the improvised steel plating defending the heavy weapon. The KPV swung down upon the Hummer, and the two machine gunners exchanged fire. Roldan's 7.62 mm was no match for the Russian 14.5 mm KPV, which had been designed to kill Nazi tanks. Roldan smeared across the top of the Hummer, and his weapon screamed with the sound of rending metal as it was ripped from its firing ring.

Juanito was screaming across the radio as the Hummer's gears ground into reverse. "Roldan is down! I am taking fire! I'm—"

The driver's window smashed inward, and the rest of the windows splattered red. The vehicle slowly rolled backward as the KPV cut it into Swiss cheese. It crunched to a halt against a hitching outside the cantina and sat steaming and ticking. Bolan rolled to his feet and shot an AK-armed man in the alley across the street. He looked for Scott and saw him ten yards ahead on his hands and knees in a pile of shattered wall clutching his bloody head dazedly.

Bolan thumbed his throat mike. "Hummer 3, this is Coop. Scott is down. Repeat—Scott is down. Requesting immediate fire support. Target bell tower. Repeat—target bell tower!"

Ruzzo was in command of Hummer 3 and he came back instantly. "Understood. Take cover." The ridgeline lit up in a flash of orange light as the launch motor ignited. "Missile away!"

The TOW antitank missile blasted forth from its tube, and the flight motor ignited, spewing yellow fire from the twin flight nozzles and trailing its guide wires. This development did not go unnoticed in the bell tower, and the KPV muzzle swung around to engage.

"Hit the tower!" Bolan snarled across the battle link. "Everyone hit the tower with whatever you got."

Hummer 3 was in easy range of the KPV. Its missile flew under the speed of sound and had to be guided all the way to the target. Bolan and every other Raptor still standing emptied his rifle into the tower. Dundee's grenade launcher thudded, and yellow fire and black smoke erupted as the grenade detonated against the KPV's improvised armor shell. Another grenade hit from Chavo's group up the street. Green tracers streaked across the desert night from the bell tower, but they were slightly off target.

The missile roared in. Ruzzo knew his business. He wasn't rattled, and he knew his survival depended on his guiding the missile in. There would be no time for a second shot. The fifty-pound antitank missile hurtled in out of the dark like an angel of death borne on twin wings of fire.

The missile hit just under the KPV, and the entire top of the bell tower blew like a volcano. The bell chamber holding the weapon and the steeple disappeared in fire. One of the KPV's crew arced through the air like a burning mannequin and flopped smoldering to the street.

Raptors howled in savage exultation as they reloaded.

Charros were spilling out onto the top of Hidalgo's villa.

Bolan thumbed his mike as he ran to Scott. "Hummer 3, this is Coop! Top of Hidalgo's villa—engage!"

"Affirmative. Target noted," came back Ruzzo. "We are reloading. Will engage immediately."

Bolan yanked Scott to his feet and quickly scanned him. He didn't appear to be shot. He did look like man who'd had a wall fall on him. "You all right?"

"What?" Scott wiped blood out of his eyes. "Yeah!" He looked down the street at the ruin of Hummer 1. It looked as if a giant had savaged it with an ice pick. "No, fuck that, now I'm mad."

The Raptors were exchanging fire with the Charros crouching on the top of the villa. Ruzzo shouted across the web, "Missile away!"

Scott blinked at the orange glare in the east as screwed his earpiece back in and then noted the flaming bell tower. "Coop, you call that in?"

"You were busy eating a wall."

"Fair enough." The top of Hidalgo's villa detonated. Heat and smoke funneled down the narrow street in an eyebrow-singing wave. Ruzzo was firing BLAAMs, or Bunker Light Armor And Masonry rounds. The BLAAM was the TOW antitank missile adapted for urban warfare.

Scott gave the fiery top of the villa a bloody smile and his middle finger.

A voice spoke across the battle net, and Bolan heard Omega for the first time. He spoke English without an accent. "This is Omega. Scott, what is the sitrep?"

"The enemy had floodlights we didn't know about. Once the alarm went up, we were caught in the open. They had a crew-served weapon in the bell tower."

"Casualites?"

Scott grimaced behind his greasepaint. "Hummer 1 is totaled. Juanito and Roldan are both KIA." Scott glowered at the blood-swathed adobe across the street. "You could bury Heinricht in a thermos."

"Chavo, you have casualties?"

The giant's voice rumbled low over the radio link. "They had a goddamn 20 or something in that tower. Larry and Uncas got caught running for cover. Larry took two to the pelvis, tore his shit to shreds. He bled out in seconds. Uncas had both his legs ripped off above the knee. We got him stable, but he's in a real bad way."

"Scotty, you okay?"

"That fuck with the machine cannon managed to drop a wall on me. Coop stepped up and called in fire support from Hummer 3. Ruzzo nuked the bell tower."

The voice on the other end considered the news. "Ruzzo, what can you see from the ridge?"

"The heavy weapon in the tower is eliminated. No hostiles remain on villa roof. The shitheads in the villa look to have buttoned up for a siege. I have an estimated twenty to forty refugees fleeing the pueblo south. They're heading for the mountains."

"Are you all right?"

"A few rounds came close, but Coop and the boys distracted them long enough to give me the shot."

"Good enough. Nico. Manolo. Advance to three hundred yards of the road leading into road into the mountains. Let the citizens flee. Shoot any man with a rifle."

Nico and Manolo were Operation Strongarm's sniper team. Nico came back. "Affirmative, Omega. We are deploying."

"Ruzzo, how many more TOWs do you have?"

Bolan knew that Scott was right as he listened. Omega was their invisible friend. He could feel him watching. Mexico didn't have any military observation satellites to speak of, but they did have a number high-altitude reconnaissance planes. Bolan's spine told him Omega was close.

Ruzzo came back. "Omega, I have six more missiles. Four more BLAAMs and two dedicated antitank. We also have the 81 mm mortar with twenty bombs, but we haven't deployed it yet."

Omega's voice was as cold as the grave. "Level the villa. Once we have a confirmed kill on Hidalgo, level the pueblo. Scotty, you burn what Ruzzo can't blow up."

Bolan spoke across the web. "I thought this was supposed to be surgical. Just the head of the hydra, then win hearts and minds."

"You know something, Coop?" Scott prodded Bolan in the chest with the muzzle of his rifle. "You done real good up to now. So, word to the wise. Shut the fuck up!"

The voice spoke calmly over the battle web. "Coop? This is Omega. The mission has changed. I want an example made. No one messes with *Los Untouchables*."

Bolan frowned at the implication. *Los Untouchables*. The vowels were spoken differently in English and the word was the same. The Untouchables.

Omega seemed to read his mind. "That's a club you belong to now, Coop. You just got jumped in tonight. Now, are you saying you want out?"

Scott's rifle was still pointed at Bolan's chest. Bolan could feel Dundee's eyes and the muzzle of his weapon in his back. Bolan let out a long breath. "Naw, I don't want out. I'm in."

"Good. Good to hear. Ruzzo? Start your bombardment. I want that pueblo turned into a parking lot."

Scott's greasepaint split from ear to ear. "You heard the man, Ruzzo. Knock this Popsicle stand to the ground."

"Affirmative, Hicks and Mannetti are deploying the mortar. Beginning missile bombardment."

"Yo-yo, your public-address system still operational?"

"Yo-yo" Yotuel was the driver of Hummer 2. "Yeah, what do you need?"

"Take a slow roll up and down the town. Tell everyone to leave their homes. Throw down any weapons and leave. Clothes on their backs. Nothing else, and to start walking for the southern end of town. Shoot anyone who resists."

"Affirmative."

Hummer 2 began to roll down the street. The megaphone began blaring out the orders in Spanish. The first missile hit the front of the villa like a fiery sledgehammer. The entire second-story front wall collapsed. Men with rifles were crushed or fell burning and screaming to the street. The front door of the villa flew open and women and children ran out screaming into the street. They saw the men in black with automatic weapons and ran up the street for the hills.

Hummer 2 had circled to the front of the pueblo and was herding an ever increasing, weeping mob of villagers up the street. They flinched and stared in horror as they were marched past Hidalgo's villa. The rifles of the Raptors cracked and fired into any open window or terrace. The villa was beginning to burn. The villagers flinched and screamed at the thunder and the wash of heat as the next missile slammed home.

Sporadic riflefire came out of the stricken building but was met by waves of return fire by the Raptors. The third TOW hit the villa, and its entire eastern corner collapsed into smoking ruin.

Omega spoke. "Scotty, what's the situation with the villa?"

"Cracked like an egg and open to the sky, but Hidalgo and some boys are still in there. Dug in like ticks and still salty."

"Ruzzo? You got that mortar deployed yet?"

"You bet."

"How many tactical CS bombs you got?"

"Six."

"Drop all of them in. Bug-bomb the place. Let's see if we can smoke Hidalgo out."

"You got it."

Moments later a mortar thumped on the ridgeline. Amid all the fire and smoke pouring out of the villa, the pyrotechnic effects of the bombs were negligible. To anyone inside, however, six battlefield-sized tear-gas bombs were filling the warren of clay cube rooms with lethal concentrations of CS gas.

Charros began to spill out in ones and twos from the doors and sections. They came out choking and weeping. Some came forth screaming ragged obscenities and firing their rifles blindly. Others came throwing down their weapons and begging for mercy.

The Raptors burned them down.

Scott's voice came across the link. "Hold your fire. This one's mine."

A man stumbled out of the shattered eastern wall of the villa. He wore black cowboy boots, jeans, a black leather jacket and the leather hat of a Mexican cowboy. His belt, boots and hat were studded with silver conchas and blue turquoise. His left arm hung at an unnatural angle, and blood dripped from his limp fingers. In his right hand, he held the nickel-plated, ivory-handled six-gun of a cowboy.

Scott stepped out of the doorway he was using for cover. "Hidalgo!"

The Charro leader whirled at the sound and thumbed back the hammer of his revolver.

Scott's shotgun roared and cut Hidalgo's left leg out from underneath him. Hidalgo fell to the street. Scott walked up and kicked the revolver out of Hidaldgo's hand. "Yo-yo, stop the parade. Tell everyone to get on their knees."

The loudspeaker blared out in Spanish. Yo-yo's gunner, Diaz, fired long bursts from the machine gun over the villagers' heads to emphasize the order. The villagers screamed and fell to their knees, clutching one another.

Scott grabbed Hidalgo by the collar of his jacket and dragged him up the street toward the kneeling mob. He spoke into his radio. "Ruzzo, resume bombardment of the villa. Start marching high-explosive bombs into the houses, starting at the north end of town."

"Affirmative, Scott. Beginning bombardment."

Another missile roared out of its tube. The mortar began slowly and methodically thudding out its ordnance.

Scott walked along as explosions began erupting behind him on the far edge of the pueblo. He jerked his head at Chavo. "You're with me."

Scott stopped in front of the villagers and forced Hidalgo into a kneeling position. "Chavo, translate for me." Scott filled his lungs. "One word!"

"¡Uno parablas!" Chavo bellowed.

"Omega!"

The Raptors roared back in response. Bolan knew they had done this before. "Omega!"

"Omega?" Scott continued. "He owns this town! He owns these mountains! He owns this desert! He owns you, your wives, your daughters, your children!"

Chavo roared out the translation.

The villagers screamed as Scott suddenly raised his shark-toothed shotgun and rammed it into the back of Hidalgo's skull. The Charro hung from the doorknob, ripping teeth embedded in his skull. He jerked, twitching and shuddering, pithed at the end of Scott's weapon.

Scott surveyed the villagers for a moment, reading their mood as he held Hidalgo's brain-dead body twitching in place. His teeth flashed in a gruesome smile. "We'll come back."

Scott retrieved his shotgun from Hidalgo's head by pulling the trigger.

Hidalgo sagged forward, faceless, to the dust. A collective moan shivered through the kneeling villagers. Scott wiped off the muzzle of his weapon against Hidalgo's back and turned to Chavo.

"Burn this place to the ground."

16

Nuevo Laredo

To the victors went the spoils. The men from Operation Strong-arm lined up while Chavo doled out money. Bolan took his share. Eleven thousand Mexican pesos and around another four thousand in U.S. dollars. All told, a little over five grand. Not bad for a night's pillaging, and pillaging there had been. The villagers had been forced out into the night with nothing but the clothes on their backs. Like a lot of poor villagers around the world, what little wealth they did have was in gold and silver, and usually worn. The Charros themselves were bandits and warlords, and they carried their wealth in fat rolls of cash and expensive jewelry and accessories.

Dundee sat gleefully, setting the time on his new titanium Yacht Master Rolex watch. The little Australian had shown no reluctance whatsoever in scampering up to Hidalgo's nearly headless corpse and stripping it of all valuables before it was cold. All money the Raptors had collected went into a common pot that was now being shared out equally so that the snipers and fire-support crew wouldn't get stiffed. It was all very democratic.

Jewelry, watches and guns, however, were strictly a finders-keepers situation.

Bolan turned to Ruzzo. The commander of Hummer 3 was first-generation Cuban immigrant. He was wiry, black, perpetually grinning, perpetually smoking cigars and wore an Oakland Raiders baseball cap indoors and out, rain or shine. Ruzzo had learned how to fire a TOW in the United States Army and gone on to be a "snake eater" in the Seventy-fifth Ranger Battalion.

Bolan's cover had him as a French Foreign Legion veteran, and it was starting to look as if Omega had his own little legion of strangers in the Mexican border country. He had brought together a trusted inner core of men who weren't criminals or drug muscle, nor Mexican soldiers or renegade police whose loyalty could turn on a dime depending on the current political wind. They were *Los Untouchables*. They were being paid to be soldiers. Being paid to do what they were best at, and being paid far more than they ever had in the respective armies they had served in. They were given the latest and best equipment. Their prey were criminals, and that made them justifiable targets in their minds. Any twinges of conscience over burning an entire pueblo to the ground and turning its people out into desert night were salved over by the opportunity of loot.

"Yo, Ruzzo." Bolan tossed him a gleaming S.T. Dupont 007 lighter he had taken off a dead Charro. Bolan had looted the dead many times, for fresh weapons, for supplies, for survival. Doing it for profit turned his stomach, but his cover had demanded it. It would serve him now. Bolan cracked a smile. "Thanks for saving our asses out there, man."

Ruzzo caught the thousand-dollar lighter and grinned delightedly at the signature Dupont ping it made as he flipped it open. "Thanks, Coop!" Ruzzo sparked up the stub he'd been gumming and grinned benevolently at the rest of the men in the room. "You assholes see that? Now, that's class. That's respect."

Scott walked into the room. He snatched Ruzzo's cap off his head and held it out. "Let's talk a little class and respect. Uncas doesn't have any legs, and he's going to need a lot of professional help. I guarantee you he's going to be well taken care of, but I'm sure it would cheer him up some if you boys kicked in a little something for a retirement present."

Ruzzo grinned and put a thousand dollars into his own hat. "Respect, boys. Class and respect."

The dozen men in the room began peeling large wads of money into the cap. Some watches, jewelry and a gold-plated .45 pistol made it into the hat, as well.

Scott handed the hat back to Ruzzo. "Since you're the only one here with any class, I'll let you handle it."

"Coop's got class!" Ruzzo grinned.

"Coop's coming with me." Scott turned to Bolan. "You paid? You happy?"

Bolan shoved his four grand into his pocket. "Oh, yeah, I'm happy."

"Good, you've got an appointment."

OMEGA SAT SMILING at the Butcher mildly. Chapa squirmed under his gaze. If he turned his head, Scott was looking at him, which was almost as bad. He fervently wished for another drink but didn't dare go to Omega's bar and serve himself. Omega could smell the fear on Chapa, and it was well deserved. The diminutive little gangster had just about exhausted his usefulness. His machine was shattered, his goon squad shattered and he had been publicly beaten and humiliated on several occasions.

"Nino?" Omega swirled the ice in his glass.

The Butcher squirmed at the hated name but said nothing.

"What am I going to do with you?"

Chapa's mouth opened and closed.

Omega's adjutant buzzed the intercom. "Commander, Balbi and Carvalo are here."

"Send them in."

The two psy-war operators came in and gave Chapa a thinly veiled look of disgust. They could tell he was a dead man.

Omega glanced at the file in Balbi's hand. "You have something for me, Bebe?"

Pedro "Bebe" Balbi looked like his nickname. He had a shaved head and a round pink face. Carvalo was blade thin and dark with a lot of Indio in him.

Balbi put the file on Omega's desk. "We have a lead."

"The blood typing?"

Balbi and Carvalo walked toward the couch. Chapa goggled as it appeared they were about to sit on him and leaped up. He scampered over to the bar and reached for the whiskey bottle with shattered nerves.

Balbi and Carvalo ignored him. "Yeah," Balbi confirmed. "Scotty was right. Only about four percent of the population are O-negative. Given the age range you gave me, this guy Esteban Buriche would be about right. He was admitted to the hospital ten years ago, beaten real bad. Required multiple surgeries. Numerous blood transfusions. His sister, Griffin, had to donate the maximum allowable amount and even then more had to be flown in from Mexico City."

"Griffin?" The Butcher looked up from his triple Scotch.

Balbi blinked and nodded at the file. "Griffin Buriche."

Omega peered at Chapa. "You know her?"

Chapa became excited. "Tall, skinny bitch! Long brown hair?"

Balbi glanced at the file. "All we have is her high-school photograph." He took it out and handed it over to the Butcher.

Chapa beamed. "Oh, I know this bitch!"

Omega leaned forward. "How?"

"Man!" Chapa spread his skinny arms. "I turned her out!"

"She's a prostitute?"

"Her father, Lorenzo? He was a police inspector. He wouldn't play ball with the Gulf Coast Gang. Supposed to be a real tough guy. He wasn't so tough after we cut off his hands and feet and did his wife in front of him."

"You did this?"

"Oh, yeah, it was one of my first jobs. The kids were in Mexico City with their grandparents or something. So the snot-nosed little punk tried to come after us. I wasn't there, but the boys took his gun away from him and beat him half to death, put him in the hospital. A couple of days later, we went and had a little party with his sister. When she healed up, we put her to work. I think Tavo was pimping her. Her brother lived. He became a mariachi or something."

Scott stared at Chapa and shook his head. "I don't know whether to kiss him or kill him."

Carvalo flipped through a skinny file marked La Guitarista. "Yeah, that's it. Tavo Sanchez. He was murdered about a month ago. That was the first killing attributed to La Guitarista by witnesses."

Omega sighed. Wonders never ceased. "I want this Esteban. I want him now."

"Yeah, but it can't be him." Chapa slugged back a huge swallow of whiskey, relieved that his appointment appeared to have stopped being a tribunal. His blood froze as Omega locked his gaze with him and held it.

"Why not?"

Chapa fortified himself with another shot of whiskey. "Well, he's retarded."

Balbi frowned and flipped back through his notes.

Omega wasn't blinking. "Retarded."

"Well, not retarded. I mean…" Chapa tried to sip his drink, but all he had left was ice. "The boys, they took his gun away from him, and they beat him with it. I mean they beat his goddamn brains out. They thought he was dead when they left him. He was all messed up, and I mean messed up. He was a joke in every bar in Nuevo Laredo. The retarded mariachi and his sister the whore."

Balbi scanned the medical file. "Traumatic brain injury, incurred by blunt trauma during an assault. Weapon unknown, multiple concussions, skull fracture and associated bleeding in the brain, particularly the left side and frontal lobe."

Omega's eyes narrowed. "You got a psych report in there?"

"Yeah, our boy suffers from severe posttraumatic stress disorder." Balbi laughed unpleasantly. "That's a no-brainer. He's been diagnosed as obsessive compulsive with low impulse control and disassociative disorder. Amnesia, believed to be both organic and selective. Loss of the ability to read and write and adult social skills attributed to physical trauma rather than psychological damage." Balbi shrugged. "It goes on."

Scott frowned. "Yeah, but if they beat him retarded and he

can't read and write, how the hell can he pay the guitar or shoot with a gun in each hand?"

"Because they didn't beat him retarded." Omega calculated. "They beat out his brains. There's a difference. He doesn't have a disease or some syndrome because he didn't get a bicycle when he was a kid. Our boy, Esteban? He's got pieces missing. Pieces that were beat out of him with the barrel of a Government Model .38 Super."

Scott nodded grudgingly at the summation. "Yeah, well, you said he had to be crazy to take on forty guys. They must have beaten out the part of his brain that gives a fuck."

"That's exactly what they did." Chapa pulled Griffin's picture out of the file. It was four years old. "Doni, you think you'd recognize the girl now?"

"Oh, yeah, you can't miss her," Chapa enthused. "Two meters tall and worth the climb. Brown hair down to her ass. Man, there wasn't nothing we didn't do to her. I'm telling you we…" Chapa trailed off as the hardmen regarded him in stony silence. "Yeah, I'd recognize her."

"Good. Bebe, you got an address on this girl?"

Balbi smiled unpleasantly. "Yeah, her and her brother both get their mail at the same address."

"Bebe, tell me you have a guy watching the place."

"Boss, I got two men watching the place."

"Good. Then take the rest of your team, and take Chapa. Stake the place out. I'll send you reinforcements directly. I want to get them both together. This brain-damaged asshole might not give up who's helping him no matter what we do to him. But all this *Desperado* crap? He's doing it for his sister. We dangle her screaming in front of him, and he'll sing for us. I want whoever's helping him. So don't move in until I tell you.

"If Buriche and his sister separate, then by God, Bebe, you put your best guys on tailing detail. You lose either one of them, I'll let the Butcher regain his confidence on your fat ass. You got me?"

Chapa swelled with pride.

Balbi put his remaining files on Omega's desk. "You got no

worries on my end, boss." He scowled and crooked a finger at Chapa. "You, shithead. You're with me."

Chapa deflated and followed Babli and Carvalo out of the office.

Omega turned to Scott. "Where's Cooper?"

"I think he's down in the kitchen grabbing some grub with Chavo."

Omega buzzed his adjutant. "Ochoa, send up Mr. Cooper and Chavo from the kitchen."

"Right away, Commander."

A few moments later Bolan and Chavo entered the office.

Bolan beheld Omega. He was as tall as Bolan, with a heavier build. With his black hair pulled back in a ponytail and the black silk suit and heavy gold jewelry, he was dressed from head to toe like a South American crime king. But that was all window dressing. The disturbing gray eyes and the way he held himself said it all.

Everything about the man screamed Special Forces.

"Listen, Coop. We have a situation here. Scotty and I have to go and take care of some business. I like the way you handled yourself at the Perro Bar, and you really impressed me during Operation Strongarm. You're a cool hand, Coop. And that shit can't be begged, borrowed or stolen."

Bolan smiled modestly. "Thanks, boss."

"So I got a job for you."

Bolan nodded. "What is it?"

"We got a line on that Guitarista son of a bitch, and his whore sister."

Bolan grinned even as his blood went cold. "I owe that fucker."

The giant's smile matched Bolan's. "You and me both."

"I've got Balbi and some men staking out their place, but Balbi's boys are interrogators and door kickers rather than real soldiers. I want both the Guitarista and his sister taken alive. That's going to take some finesse. Chavo's going to put together a team."

Bolan leaned back with a cautious smile. "You're making me second in command?"

"I'm saying you're gonna be Chavo's right arm on this one. This Guitarista is a nut job, and taking him alive is a job that could go south in an eye blink. I want you and Chavo to go scope the situation, and then you're going to come up with a plan."

"Got it."

"You guys don't move except as tails until I approve it."

"You got it."

Omega rose from his chair. "I want a mission profile on my desk in an hour."

17

There wasn't much time. Bolan swiftly tapped out Morse code on the bezel of his watch. He had to pray that Esteban was monitoring his black box.

"Where are you?"

Esteban came back immediately.

"The cave."

"Where is your sister?"

"Home. Why?"

Bolan considered his options. None of them were good.

Esteban signaled back again, the buzzer pulsing against Bolan's wrist ever more rapidly.

"Why?"

Bolan grimaced. "I'm going to pick her up."

"Why?"

Bolan knew he had to calm Esteban. If he was going to save Griffin, he couldn't have La Guitarista blowing up in his face.

"I need—"

Esteban interrupted his transmission.

"They know."

Esteban had a lot of malfunctions, but his battle instincts were spot on.

Bolan dotted and dashed. "Wait."

Bolan knew what the response would be before it pulsed against his wrist.

"No."

Bolan could hear Chavo's huge footsteps walking up the hall towards the bathroom.

"Wait."

"No."

"I need you to—"

"I'm on my way."

Bolan furiously tapped instructions to wait, but there was no response. Esteban would be on his motorcycle. He was going to save his sister, and he would be riding straight into an ambush. He might be able to shoot his way through Balbi, Carvalo and their crews, but once Chavo and the strike team were in place the sniper would shoot him out of the saddle before he ever saw a target or could slap leather. Bolan's only hope was that Esteban had strapped his signaling device in place onto the tank of his motorcycle and was still receiving.

Chavo banged on the bathroom door. "Christ, Coop! You coming or what?"

Bolan groaned through the door. He tapped in his last message to Esteban. He wouldn't be able to get away with tapping morse code sitting next to Chavo.

"Four men currently stalking out house. Four more coming or already there. Strike team with sniper inbound. I will be with them. Signal me when you are within two blocks. Will assist as best I can."

Bolan waited.

Chavo fist shuddered the door. "Coop!"

Bolan ran water in the sink and waited a few more seconds, but no response came. Bolan opened the door and wiped his brow. "Man…"

Chavo thudded a hand the size of a catcher's mitt on Bolan's shoulder and propelled him down the hall. "We gotta go, Coop."

Bolan nodded. "Let's do it."

They walked back into the room where the money from Operation Strongarm had been doled out. The strike team was assembled. Bolan recognized most of them. Dundee, the Australian, grinned at Bolan.

There was a wiry, bullet-headed little Russian guy named Svarza. Then there was Nico, the sniper from the Strongarm operation, and a white-haired scarecrow of a Dutchman named Sybo who had checked the heavy weapons.

Bolan nodded inwardly to himself. Balbi and his boys were all Aztec Raptors. Other than Chavo, the strike team were all *Los Untouchables*.

Omega's Mexican Foreign Legion.

Nico was giving Bolan a funny look. Eyes slitted. Calculating. Bolan knew the look. He'd worn it on his face many times staring through a telescopic sight. Nico was a sniper examining a possible target. Bolan grinned. "You want to earn a lighter, too?"

Nico Torrez had learned the sniper's trade in Expeditionary Unit 24 of the United States Marine Corps. He still wore his thick black hair in the regulation buzz cut. He was hook-nosed, hawk-faced, and had the flat black eyes of a shark. He shook his head at Bolan and smiled. "No, you just look familiar for some reason."

There was only one way an Aztec Raptor sniper would think he'd seen Bolan before. Nico Torrez had been the shooter with the .50-caliber rifle overlooking General Lothario's compound. Bolan had been wearing a suit, his skin had been darkened, his hair had been black and contact lenses had made his eyes brown. But he couldn't depend on that confounding Torrez forever. Bolan was a sniper himself. They were finicky for details.

Bolan cocked his head. "You been to Somalia?"

"No?"

"France?"

"No."

"Canada?" Bolan tried.

Nico grinned wearily. "Uh…no?"

"Then fuck off, you're creeping me out."

Nico laughed, and so did the rest of the team, but the sniper's eyes lingered on Bolan. He was trying to figure out the math. Nico was a very dangerous loose end that would have to be dealt with quickly. Bolan turned to Chavo. "You get the stuff?"

"Oh, yeah. Your Old Uncle Omega's candy store has every useful flavor, including ones you haven't even thought of yet." The giant bent and opened up a rubber-armored luggage case. Inside lay a pair of modified FN 303 Less Lethal Launchers. The FN 303 was simply a military-specification paintball gun, featuring a pistol grip, a skeleton stock and a compressed-air tube with a 15-round drum magazine. An X-26 Taser gun was mounted where the optical sight might have been.

Bolan took out the weapon and checked the action. "Omega wants this Guitarista punk alive. So here's how I want to play it. Me and Svarza are going to walk up to the door. Forcing our way in should be no problem. We juice the sister a couple of times, and she'll do anything we want. When her brother comes home, she opens the door, Svarza has Taser probes already in her body. She lets her brother in, and then we hammer him to the floor with baton rounds. When he goes down, we hit him with the Tasers, hog-tie his ass, put him and his sister in a van and take them to Omega. Whoever's babysitting them on the ride has stun guns. I don't care what kind of nut job this Guitarista guy is, he can't take forty thousand volts up his ass and stay salty."

Bolan put the weapon back in its case and checked the second one. "That's if everything goes right. If there's a problem, Balbi and Carvalo's teams come in guns blazing. If this little shit Guitarista breaks through or it looks like he or his sister is going to break out—" Bolan sighed and shook his head at Nico "—then you're green light. Take them out."

Nico nodded, temporarily distracted by the mission.

Everyone tensed as Omega's voice rumbled through the room through hidden speakers. "Good enough, Coop. Chavo? Do it."

Chavo raised his massive frame. "You heard the man, let's do it."

BOLAN RODE next to Nico in the Land Rover's second bank of seats. It was an armored VIP model with tinted windows. Dundee and Svarza sat in the seats behind them. Chavo sat in front and Sybo was driving. Nico rode with his rifle case standing up between his knees and every few seconds gave Bolan a searching look out of the corner of his eye.

Bolan checked the loads in his Browning and loosened his knife in its sheath. There had been no time to get any of his own special weapons and gear. He would have to work with what he had.

Svarza checked his stun gun and then took out a Beretta 92 and screwed a sound suppressor onto the muzzle before snapping it into a shoulder holster. He grinned at Bolan to show yellow, crooked teeth. "You ready, Coop?"

Bolan checked FN 303's cassette of projectiles and then slid the weapon into a big red duffel. "Ready."

Chavo craned around in his seat. "We're here."

They were in a run-down neighborhood in a bad part of Nuevo Laredo. The houses were small and crooked, with narrow doors. The narrow alleys between them were strewn with plastic bags, cardboard boxes and trash that feral dogs lazily surveyed.

Chavo pointed at a billboard with two girls in bikinis emoting openly about a giant bottle of beer between them. The billboard was covered with graffiti. "Nico, you're going to deploy from there. It should give you a clear shot of the streets both in the front and back of the house, as well as the west alley. Only the east side will be out of your view, and there's nothing there but five meters of sewage and garbage cans."

Nico nodded once. "Got it."

"Go."

Nico took his rifle case and slid out of the Land Rover. The sniper hopped a fence and disappeared. Seconds later he was scrambling up to the billboard's platform like a spider.

"Coop, Svarza. Balbi's got men in the house across the street and the one behind. Chapa gave us a positive ID on the girl. She's in the house."

Bolan's blood went cold. Chapa was here. Nico was suspicious and would be watching his every move with a sniper rifle. Esteban was roaring in on his motorcycle screaming for vengeance. The whole thing was going FUBAR. "Chavo, which way did she go in?"

Chavo's massive brow furrowed. "What?"

"The girl—did she go in the front or the back? How did she look?"

Chavo clicked his tactical radio. "Bebe, the girl. How did she come in?"

Balbi's voice crackled across the link. "She snuck in the back. Looking both ways. Nervous."

"Roger that." Chavo nodded at Bolan. "Good thinking." He glanced around the Rover. "All right, she's on a high state of alert. That's why you nice, fresh-faced white boys are going to do the knocking. Coop, Svarza, all you gotta do is get her to open the door and then push your way in. When shithead comes home, we can't afford to have windows or doors smashed in or any bullet holes anyplace. Nothing suspicious. We need the girl compliant and welcoming her brother home. Got it?"

Bolan and Svarza nodded.

Chavo lifted his chin at a dilapidated little house three houses down. "Go."

Bolan slung his duffel and jumped out. Sliding out of the air-conditioned Land Rover into the noon heat of the Mexican border town was like jumping into an oven. There was no sidewalk, just a gutter that abutted the houses. As they walked up to the house, Bolan waited for the bullet between his shoulder blades. His only hope was that since Chapa had seen her sneaking in the back, he was still stationed in the house behind.

Bolan pressed the door buzzer.

A few moments later the door opened a crack. Griffin peered out past the chain and looked at Bolan in surprise.

Bolan winked at her. "Ma'am, may we speak with you for a moment? It's very important."

She looked back and forth between Bolan and Svarza. "Well, okay…"

The door partially closed as she undid the chain, and Bolan shoved the door hard. Griffin fell back, and Bolan and Svarza swarmed into the room. Bolan slammed the door behind them.

Svarza yanked Griffin to her feet and pinned her against the wall. Bolan clicked on his radio. "We're in. We've got the girl."

Chavo came back. "Excellent, Coop. You and Svarza sit tight. Will advise."

"Roger that."

Svarza lifted Griffin up and slammed her back against the wall. "When's your brother coming home?"

Griffin looked wide-eyed over Svarza's shoulder at Bolan. Bolan unzipped his duffel and took out the FN 303. He nodded at Griffin.

Svarza snarled and slammed her against the wall again. "Don't look at him, bitch! He ain't gonna help you! When you expecting your brother!"

Bolan winked and held up two fingers behind Svarza's back.

Griffin sobbed. "Two hours! He's coming home in two hours!"

Svarza put a hand on her throat and squeezed. "You expect anyone else?"

Griffin's eyes rolled in terror. "No!"

Bolan glanced around. "Tell Chavo I'm going to sweep the house real quick."

Svarza hurled Griffin onto the couch and checked in. "The girl says she expects her brother in two hours. No other callers expected. Coop is sweeping the house."

"Affirmative," the giant rumbled.

Bolan swept the house. There wasn't much to sweep other than the little parlor, a shoebox of a kitchen, a bathroom and a single bedroom with nothing but a curtain of hanging beads for a door. On the west end of the house, a sliding glass door led to a tiny patio separated from the shack next to it by a rickety fence. "House is clear!"

"Coop says the house is clear," Svarza relayed.

"Good." Chavo grunted in satisfaction. "You two settle in, but don't get too comfortable. We have the neighborhood under surveillance. We'll intercept any unexpected callers and let you know when the target is in sight."

"Affirmative."

Bolan came back into the parlor. Svarza had his silenced Beretta out. He was smiling ugly at Griffin. He turned the smile on Bolan. "Hey, Coop. Wanna have some fun?"

Bolan regarded Svarza coolly. "We're supposed to stay frosty on this one."

"Yeah, and we got two hours to kill."

Bolan snorted in disgust. "If Chavo finds out, it's gonna be both our hides."

"What Chavo don't know won't hurt him, and Chavo ain't gonna find out." Svarza tossed his Beretta onto the armchair and loomed over Griffin. "Is he, baby?"

Bolan brought the FN 303 to his shoulder and fired. The .68-caliber finned polystyrene ball was filled with bismuth and designed to bring rioters down with body blows rather than killing them. Its maximum range was one hundred yards. Bolan shot Svarza in the forehead from five feet.

The compressed-air launcher made little more than a snapping noise as Bolan pulled the trigger five times. The baton round didn't have the power to crack the frontal arc of Svarza's skull, but the 8.5-gram projectiles still delivered every ounce of their energy.

The would-be Russian rapist fell twitching to the floor with his skull exposed and nothing but hemorrhaging applesauce between his ears.

Bolan scooped up the silenced Beretta and checked the loads as he checked in on the radio. He had one bad guy down, but he needed to even the odds more if there was to be any chance of getting Griffin out alive. "Chavo, this is Coop."

"What you got, Coop?"

"Dunno." Bolan put some uncertainty into his voice. "I think maybe you should give me another couple of guys."

"Why?"

"Because this Guitarista guy, he's…" Bolan chose his next words carefully. "I don't know, Chavo. I'm getting a real bad feeling."

There was a moment's pause before Chavo answered. "Yeah, I hear you, Coop. I'm gonna send you Carvalo and two of his men. He's the fastest I've ever seen, and all of them know something about restraining suspects."

Bolan let out a long breath. "Thanks."

"Hang tight, Coop. I got your back."

"Roger that." Bolan clicked off and dragged Svarza into the bedroom. Blood leaked from his torn scalp but there was no time to do anything about it. He patted the Russian down and found a snub-nosed .38 in a shoulder holster. He shoved the pistol into Griffin's hands. "Stay in the bedroom until I tell you to come out. Shoot anyone who isn't your brother or me."

Griffin stared at the pistol, but nodded. Bolan just got back to the parlor as a rapid two taps knocked on the door.

"Coop! Svarza! It's Carvalo!"

"It's clear."

Carvalo came in. Wearing a black suit, black sunglasses and a black hat, the blade-thin former Mexican military policeman looked like something out a bad B-movie. Bolan noted the Colt pistol tucked into his waistband and the rubber bands wrapped around the grips to hold the weapon in place. It wasn't the securest way to carry a gun, but it was one of the fastest draws there was, and had earned the nickname "the Mexican Carry." If Chavo said Carvalo was the fastest he'd ever seen, Bolan didn't doubt it.

The two men with Carvalo were classic military police muscle. They were big men in bad blue suits with big hands and scarred knuckles. Their cold eyes scanned the room like cops rather than soldiers. They each carried an army-issue P-7 M-13 in a shoulder holster.

Carvalo glanced around the tiny parlor. "Where's Svarza?"

Bolan jerked his head down the hall. "In the bedroom."

Carvalo straightened out of his slouch. "Where's the girl?"

Bolan rolled his eyes. "Where do you think?"

Carvalo's face darkened. "Goddamn it."

"Yeah, I told him I wasn't gonna tell Chavo, but if that's how this asshole operates, then I want some backup when the guitar freak shows up."

"Oh, Chavo's gonna find out, all right." Carvalo's face was

turning purple with rage. "After we take Guitarista down, Chavo's gonna stomp him down to China." Carvalo jerked his head at one of his men with a snarl. "Lalo, bring me that goddamn Russian."

Lalo rolled his head around his shoulders with a snap-crackle-pop and marched down the hall with a grim smile on his face.

His partner frowned at the floor. "What's with the blood?"

"The girl." Bolan spit in disgust. "She didn't want to go with him."

Carvalo went livid. "Goddamn it!" He unclipped his tactical radio from his jacket.

Bolan drew.

Chavo was right, Carvalo was more than fast. He was sudden.

Bolan slid the Beretta and its long suppressor tube from under his belt with oiled speed. Carvalo dropped his radio and his right hand snatched out his .45 like a snake striking, but Bolan had the drop on him. The suppressed Beretta chuffed twice as Bolan shot Carvalo in the face. The other big man spent a fatal second staring agog before clawing for his pistol. Bolan doubled-tapped him twice through the skull. Lalo turned at the sound of the two men falling and met a pair of 9 mm hollowpoint rounds that emptied the space between his eyes.

Bolan lowered the smoking pistol. Four down, but by his unofficial count there were probably still thirteen more to go. He had to draw a few more in. Bolan calculated. There was a chance he might be able to get out of this with his cover story intact, but Chapa was going to be a problem as long as he ran his present ruse. He'd promised not to kill the Butcher at General Lothario's compound, but now it turned out Chapa had victimized Griffin and her family and now he was doing it again. The Butcher was a loose end that needed to be dealt with, and dealt with now. The question was how to suck him in without arousing suspicion and how to do it before time ran out.

Bolan's watch pulsed against his wrist in Morse code.

"I'm here."

Time had just run out.

Bolan pumped code into the bezel of his watch. "Wait."

The reply came back instantly. "No."

The situation had changed. There was still a slim chance to get Griffin and Esteban out of this alive. Bolan played his last card. Esteban had loved the lingo, what he called "the secret agent stuff" during their last operation together. Bolan tapped code.

"You need sitrep."

There was a pause as the military acronym had its effect. "Waiting."

Bolan dotted and dashed. "Sister safe with me. Am in house. Four targets inside neutralized. Estimate thirteen more on either side of house. Enemy currently unaware. Sniper still in play. Sniper positioned on beer billboard. East alley of house sniper blind spot. Acknowledge."

Bolan could almost hear Esteban's mind processing.

"Acknowledged. What is plan?"

Bolan allowed himself a slight sigh of relief.

"Will have sister in east alley. Will engage sniper. You and Griff extract. Go to cave. Use code I gave you on computer. Tell who answers who you are and what happened. They will advise you."

Bolan's watch buzzed back.

"Acknowledged. Inbound."

Bolan went to the bedroom. "Griff, your brother's coming to get you. You're going out into the alley when I tell you."

Griffin stared at Bolan shakily, still clutching the pistol. "Okay."

Bolan took Svarza's three spare magazines and reloaded the Beretta. He put his Hi-Power in his other hand and vainly wished that Carvalo or one of his men had brought a rifle or a bucket of grenades with them. Bolan waited for the radio to start blowing up. It didn't take long. Voices were shouting in a mixture of English and Spanish.

"He's here!"

"Jesus Christ!"

"What the hell!"

Bolan called to Griffin. "Stick close to me! Get ready to run!"

Chavo's voice boomed across the radio in disbelief. "Can't be! He's dead!"

Bolan cocked his head as he considered that last exclamation. *"Can't be! He's dead!"*

Interesting.

There was only one person Bolan could imagine they were referring to. A slow smile crept across Bolan's face as heard the confirming sound of an engine. Just as it became audible, gunfire erupted out on the street. It was not the high-rpm snarl of a Honda CX 500 motorcycle. The sound was the unmistakable thunder of a supercharged, 400-horsepower '68 Chevy.

Esteban had borrowed the black El Camino.

Bolan tapped on his watch.

"New plan. Ram fence and glass door to patio. Acknowledge."

Automatic weapons, pistols and shotguns were unloading in a cacophony out on the street. Tires were screaming on pavement. Esteban's response was slow, and he lost his English in the excitement.

"Sí."

The house shook as a 1968 El Camino smashed through the side fence, the sliding glass door and rammed the bathroom. Esteban popped out of the driver's door like a jumping jack with a gun in each hand and a beatific grin on his face. "Matt!"

Bolan pointed to the bedroom. "There's a guy on the floor! Shoot him in the face four times!"

Esteban didn't blink at the order. His pistols banged out four times in the bedroom, and he charged out with Griffin in tow. Bullets began hammering into the house.

Bolan considered their options and finalized his plan. "Get Griffin in the car and shoot the other three guys in the parlor, then get out! Drive west. I'm going to jump in the back and shoot at you! The car is bulletproof. A few blocks away, I'll jump out!"

Esteban blinked three times slowly and suddenly snapped into action. *"Sí!"*

Griffin jumped into the car without being asked. Esteban slid across the hood and began firing into the cadavers in the parlor. Chavo and his men would be charging the house. Esteban slid back across the hood.

Bolan spread his arms. "Hey!"

Esteban looked up puzzled. "What?"

"Shoot me."

Esteban grinned like Satan himself and shot Bolan four times in the chest. Bolan grunted and staggered back against the wall as his vest took the impacts. Esteban slid behind the wheel. Bolan drew his Hi-Power and began shooting into the windshield. Esteban stomped on the gas, and the back tires screamed on the patio brick as the car shot backward and turned sharply in a half bootlegger's turn onto the street in front of the house. Bolan pursued, firing all the way.

Dundee went flying over the tailgate and into the El Camino's truck bed. Sybo wasn't quite as lucky and went under the wheels.

Bolan emptied his pistol and slammed in a fresh magazine. He jumped and ran up the top of the hood. The El Camino screamed forward beneath him, and he ran across the roof and fell into the truck bed. He rose up and began firing into the El Camino's narrow rear window. Bolan almost flew out as Esteban played his part too well and tried swerving to throw him. The Executioner fell down, rose once more and emptied the rest of his magazine. Esteban screamed down the boulevard for ten blocks, and his tires burned to a shrieking halt at a red light, where cross traffic blocked him.

Bolan grabbed Dundee. "We gotta get out of here! We don't want to take this ride!"

"Too bloody right!" The little Australian gasped but wrapped an arm around Bolan's shoulder. Bolan leaped from the El Camino's bed as Esteban stomped on the accelerator and roared into traffic. The car shot out from underneath them. Dundee howled as Bolan landed on him. Esteban disappeared into traffic like a NASCAR driver on crack.

"Ya saved me, Coop!" Dundee wheezed.

The Australian groaned as Bolan slung him over his shoulder in a fireman's carry.

"C'mon, Lucky. We gotta go."

18

"Coop, where the hell are you?"

Bolan was pleased that Chavo actually sounded more concerned than angry. "Me and Dundee are in some shit hole motel downtown."

"What happened?"

"We were two bloody white guys laying in the middle of the road with guns. I figured we'd better get off the street. I gave the guy at the desk five hundred to keep his mouth shut."

"Which shit hole?"

"I don't know." Bolan paused a second or two. "El Torro Valiente? The Brave Bull? Something like that."

"I know it. Pick up is on the way."

"Thank God for that."

"So what happened, Coop?"

Bolan let anger come into his voice. "La Guitarista shot the hell out of everybody and everything, that's what."

"Coop? This is *muy importante*. Was it the guitar player? Or some big nasty white guy?"

"Naw, man. It wasn't El Hombre. It was La Guitarista. Same little son of a bitch that tried to take us down at the Perro Bar. He killed everybody in the house. Then he took me and Dundee for a sleigh ride. We jumped out at a red light, God knows where, and let me tell you something. That car? It was armored. I put three magazines into it, and I didn't even scratch it."

"I know. We were all shooting blanks on that sled. Nico says he put four rounds into the driver's side that should have been kills. How's Dundee?"

Bolan looked across the room. Dundee was reclining on the couch, watching bullfighting on cable. Bolan had taped his ribs with a ripped sheet, and the little Australian was swilling beer like mother's milk. "The tailgate didn't do him any favors. I think he's got some cracked ribs and some other bumps and bruises. Tell me, did Sybo make it?"

"Sybo got crushed like a bug." Chavo's voice lowered a notch, and again Bolan noted concern. "What about you, Coop? You all right?"

"The son of a bitch bounced me into the bathroom with that goddamn chrome grille. I think my armor saved me."

"Yeah, and?"

"And when I sat up, I took four in the chest. I don't know man. It's hazy. But my armor held. I sat up. I saw red. He just…pissed me off. I started chasing him down the street."

"Oh, I know. Don't think I didn't see that."

"He got the girl. That much I saw."

"Yeah, I know. Don't worry about that for now. You just take care of Dundee."

"You got an ETA on extraction?" Bolan asked.

"I'll be there in five minutes."

"Where's Chapa?"

"That little shit? Why?" Chavo queried.

"Because that little shit is major trouble. La Guitarista? El Hombre? They follow him around like the plague. Wherever he is, people get whacked."

"He wasn't with us at the Perro Bar."

Bolan let anger creep back into his voice. "Weren't we doing his collections that day?"

"Yeah."

"Yeah, and the girl? The Guitar Player? Isn't this whole thing one of his messes?"

"Yeah—"

"Yeah, and we got hammered trying to clean up his goddamn mess today."

Chavo's voice dropped an ugly octave as his own anger with the situation kindled. "Yeah, Coop. We did."

"So put him in the river or cut him up for bait. But you keep him the hell away from me! Hell, I'll shoot him." Special Forces operatives were the deadliest men on Earth. By the same token, they were notorious for Byzantine sets of superstitions. Bolan spit and pulled out the magic one-hundred-dollar word. "The Butcher, I'm telling you, Chavo—he's bad luck."

"Coop, you're just saying what everyone else is thinking, and it's about time someone goddamn did. You sit tight with Dundee."

"We're sitting tight in room 12. Gimme three knocks and five knocks again."

"Noted. Out."

Bolan turned to Dundee. "You get most of that?"

"Three knocks and five, Coop. Someone gives the wrong knock…" Dundee raised an Egyptian 9 mm Helwan pistol.

Bolan grinned and checked the loads in his Hi-Power. "Good enough." He went into the bathroom and turned on the water. He hadn't told Chavo or Dundee that he'd given the guy at the front desk two hundred dollars American for his cell phone. Bolan clicked it open and hit buttons. The Farm had about a dozen cutouts, but Bolan rowed through them and gave his current call sign.

Kurtzman picked up instantly. "Striker!"

"Bear, I don't have long and won't be able to use this phone again. I need a sketch artist to work on this description."

"Hold on." The phone made a click. "We're recording."

Bolan gave a very swift, concise description of Omega. It was the kind of description a police sketch artist would have killed for. Many times, Bolan's life had hung on his ability to have someone identified. His description was precise down to the distance between the eyes, length from brow to chin and width of cheekbones. A phrenologist would have enthused about Bolan's description of Omega's skull. "Got it?"

"Got it. What's your situation?"

"The enemy knows who Esteban and Griffin are. They extracted to the cave. Esteban will probably try to contact you using my codes. Tell him to sit tight. I'm in pretty good, but Chapa can identify me. What can you tell me about Scott?"

"I've got news for you there, Striker. Given your description, I've got Leland Scott. United States Army Green Beret."

"Let me guess, Seventh Special Forces Group."

The U.S. Seventh Special Forces group was officially responsible for all operations south of Mexico. Unofficially, Mexico was one of their biggest spheres of operation.

"On the nose, Striker. But Leland Scott is officially dead."

"He's pretty salty and sadistic for a dead guy. Let me guess. He died in Mexico. Tell me, was he in Desert Storm?"

"Bingo."

"Afghanistan?"

"Give the man a cigar."

Bolan's instincts spoke to him. "Bear, we've got a hard core of international mercs doing the deep and dark with this outfit, with the most trusted elements of the Aztec Raptors making the inner circle. Omega is of Latin extraction, but he acts American. Give me an American Special Forces operative who fits the description, and check all the services, no matter how cryptic. Check for Mexican deployments." Bolan considered what he'd heard about Scott. "And Bear?"

"Yes, Striker?"

"Assume Omega is officially dead."

"That should narrow it down a bit. Nice work."

"Thanks. The next single malt is on me. I'll contact you again when possible."

"Affirmative, Bear out."

Bolan clicked the phone shut, smashed it beneath his heel, opened the tiny bathroom window and hurled the remnants into the heaps of refuse in the alley below.

Bolan tapped his watch. "You all right?"

Esteban came back instantly. "In cave. All right. Advise."

Bolan coded back. "Stay put."

Bolan breathed out in relief at the answer.

"Staying put."

Bolan grimaced at a red light that blinked atop the numeral 12 on his watch. His battery was running low. He needed to find some more power fast, and there would be no foreseeable opportunity to go to any of his equipment caches or a CIA safehouse in the city. The end game on this mission was getting thinner and thinner.

At the moment there was nothing to do except wait for extraction. Bolan took a shower and shaved with his Canadian army knife and a bar of Mexican soap. He'd picked up a bruise on his left cheek when he'd fallen in the El Camino's truck bed. With the top of his face sunburned and the lower half shaved and pale, the blue bruise stuck out along the equator in spectacular fashion.

It could only add to his credibility.

Bolan came out of the bathroom feeling half human. He knew he had company before he opened the door.

Chavo and Scott were sitting in chairs waiting for him. Dundee was still sprawled across the couch with his pistol lying on his belly, a sea of beer bottles surrounding him, the TV blaring away and snoring without a care in the world.

Bolan rolled his eyes and slowly shook his head. "He never heard you come in."

Scott gazed at the little Australian in fond irritation. "No."

Bolan nodded. "He's had a hard day."

"So I hear." Scott took in Bolan's bruise and his swelling cheek. "You okay?"

"It hurts when I laugh. But nothing much is goddamn funny today." Bolan lifted his chin at Dundee's snoring form. "Except maybe him."

Scott leaned back in his chair. "Well, he had a hard day, but I was pleased to hear you pulled him through it."

Bolan took a deep breath and looked at the former, officially dead Green Beret. "Scott?"

"Yeah, Coop?"

"Get us the hell out of here."

Scott nodded. "Done."

19

"So La Guitarista showed up." Omega seemed more speculative than displeased.

Scott sighed as he sat on the couch and cracked a beer. "Yeah, in the armor-plated El Camino. Chavo says the thing looked and sounded like doomsday." Scott tossed back a few healthy swallows of beer. "At least, it confirms your theory."

"Really." Omega smiled. "How's that?"

"Well, you figured someone was guiding La Guitarista, and it's starting to look a lot like it was El Hombre. So, I guess the good news is that with El Hombre dead, our little guitar player pal doesn't have a handler anymore. He's running people over in broad daylight in a car everyone in the whole town has heard of. We know where he lives. I don't think the idiot can hide for long, even if he wanted to. Which, by the way, I don't think he does."

"Valid points," Omega conceded, "but there's still some things I just don't like."

"Yeah, I get that feeling, too." Scott scowled as he examined his sweating beer bottle. "And Chapa is part of it."

"Chapa?"

"Yeah, the men don't like him."

Omega shrugged. "Well, he's a man of few redeeming characteristics."

"Chavo, Cooper, Dundee, hell, most of the men want to see him dead. They think he's bad luck, and I can't say I disagree. That little shit has brought down the thunder on us, and I say he outlived any usefulness about a week ago. I say we put him out of our misery."

Omega's teeth flashed a smile even as his eyes went as flat as a shark's. "You say, huh?"

"Jesus Christ!" Scott recoiled in his seat. "You know what I'm saying!" Scott stiffened. He knew Omega despised weakness more than anything. Omega also liked to play mind games, and Scott knew he'd fallen into a trap. Scott tried to retrieve some lost face. "After all we've been through together? That's a hell of a thing for you to say to me! You know I was under the impression I had permission to speak freely."

"Sorry." Omega shrugged dismissively. "I've got a lot on my plate right now. Perhaps I overreacted."

"Uh…" It was such an unusual admission it caught Scott flat-footed. In the same second, Scott realized he'd been disarmed and played again. Omega changed the subject. "So Coop did okay again?"

"That Canadian is goddamn Superman."

"Mmm." Omega nodded. "Everyone in the house was killed but him?"

"Well, yeah, I admit it sounds fishy, but you weren't there. Goddamn guitar boy rammed the house. Coop went flying. Then the SOB shot him four times. I saw the blunt trauma on his chest, and his face looks like he went five rounds out of his weight class. And you didn't see him hit that El Camino running. He was a man on a mission. If it wasn't for Coop, Dundee would be in La Guitarista's hands right now having God knows what kind of retarded shit inflicted on him."

Omega examined the ice in his whiskey glass. "Nico says he knows him."

"Yeah, I know Nico says he's seen him someplace before, and that bothered me." Scott reached into the bucket for a fresh beer. "But I checked. They never served together in the same theater. Never been in the same state or province at the same time."

"I trust Nico's instincts."

"I do, too. But he can't say where he knows Coop from.

Coop's been a hard-charger since day one. The men like him. Chavo trusts him, and so do I. Nico's mistaken."

"He's a sniper."

"Even snipers make mistakes. Hell, even you made a mistake once."

Omega's face went flat.

Scott paled, knowing he'd gone too far. "Uh…" He tried to think of something to say but there was no backpedaling. Scott knew from long, hard experience you couldn't unring a bell. He had brought up, however mistakenly, that which was never to be mentioned.

The blood drained from Omega's face, and then color returned in a red veil of imminent violence. Omega stared at Scott, and his right cheek muscle ticked. Omega seemed unaware of it. His black eyes bored holes into Scott. Scott knew he was a dead man. For one ill-considered second he contemplated the SIG-Sauer P-220 in the cross-draw rig at his waist. Scott was a very dangerous man and knew it, but Omega was an animal of a higher order, and Scott knew that, too.

He was dead.

Scott slowly reached for his piece. Omega never moved. The retaining strap of Scott's holster popped off with a snap as he drew the pistol. Swiss steel rasped against Mexican leather. Scott never broke eye contact with Omega as he brought the SIG-Sauer to his own temple. "You want me to do it? Or you want to?"

Long seconds passed as Omega's face relaxed fiber by fiber and resumed its normal cool mask. He suddenly flashed a disarming smile. "You know something, Scotty? I'm just going to let that one go."

Scott lowered the pistol and covered his relief with a laugh. "Nothing I don't owe you, main man."

"No." The shark look was back in the flat black eyes. "Nothing you don't."

Scott kept the shiver in his spine to himself with effort. Omega had saved his life, and now he'd spared it. Scott steeled himself for the unpleasant part of his job. "You want me to whack Coop?"

"No. But I want him tested."

Scott chose his words very carefully. "I'm not contradicting you…"

"No?"

Scott fought the frog in his throat and stuck to his guns. "But Coop is battle proven. Dundee? Ruzzo? The rest of the boys? Hell, even me. I like him. Even Chavo likes him, and there's a guy whose instincts will keep your ass alive. We all swear by the guy." Scott tossed his empty into the beer bucket. "And Nico *thinks* he saw him someplace?"

Omega nodded. "Chavo had a feeling something was wrong with the guy."

"Chavo's first impression was he liked him, and I admit he had a bad feeling at the Perro Bar, right before *La Guitarista* put a bullet upside his head and Coop saved his life."

"Mmm." Omega nodded and smiled. "So we have a conundrum."

Scott let out a long sigh. "Okay, boss. You got me. What's a conundrum?"

"It means Coop goddamn rocks, Scotty. Just like you and Chavo and Dundee and all the boys say, but…"

Scott picked up the ball. "But let's test him."

"Yes, Scott." Omega nodded. "Let's test him."

R AND R ON OMEGA'S expense account was good.

Bolan climbed out of the pool and reclined back in his deck chair next to Scott. He didn't know where he was, except that when he scanned the horizon it looked a hell of a lot like border country. He'd been blindfolded at the Nuevo Laredo private airport in a Huey civilian AH-12 helicopter. The flight had been about twenty minutes by his internal clock. He knew Hueys, and the engines hadn't been at top speed. Bolan guesstimated he was within fifty to seventy-five miles of Nuevo Laredo.

"Milk and honey, Coop!" Dundee stood naked on the diving board with a shot of tequila in each hand. He held out his arms in a cross, displaying a body that was nothing but knotty muscle, tattoos and scars. He tossed back both shots and then flung the glasses behind him to shatter on the deck tiles. "Bloody milk and honey!" He bounced three times to gain altitude, and the topless women in the pool shrieked as he cannonballed into the blue water among them.

Scott sprawled his frame back in his chair and soaked in the sun. "You know, I could have gone my whole life without seeing him naked."

Bolan snorted.

Scott peered at his empty beer bottle and waved at one of the women. "So how you doing, Coop? You like?"

Bolan watched the woman approach. "Oh, I like, all right."

"Señor Coop?" Citlalli knelt beside Bolan wearing a Brazilian bikini that left nothing to the imagination and proffered him a fresh pair of beers with lime. Her huge, dark slanted eyes, wide cheekbones and pointed chin tilted invitingly at him over a body that was petite, lush and languorous all at the same time.

"Gracias." Bolan took the beers.

The compound was more of an estate than a traditional Mexican hacienda. Everything was modern. It stood out in the middle of the rocky, hilly desert like an oasis. A nearly completed golf course stretched out in low, rolling cool green just to the east. Palm trees and almost hidden bungalows dotted the landscape. An airstrip capable of handling jets lay just behind the estate. Beautiful girls were everywhere. So were most of Los Untouchables, or at least, the ones Bolan had met. It looked a lot like a Club Med all-inclusive, except for the dangerous clientele and the out-of-uniform Aztec Raptors patrolling the grounds with G-36 rifles. Bolan's instincts walked up and down his spine as he reclined in paradise. He was in danger, and he was getting a bad feeling.

There wasn't much to be done about it at the moment. He'd been allowed to bring his personal gear, but lolling around the pool packing a 9 mm pistol over his khaki shorts would have attracted all the wrong kind of attention. However, he was far from unarmed. In a concealed pocket in his shorts, he had a cheap, stiletto style switchblade he had pocketed during col-

lections with Chavo. He had also looted a pair of French Alse-
tex Number 1 offensive hand grenades from Hummer 3 during the cleanup operations after the battle for Diablo Cabra.
Perhaps it was their Gallic heritage, but the two little French
grenades looked very much a like a pair of tiny brandy bottles
with cotter pins and fuses replacing the corks. The grenades
were rolled into the towel Bolan wore draped around his neck.

The weapon Bolan needed most was a phone. They seemed
to be on an unspoken, restricted basis. Bolan could use the land-
line in his bungalow, but he suspected it was tapped. Scott had
one and if anyone besides Omega wasn't bugged, it would
have to be Scott. Bolan lifted his head at a blonde in the pool.
"Hey, Citalli. Who's your friend?"

Both Scott and Citlalli looked at giggling blonde as she pre-
tended to fend off Dundee's advances. Bolan palmed the little
plastic bottle of eyedrops he had taken from his medicine cabinet and squeezed half of it down the neck of Scott's Corona
beer.

Citlalli turned back with an unhappy look. "That is Nona.
You like her?"

"Naw." Bolan grinned. "I only love you."

"Aww…" Scott took his beer and poured half of it down his
throat at a go. "You Canadian schemer, you."

Bolan sipped his beer and waited. The human body did not
tolerate the active ingredient in most eyedrops. In rare cases,
it could cause seizures, difficulty in breathing or even a coma.
However, the most common effect was nausea and vomiting.

Bolan didn't have long to wait.

Scott let out a groan and clutched his stomach. "Jesus…"

Bolan cocked his head questioningly. "You all right?"

"Yeah, I mean…no!" Scott lurched upright and dashed for
the patio door.

Citlalli stared after him in concern. "Is Señor Scott all
right?"

"Dunno." Bolan poured out his and Scott's beers. "Maybe
I'll switch to another brand."

Citlalli rose to fetch Bolan a fresh beer. Bolan snagged

Scott's cell phone and watch from the little table. "Dundee! I'm gonna go see if Scott's all right!"

The Australian draped his arms happily about Nona and her friend. "I'll manage as best I can, Coop!"

Bolan went inside. He could hear Scott hurling away in the bathroom down the hall. He went a side door and dropped down behind a hedge of sculpted juniper. There wasn't much time. The switchblade snapped open, and he popped the back of his watch and Scott's and swapped batteries. He put them back together and then dialed the Farm. He spent a few seconds jumping through the usual hoops of codes and call signs and suddenly the Bear was on the line.

"Striker! Where have you been?"

"My watch ran out of power and I have to make this fast. Something bad is about go down."

"I've got Omega, and you're right. It doesn't look good."

"Give it to me. I can receive."

"Sending."

Bolan watched the phone's display and a picture appeared. The shoulder-length black hair was cut short and the beard and mustache were gone, but there was no mistaking the piercing gray eyes and the satanic eyebrows. It was a picture of Omega. It was the United States Air Force ID photo of Captain Moses Xavier Raza, deceased.

Bolan scrolled down and squinted at the tiny text, culling out the important facts. Raza had been an air commando, the USAF's own Special Forces unit. He'd earned the Air Medal three times, which meant he had flown at least eighty combat missions. In Operation Desert Storm, he had won the Distinguished Flying Cross for bravery. His death in 1998 was declared a "training accident" with no further elaboration.

Bolan did the math. "Raza got seduced by the black operations boys, didn't he?"

"It seems he went to work for the CIA, paramilitary branch, during the War on Drugs years. The exact nature of most of his missions are classified, but you can guess the kinds of things he would have been up to."

Bolan could easily guess. As an air commando, Raza's main missions for the USAF would have been insertions, extractions and search and rescue, as well as securing or retaking airfields. When he'd gone contractor for the CIA, such missions would have turned into inserting and extracting intelligence assets, as well as snatches, kidnappings and organizing and leading raids against the crime lords. Those kinds of raids would never be reported in the media and that would have been considered illegal, at least publicly, by all countries involved. Raza's Air Force training made him a lethal Special Forces soldier. His missions for the CIA would have taught him everything there was to know about crime south of the border.

"It wasn't any training accident, Bear. Raza died doing something the U.S. government, particularly the CIA, didn't want to 'fess up to. Something went wrong, and bad wrong."

"This is what I could get officially. Raza was supposedly running a training mission in conjunction with Mexican special forces. His HH-53H went down in the deserts of Northern Mexico. The entire crew and all passengers were killed or presumed dead."

The H-53 "Super Jolly Green Giant" was the largest, most powerful helicopter in U.S. inventory. It had a habit of "going down" just about never.

"That's official story. Now tell me the rumors," Bolan said.

Kurtzman took a long breath. "I called in a few markers at Langley, and this info cost me. This is one no one likes to talk about. The rumor is this. Raza and his team were shot down, by black market Stinger missiles. Someone on the inside—the prevailing thought is that it was on the Mexican end—had tipped off the bad guys that Raza and the boys were coming. The bad guys were waiting, and they had been given the right tools for the job. The rumor is not everyone died in the crash. The survivors fought in the desert for three days, without food or water, trying to shoot their way back to the U.S. border before they were overwhelmed. Rumor is the bad guys had the support of certain Mexican army units." Kurtzman let out a long breath. "The rumor is that despite repeated calls for aid, no rescue was attempted by either the U.S. or Mexican governments. Prisoners were taken, and they were extensively tortured. The bad guys made examples out of them. Pictures of what was left when they were finished were sent to CIA headquarters as a warning not to meddle again."

Bolan had been a part of operations that had gone wrong. He knew all about being betrayed, being left behind and denied. That and a healthy dose of torture was the kind of thing that could give a man a bad attitude. He glanced at the photo again, comparing it to the man he had recently met. "Raza was captured and tortured, but he escaped."

"If there's any guy who could do it, would be him," Kurtzman agreed. "Escape and evasion was part of his stock-in-trade."

"But rather than going home, he stayed south of the border. Probably got his revenge."

"That's another interesting tidbit. The cartel he was operating against? A year later, the four brothers who ran it were all kidnapped and killed over the course of three months."

"They were tortured first."

"Extensively, and a certain Mexican colonel, who rose to the rank of general in the intervening year, was killed in a similar fashion, as well."

"The same Mexican army colonel involved in the raid."

"One of two, but yeah."

"Two?"

"Can you guess who the other one was?"

Bolan could. "Lothario."

"That's right."

"So he killed the one he blamed and aided the other in his rise to power. When Raza went into business for himself, he had a built-in ally in the Mexican army. One who respected him and owed him favors." Bolan's brow furrowed. "Bear, before we hit Esteban's house, Raza and Scott said they had business to attend to and put Chavo in command. I think they're up to something big, and it's going to go down soon."

"Any idea what?"

"No, but I think I've got an interview with Raza today. With any luck, they're going to teach me the secret handshake. You heard from Esteban?"

"Yeah, he and his sister are at the mine. Awaiting word from you."

"Good enough. I'll contact you as soon as I have anything new. Striker out."

"One other thing, Striker."

"What's that?"

"Last night a body washed up on the U.S. side of river. Latin American with what looks like a lot of yanqui blood. He'd had both of his legs blown off above the knee. That mean anything to you?"

Bolan's blood went cold as he thought of Gabriel Uncas losing his legs on the pueblo raid, and the retirement present he and the rest of the men had all chipped in on for him. "Yeah, I think it means something. I think it means Raza doesn't leave any loose ends behind."

"That's what I was thinking, too, and here's why. The cause of death was a .38 Super hollowpoint to the back of the head. So you watch yourself, Striker."

"Thanks, Bear. Striker out." Bolan went back inside and went to the bathroom door. "Scott, you all right?"

Bolan was surprised to see the door open. Scott looked green around the gills, but he was standing. "I don't know, man. There must have been cat meat or something in those *huevos rancheros* this morning."

Bolan grinned. "I had seconds."

"Yeah, well, you go to hell, and you die."

Bolan held out Scott's phone and watch. "I brought you your stuff."

"Thanks, Coop." Scott checked the time. "We gotta go. We've got a meeting with the man."

"I'm still a little wet—let me grab my towel."

"Grab your towel, grab your pants, and let's go. Believe me, you don't want to keep the man waiting."

20

Bolan draped his towel around his neck and took a seat before Omega's desk. Nico was in the room, and the sniper was still giving him the hard stare. So was Chavo, Ruzzo and a couple of guys Bolan didn't recognize. Scott had dropped him off at the door and gone off to the bathroom again. Bolan could sense some anticipation in the spacious den, but he couldn't read an immediate threat from anyone in the room. Bolan returned his attention to the man behind the mahogany desk.

Seeing Omega again only reconfirmed Bolan's suspicions. Omega wore a mask of relaxed cool for the world to see, but beneath that mask was a rage that still seethed and burned. It was a rage that revenge had not satisfied. Bolan knew that rage all too well. It had turned him into what he had become. For him, it had set the course for his War Everlasting. Bolan had taken his rage and loss and turned it into a war against that which had taken his family. Betrayal and abandonment had twisted Moses Raza, and he had let his rage turn him into a crime lord and a sociopath. But Omega had skills and connections that would let him take his hatred from the local, tactical arena to the international stage. Bolan knew he was going to have to take him down.

Bolan smiled at the man he had come to kill.

"Morning, Coop. You enjoying the hospitality?"

Bolan nodded and accepted a beer from the bar out of Scott's hand. "I gotta admit. You live pretty plush."

Omega smiled and leaned back in his chair casually. "Listen, Coop. I'll cut to the chase. We've taken some losses lately. I've got some things coming up, and we need some new men."

Bolan shrugged. "I'm your boy."

"I'm thinking you need to prove yourself before you get your decoder ring."

Bolan put a frown on his face. "You know, maybe I got my ass kicked twice, but I thought I did pretty good against that Guitar Player punk."

Omega nodded in agreement.

"I pulled my own weight in the fight at the pueblo," Bolan continued, "and you know it."

"Indeed." Omega raised a finger in point. "But you weren't very happy about it."

"No, no, I wasn't." Bolan raised his beer in counterpoint and circled it at his present environs. "But it put four grand in my pocket, cold beer in my hand and a pretty plush roof over my head. So I'll tell you flat out. You want to burn another village? I'll do it again. I'll do it tonight, and I won't lose a wink of sleep over it."

Chavo made a rumbling noise of approval.

Omega sat back. "Fair enough, but I want you solve a little problem for me."

"What kind of a problem?"

"Oh," Omega said, "a mutual one. I hear you and the boys don't like Chapa much."

"No, he's bad luck, and everything that's happened is his fault."

"Would you kill him for me?"

Bolan frowned. "I never just…shot anyone, if you know what I mean. I mean I shot a lot of guys, but that was…"

"That was in combat." Omega nodded. "Oh, I understand."

Chavo grinned from his seat on the sofa. "The first one is the hardest, then it gets easier real fast, and brother, you couldn't ask for a sweeter first time than a scumbag like the Butcher. I can't begin to tell you the vile crap he's dirtied his hands and other extremities with."

Omega spoke quietly. "This would be more than just a random slaying to prove yourself, Coop. This would be you tying up a loose end for me, and your way in."

Bolan looked around the room. It was a pass-fail situation. In was the only way to go. Out would be a bullet in the back of his head and an unmarked hole in the desert. It was also an opportunity to get out of the compound and call in reinforcements. Bolan set his jaw. "Chavo said he's someplace deep and dark. Tell me where. I'll bring you his head."

"Good man!" Chavo was pleased.

Omega waved his hand dismissingly. "No, no need for that, Coop." Omega snapped his fingers.

The side door of the den opened.

Omega took a nickel-plated, silver-eagle-gripped Colt 1911 pistol out of his desk.

Balbi and one of his goons walked in, escorting a confused and frightened-looking Donato "The Butcher" Chapa between them.

Chapa looked around the room and his eyes fell on Bolan. Every ounce of blood drained from his face.

Omega put a single Winchester 125-grain Silvertip hollow-point bullet on the desk beside the pistol. "Just shoot him, Coop."

Chapa squeaked at Bolan. "You!"

The pistol on the desk was a dead issue. Its presence confirmed everything, but it had only one bullet and Bolan knew he would never live to load it and fire it in time.

"Him!" Chapa began pointing violently at Bolan. "It's him!"

Balbi slapped the Butcher in the back of the head to shut him up. "Be a man."

Chavo rumbled in amusement. "That's the face of death, Doni. *Vaya con dios, amigo.*"

The men in the room laughed, except for Nico and Omega. They both sensed something was wrong and turned to look at Bolan. There was no one close enough to strip a pistol from. The scream ripped from Chapa's throat.

"El Hombre!"

Bolan went into motion. He threw his beer in Omega's face.

He whipped the towel from around his neck and took the ends in his right hand. Chavo began to rise just in time to take the grenade-laden towel in an uppercut that knocked him over the back of the sofa. Bolan lunged and whipped the improvised weapon around in a backhand for Omega's temple.

Omega moved with liquid speed. He pushed himself back and toppled his chair over. The bludgeon whipped inches from his skull as he toppled backward.

Bolan continued his spin. His blow hit Ruzzo like a ball and chain and smashed him back into his seat.

Nico was up, and his right foot lashed out in a high kick into Bolan's ribs. Bolan took the shot and swung low, whipping the weighted towel into Nico's standing leg and scythed him off of his feet.

Balbi had shoved Chapa aside and was drawing his pistol. Bolan snapped the towel open, and grenades fell into Bolan's palms like a magic trick. He ripped out the pin of the grenade in his right hand and hurled it like a baseball into Balbi's chest. The ex-MP wheezed and staggered back two steps.

Chavo roared, "Grenade!"

Bolan took three running steps and threw his shoulder into the door. He exploded into the hallway like fullback breaking a tackle. Chavo gave out a wordless roar of effort and more wood broke within the den. The house shook as the French grenade detonated and the den's windows blew out. The offensive hand grenade had a thin plastic sheath rather than metal and did its damage concussively with its high-explosive charge rather than ripping men apart by spewing shrapnel.

Bolan felt the wave of force wash out of the den and spill into the hallway. He rolled to his feet as Scott burst out of the bathroom door, pale and sweating, but with his saw-toothed shotgun in hand.

"Coop! What the hell—"

Bolan flung his second grenade in a softball pitch. He was throwing left-handed and it lacked power and speed, but the French grenade still managed to clack off Scott's shotgun and the blast of buckshot meant for Bolan's head ripped nine .38-

caliber holes in the wall behind him. Scott pumped the action of his shotgun for a second shot. Bolan's switchblade clicked open in his hand as he moved in for the kill.

The Mexican steel slid under Scott's sternum, but the three-and-three-quarter-inch blade didn't have the length to reach the heart for the quick kill. Scott still groaned horribly as Bolan twisted the blade inside his rib cage. The big man punched the shotgun into Bolan's face with both hands and knocked him back across the hall. Bolan took his knife with him and whipped it up at Scott's face in a shovel throw.

Scott screamed, and his shotgun blew a hole in the ceiling as the Mexican switchblade sank into his eye.

Bolan lunged forward and grabbed the hot barrel before it could be lowered. He ripped the shotgun out of Scott's hands. Scott screamed in agony and rage, and his finger's closed around Bolan's throat. Bolan rammed the toothed, door-ripping teeth of the muzzle into Scott's neck. Scott gagged on his own steel, and his grip loosened. Bolan pumped the action and pulled the trigger.

The wrestling match ended abruptly in an arterial spray that covered Bolan and about half the hallway.

Bolan stripped Scott of his phone and scooped up his fallen grenade. He pulled the pin as he heard movement. Chavo appeared in the doorway of the den. He weaved drunkenly, but his Russian Gurza pistol was in his hand. Bolan bowled his grenade down the hallway.

Chavo's eyes flew wide as he hurled himself back. "Grenade!"

Bolan reached the end of the hall and hit the stairs running as the grenade detonated behind him.

OMEGA ROSE from the floor. His ears rang from the grenade, and his nose was bleeding from the bottle he'd taken to the face. Just about everyone in the room was a bloody mess. He instantly understood that the grenades had been in the towel and that El Hombre had beaten his best men, all armed, as if they were rugs. Through his pounding head, he could hear the pop and crack of gunfire out in the compound. He looked at the shattered remnants of his desk.

Chavo had picked it up and dropped it on top of the grenade.

That had saved the life of just about everybody in the room. The second grenade had slapped Chavo back into the den like a giant, invisible hand. He pushed himself up to his hands and knees. Ruzzo's face was a mess, and he sat with his head hung and spitting teeth into his hands. Nico was up and hopping on one leg. Balbi's man, Leto, was helping him to his feet.

Chapa sat on the floor. Legs outstretched like a little kid. He blinked and yawned at the grenade's effect and stared around in a daze.

Omega was on him in two strides. Chapa howled as he was yanked to his feet. Omega pressed his face into the little killer's. "That was El Hombre?"

Chapa shrieked like a trapped rat. "It was! I swear it! I swear it!"

"He's right." Nico hopped over to the bar and propped himself up. "*That* was him. That was the son of a bitch at the general's compound I was shooting at. Same one who stole the armored vehicle. The hair and skin and eyes are different, but that's it. That's where I saw him."

Omega still held Chapa off the floor. "Scotty says he sank El Hombre with a salvo of rockets. Said he saw him burn and sink."

Chavo had risen. His voice was stone cold. "Scotty's dead."

Omega took out his phone. The phone and the walkie-talkie feature were all lit up like Christmas trees. "This is Omega."

Orlandivo, Omega's head of compound security, shouted breathlessly into the phone. "What the hell happened? That guy! Cooper! He shot three of my men!"

Omega did a mental count. Two rounds fired in the hallway. Three more out on the compound. Scotty's shotgun was empty. "Did he get their guns?"

"No! We drove him toward the golf course!"

Omega sighed. "So he got to his bungalow."

"Uh…yes!"

So El Hombre now had a loaded Browning Hi-Power and a spare magazine. That wasn't good, but there was a rule about gunfights. The first rule was to bring a gun. The second rule was to bring a rifle.

"Secure the perimeter. Don't have anyone go after him. It's 110 and rising out in the desert. Let him run. Keep security in tight and in communication at all times. I'm assembling a team. Keep me advised constantly."

"Yes, sir!"

Omega rummaged through the shattered remnants of his desk and found his pistol, spare magazines and a box of ammo. He loaded the .38 Super and racked the action. "I need you men to get to the infirmary. Have the doc give you the once-over, and then shoot up with whatever you need to get frosty. We're going to have a little hunting party. This El Hombre asshole really only has one choice, and that's to run for the border. Even if he knows where that is, that's a hard thirty-mile hump across hell's half acre."

Ruzzo dropped his broken teeth and rose with his pistol in his hand. "What if he calls for help?"

Omega shook his head. "Help won't come."

"How do you know?"

Ruzzo took a step back at the terrible smile that lit Omega's face. "He's expendable. He's deniable. Take my word for it. No one will come for him."

Nico scowled. "He could double back."

The giant's voice rumbled like breaking slate. "I hope he does." Chavo wiped blood from his face. "Because then he doubles back into us, and then God help his narrow ass."

21

Bolan doubled back.

There really wasn't any other choice. Tracing a cell phone call took some time, and everything had gone south before Bolan could get a call back from Stony Man Farm on his exact location. Bolan crouched in a ravine and looked at his only two methods of communication. The signaler in his watch was out of range of Esteban. When he tried calling the Farm with Scotty's phone, nothing went through. Apparently, Omega had the power to jam the phone frequencies in his compound. However, jamming was an uncertain science, and sometimes certain signals, particularly closer ones, could filter through. Bolan phoned Esteban at the mine.

The numbers dialed, but there was a blast of static when Esteban picked up on the other end. Bolan hung up and tried again and got the same result. The phone rang back as Esteban tried to contact Bolan, but only static came across the line. Bolan squatted in the heat listening to the sound of white noise. Then he began tapping the zero key in Morse code.

"Can you hear me?"

Bolan instantly heard the rapid peeping of the dial tone in his ear.

"Loud and clear."

The jamming was preventing any voice transmission through the receivers, but if the call went through, the phones were still receiving signals and could still relay their dial tones.

"Contact Bear. He will give you my location. Do not call

back. Am being hunted. Ring tone could give away my location. Will contact you again soon."

Bolan listened while the phone peeped back in his ear.

"Understood. On my way."

Bolan clicked the phone shut. He could hear his hunters moving in on him. Bolan had made it back to his bungalow and gotten his pistol, his tomahawk and a quart of bottled water. The desert was a death trap. He still didn't know where he was, and the temperature was climbing with every inch the sun rose. It would be noon in another hour. A blind march north would kill him while his well-supplied enemies hounded him in familiar territory. Bolan had caught a little luck. There were no helicopters at the compound for the moment, but they would be on the way, and once choppers were in the sky, he was finished.

The only chance was to dance in the jaws of the serpent and pray they didn't snap shut on him.

Nico, the sniper, was the main problem. He was out there, somewhere, on some high ground. Waiting for Bolan to make his move. The enemy wasn't making too much of an effort to flush him out. They were waiting for the helicopters and reinforcements.

Bolan crawled along the little ravine. It was barely four feet deep, but it worked its way back to the golf course and the bungalows. Not much of a chance at all but—

Bolan stopped at the sound of Dundee's voice.

"Unit 2, checking in, no movement."

It sounded as if the little Australian were right on top of him. Bolan crept backward slowly. Putting a little bit of distance between himself and the former Australian SAS man, he risked a peek over the lip of the ravine. Dundee was perched in a triangle of boulders. It wasn't a bad strongpoint. It would take a grenade to dig him out, and Bolan was fresh out. However, the rock formation also made a nice, intimate little place for the two of them to have a conversation.

Bolan slid over the top of the ravine like a snake, keeping a lump of mesquite between himself and Dundee. If Nico had more than ten or twenty feet of elevation, Bolan knew he'd be spotted. But optics narrowed one's field of vision, and Dundee had just checked in to say that his sector was clear.

Bolan rose, knife and tomahawk in hand, and moved forward in a crouch. He took one agonizing step at a time, testing his weight on each patch of dirt and sand so there would be no noise. Bolan concentrated on the last few yards of his approach. If Nico's bullet found him, he would never feel it. Bolan moved to within feet. Dundee slapped at a fly buzzing about him and mumbled to himself.

"Where the hell are the bloody choppers, then?"

Bolan's shadow fell across Dundee, but it was already too late for the little Australian. He started to rise, and his breath hissed in to shout. Both actions stopped as he felt the inner edge of Bolan's tomahawk whip around his throat. His hand started to go for his pistol but froze as he felt the tip of Bolan's Canadian army knife press into his back.

"You might get me, Coop, but I'll kick up a ruckus when I go down. I swear it. Then shit's gonna rain down on you, mate."

"Really?" Bolan pulled the sharpened inner edge of the handax harder against the Australian's Adam's apple, and the tip of his knife drew a pinprick of blood against Dundee's kidney. "You know, I think one good rip and stick, and you're going to go down as gentle as a lamb."

The Australian swallowed with difficulty against the steel pressing his throat. "Aw, bloody hell, Coop. I never did nothin' to you."

"You're out here hunting me. It's getting hot. I'm losing that loving feeling for you."

"You got nowhere to go, Coop. The choppers are late, but they'll be here soon, and you got Nico hunting you. He's the bloody devil himself with that rifle of his."

"Yeah, where is old Nico, by the way?"

"He's—" Dundee gagged as Bolan pulled hard on the tomahawk.

"I really want you to get this one right, Dundee."

"He's in that rock formation! The big one! By the edge of the fifteenth hole!"

Over three hundred yards away, with far too much open ground between them. If Bolan had a grenade launcher, he might risk a shot at him. Exchanging shots with Dundee's short assault weapon against Nico's Remington 700 sniper rifle was suicide, and with his first shot the rest of the Raptors and Untouchables would descend on him like wolves.

"How many men out there?"

"Twenty, twenty-five, I reckon. About ten of them are security, six of us Untouchables and the rest Raptors."

"You know, I always liked you, Dundee."

"Reckon I'm right fond of you, too, Coop."

Bolan calculated the odds. "How bad do you want to live?"

"Pretty fucking badly, I reckon."

Bolan nodded. "So how'd you end up in this line of work, anyway?"

"You want to squat here in the heat and have a bloody yabber about my employment history, then?"

"Sure." Bolan gave the tomahawk a friendly tug. "Let's have a…yabber. I've got nothing better to do except kill you."

"Well, if you put it like that, then. Dunno. Raised on a sheep station in Darling Downs. Went army after my schooling looking for a bit of adventure. Royal Australian Regiment, then qualified and went SAS. Had my bell rung once in training. Then again during Desert Storm. Finally had a really bad one in East Timor. You only get to have so many concussions and they sit you behind a desk. I wasn't really cut out for that kind of duty. So I went to Afghanistan as a private contractor. Scotty recruited me from there."

Bolan measured the little man. Despite appearances he had once been among the best of the best. "You like burning villages, running drugs, selling little girls?"

"Aw, hell, Coop. It didn't start like that, did it? It was all easy hits on scumbags. Then you cross the line, but you pull your weight to back up your mates, and then you've gone too far and you're in too deep. Ain't no goin' back, Coop. Not with this Omega fella."

"No, there isn't. You remember Uncas?"

"Course, I do. I went with Ruzzo to see him off. Word is, Omega gave him a sweet little beach place somewhere around Acapulco."

"Uncas got sent to the bottom of the Rio Grande, and all Omega gave him was a .38 Super in the back of the head. Just like he wanted me to do to Chapa. Just like he did to four Border Patrol agents and a U.S. federal marshall."

Dundee swallowed again. "Didn't know that."

"What do you think is going to happen to you if you get your bell rung one more time? Omega doesn't leave loose ends. No one crippled and sitting around getting embittered in their beer and shooting off their mouth about the milk-and-honey days in the wrong ear in the wrong bar."

"Never really thought about it."

Bolan lowered his ax and spun Dundee around to face him. The tomahawk blade sank in the sand, and the Hi-Power filled Bolan's hand in a heartbeat. "You have exactly five seconds to think about it. Omega is a drug smuggler and a murderer. He killed Uncas. He wants to kill me. I saved your life, Dundee, and I'm trying to save it now. Choose."

The Australian broke into a fresh sweat. "We'll never make it."

"Not out here, but together, in the compound, it'll be a free-for-all rather than a stalk. We can bunker ourselves into one of the buildings. There's a chance the cavalry is coming."

"Yeah, but how the hell we gonna make it across three hundred yards of open terrain? Even if they think I captured you, they won't let me walk you in by myself."

"No, they won't," Bolan agreed. "So I'm going to walk you in."

"They won't let you use me as a shield. Nico'll green light the both of us. Bloody even I know that."

"No, but call in. Tell them you're sick. Tell them you think I poisoned you with the same stuff I used on Scott by the pool."

"But then how—"

"Do it."

Dundee's hand reached for his tactical radio.

Bolan leveled the Browning between the Australian's eyes. "Do it slow."

Dundee clicked his radio. "This is Unit 2."

Chavo's voice came over the line. "What have you got, Unit 2?"

"I feel sick."

Chavo paused. "Sick?"

"Yeah, I've hurled three times already. I think whatever Coop put in Scotty's drink by pool, he put in mine, too."

"You all right?"

"Dunno, I feel sick. I can't keep any water down, and it's just so bloody hot out here in these rocks. I hate to be a wuss, Chavo…but think I'm gonna pass out in a minute."

"Dundee, you take it easy. Stay frosty. If you can't keep any water down, hold a swallow in your mouth and pour some over your head. Sit tight. I'm gonna send Balbi to retrieve you. We'll get an IV in you and put you in an air-conditioned room."

"Roger that, Chavo. Thanks."

"Sit tight, Chavo out."

Dundee released his radio. "How was that?"

"Not bad. Listen. We're out of time. Omega and his operation are going down. You help me, and you get a pass. You don't, and I kill you now and take my chances."

The Australian rubbed his throat and stared at Bolan.

Bolan read his mind. "You betray me? You just remember. You and the rest of the Untouchables? Your names are known, and there are certain people in this world you don't want to meet. Certain people who will come looking for payback. People who will never stop." Bolan's blue eyes burned into Dundee's. "As for me? I don't know what you believe in, but God as my witness, I'll be waiting for you in hell."

"Jesus…"

"Choose a side. Choose now."

"I…"

Dundee's radio crackled. "Dundee, this is Bebe. I'm fifty yards from your position. Coming from the south. You okay?"

Bolan made a motion of sticking his finger down his throat. The Australian grabbed his radio and gagged himself.

"Bebe...I'm bloody dyin' out here."

Bolan motioned again, and Dundee gave up the last of his breakfast.

"Hang tight, Dundee."

Bolan lifted an ear as he heard Balbi making his approach. He was a big man and a military policeman rather than a Special Forces operative. He made far too much noise. Bolan pulled his tomahawk out of the sand.

Dundee closed his eyes. "Bloody hell..."

Bolan pressed himself against the side of the rock.

Balbi called out, "I'm coming in."

Bolan spoke low. "Make it good."

Dundee let out a convincing groan. "Clear! Come ahead!"

Balbi moved into the rocks. A floppy field hat covered his bald pink head against the sun. He held a 9 mm Mendoza submachine gun not particularly at the ready in his hands. His eyes bugged as he caught Bolan's form in the corner of his eye.

The tomahawk slicked down into the side of his head with grim finality. Bolan guided him down to the ground, keeping the side of his head turned so he wouldn't bleed all over his clothes.

Dundee let out a shuddering breath, betrayal and fear getting the better of him. "Now I think I'm really gonna be sick..."

"Do it now. You won't have time later." Bolan stripped Balbi of his shirt and hat and body armor. He was a size or two bigger than Bolan, but the armor would help fill that out. Bolan checked the load in the Mendoza and strapped on Balbi's web gear. He pulled the oversize hat low over his face. "Pick up your rifle and put your free arm around my neck." Bolan splashed water on Dundee's face and chest and took his hat so observers would be looking at Dundee's face rather than his. "Drag your feet, but not too much. Try to look pathetic."

Bolan grabbed the Australian's arm and began his suicide walk.

He lowered his head, dragging Dundee along, waiting for the spray of bullets to cut them both down. Bolan muttered low, "Hang your head back. Sag a little."

Bolan risked a glance under the brim of Balbi's hat. Perhaps it was the fear, the guilt of what he had done for Omega and now his betrayal, or the two self-induced vomitings, but he looked like hell. Bolan kept his head down and trudged onward toward the compound.

The radio crackled. "Bebe, how's Dundee?" Omega asked.

Bolan gave Dundee's arm a tug. "Answer it."

Dundee slowly clicked on his radio. "I'm all right, boss. Be okay. Just gotta get in some shade."

Omega repeated his question. "Bebe, how's Dundee?"

Bolan made a show of hitching the Australian's arm better around his neck and risked a single grunt into the radio. *"Malo."*

"Get him to the infirmary."

Bolan plodded on. He passed Ruzzo thirty yards to the right but kept his head down and kept walking toward Nico's position. At fifty yards, Omega came on the line again.

"Where you headed, Bebe? I said take him to the infirmary."

Bolan hissed in Dundee's ear. "Tell him you discovered dead ground near your position. A little ravine that goes near the fourteenth hole."

Dundee radioed in. "Gotta talk to Nico. There's a little riverbed near my position. Leads close to the fourteenth hole. A man could crawl it and get close under Nico's rifle."

This bit of information caused a brief pause. Omega suddenly said something in Spanish too fast for Bolan to follow other than that it was personal and a question to Balbi. Omega spoke again in English for everyone's benefit. "That's not Bebe! Shoot them! Shoot them both!"

"Cover me!" Bolan burst into a forty-yard dash for Nico's position. He could see the glint of Nico's optics as they swung toward him. Bolan shoved out the Mendoza like a huge pistol and fired rapid bursts. Bits of granite chipped off the top of the rock formation, and Nico ducked. Rifles fired behind Bolan, but he kept his attention on the sniper. The sudden clack of Bolan's submachine gun racking open on empty was very loud.

Nico rolled to his feet and aimed his rifle at Bolan.

Bolan had already dropped the Mendoza on its sling and begun his throw. The tomahawk revolved through the air and sank deep into Nico's left bicep. Nico's rifle cracked off a wild shot and sagged in his weakened grip. Bolan ran up the sloping rock face and slapped the muzzle of the rifle away from his chest. His right fist pumped into Nico's face once, twice, three times. There was no room for mercy. Bolan yanked his tomahawk out of Nico's arm and buried it in the sniper's head. He ripped the Remington rifle away and let Nico fall.

Dundee had dropped to one knee and was exchanging shots with the men in the skirmish line. A Raptor's head snapped back, and he fell to the sand. You didn't make the Australian SAS without being a crackerjack shot.

"Dundee! Come on!"

Dundee rose from his firing crouch and broke into a run for the rocks. Bolan swept the perimeter with the Remington's optics. Ruzzo had flipped up the sights of the grenade launcher beneath his barrel. Bolan put the rifle's crosshairs on the Cuban's chest and fired. All the Untouchables and Raptors were wearing soft body armor, but it was not up to the steel-cored .308-caliber sniper bullet. Red desert dust flew from Ruzzo's clothes with the impact of the bullet, and he toppled forward onto his weapon. Dundee ran up over the rock, and he and Bolan both dived down as a hail of bullets began sparking off the red granite.

"Bloody hell!"

Bolan reloaded the Mendoza and stripped Nico's body of two 20-round cartridge wallets. "So where do you think Omega is?"

Dundee shoved a fresh magazine into his carbine and pointed.

Rising up among the bungalows and outbuildings was the sweeping white stone and black glass three-story pyramid of the main hacienda. "He's directing traffic from up top, then, ain't he?"

Bolan swept the top of the hacienda with his optics. He couldn't see anything through the polarized black glass, but he knew Omega could. Bolan lowered his rifle and estimated where he might be standing with a pair of binoculars to view the battle. He suddenly snapped the Remington up to his shoulder and fired. Bolan grimaced as a white smear of cratering marked the glass.

It was bulletproof.

Omega spoke across Bolan's stolen radio. "Nice try. Liked it. You could have worked out, Coop."

"My name isn't Cooper."

"Oh, what is it then?"

Bolan skinned a grin up at the pyramid. "My name's El Hombre."

"All units hit the rock," Omega responded. "Full attack."

Bolan slapped Dundee's shoulder. "We gotta go!"

The two men sprinted over the golf course, keeping the rock formation between themselves and their pursuers as long as they could. A golf cart came trundling towards them across the green. It stopped at one hundred yards, and the two security men jumped out and began popping off with Uzi submachine guns from behind their vehicle. It was the outer limit of an open-bolt machine gun and point-blank for a sniper rifle, and a golf cart was no cover at all against a .30-caliber rifle.

Bolan dropped to one knee, and his rifle cracked twice in rapid succession. The two men toppled back onto the manicured grass in spreading pools of blood.

Bolan and Dundee sprinted for the golf cart. "You drive." Bolan stripped the two security men of their Uzis and spare magazines and threw them in the back. What he really needed was a grenade launcher, but none was available at the moment.

Dundee jumped behind the wheel. "Where you wanna go?"

"Let's go say hi to old Uncle Omega."

"You got a real death wish, you know that, Coop?"

"My name isn't Cooper."

"All righty, then, Hombre." Dundee suddenly flashed that devil-may-care grin that was peculiar to a lot of Australians who'd seen the deep bush. "Let's go give old Uncle Omega our bloody best regards, then."

22

Stony Man Farm

"Sending the coordinates now!" Aaron Kurtzman punched a button and sent Bolan's location to Esteban.

Omega was building a golf course and casino that people could access by driving across the border from the United States. The smartest criminals always went at least partially legitimate. Kurtzman had hacked the plans, and satellite recon showed lots of construction on the site. It stank a lot like a money-laundering operation and a smuggling corridor, as well.

"I have received them, Bear! Desperado out!"

"Wait! I—" Kurtzman snarled as the connection cut. He redialed, but there was no answer. Esteban was just the way Bolan had described him. Once set in motion, he was unstoppable. But with any luck, that unstoppability might just turn the tide for Bolan if—

Kurtzman's shoulders sank. It suddenly occurred to him that Esteban couldn't read or write.

God only knew what he'd make out of a map.

Esteban's communication had been short and confused. The words *"don't call, ring tone could give away my location"* implied that Striker was in some real trouble. Kurtzman considered his options. He had a brain-damaged gunslinger driving in heaven only knew what direction. He couldn't send in the Army or Special Forces. The police wouldn't cross the border. Able Team and Phoenix Force were deployed on different continents.

Kurtzman dialed a number.

Ranger Missy Hootkins answered on the second ring. "Bolan?"

"No, this is his friend. The Bear."

"How is he?"

"I can't be sure. But he's in the lion's den, and my guts tell me he's in a lot of trouble."

"He seemed to put a lot of faith in your guts. Where is he?"

"He's on the other side of the border." Kurtzman quickly sketched out what he could of the mission and Bolan's enemy and his current location. "That's the situation. La Guitarista might be on his way. I don't know. Other than that, my hands are tied."

Ranger Hootkins didn't take the time to bat an eye. "I'm currently on medical leave. Fax me the exact location and an aerial or satellite photo if you've got one. I'm going to requisition a helicopter. I can be on the border in twenty minutes."

"No one's going to let you fly across the border in a police helicopter, Ranger."

"No, I said I'd be on the border in twenty, not across it. I'll make my own way over the river. "

"Omega will have spies on the border. Maybe even an ambush set up on the roads. He probably already has police or military in his pocket setting up roadblocks and checkpoints on the roads."

"Sounds about right," the Ranger agreed. She didn't sound very deterred by the idea of Mexican army checkpoints or police roadblocks. "But you seem to have some pull, Mr. Bear. So this is what I want you to do."

"So, what next?" Dundee looked at Bolan expectantly as a dinner-plate section of the wall collapsed beneath a storm of bullets. "You gonna pull a rabbit out your ass, then?"

"Maybe out of yours, if you don't shut up." Bolan crouched lower as a bullet whined overhead through the shattered window. They'd spent an hour playing hide-and-go-seek across the grounds. They hadn't been able to break into the main hacienda. Now they were surrounded, holed up in a bungalow whose adobe walls were being picked away by riflefire. Bolan had fired the Mendoza dry. He still had the sniper rifle and the two Uzis he'd taken from the security men, and his pistol. They'd killed six security men but hadn't been able to collect their weapons. Two Untouchables and a pair of Raptors had died rushing the house, but they were in the grass ten yards away. They might as well have been a million miles away. "How are you on ammo?" Bolan asked.

"I'm on my last stick." Dundee popped his magazine and stared at it sadly before popping it back in place. "Five rounds, I reckon."

Bolan shoved him the remaining submachine gun and the dead guard's bandolier of spare magazines. The Australian hefted the weapon and cringed as a grenade hit the house. "So what now?"

Bolan shook his head. They were just about out of options, save for the final one. "Dunno." Bolan smiled. "Pull a Gallipoli, I guess."

Dundee grinned from ear to ear. The WWI battle for Gallipoli still resonated for every Australian soldier. On August 7, 1915, the Australian Light Horse Brigades had been ordered to attack the Turkish trenches at Gallipoli in a series of suicidal bayonet charges. Wave after wave had died as the Turkish machine guns swept the no-man's land. The word Gallipoli was synonymous for bravery and suicide in the Australian military. "Blaze of glory and all that, then, Coop?"

"More like last act of defiance."

"That'll do, too. Reckon we really don't want to be captured, anyway."

Bolan unloaded an Uzi magazine and refilled the Mendoza. He'd probably never live to use it, but a second gun was always faster than reloading. Both men looked up as the firing ceased.

Chavo's voice boomed outside. "Hey, Dundee. You hear me?"

Dundee looked to Bolan. Bolan shrugged and the Australian shouted back, "Loud 'n' clear, big man!"

"Why don't you walk out of there? Maybe we can negotiate something."

"Heard about Uncas! Are my retirement benefits negotiable, too?"

Chavo didn't bother to deny it. "Chopper's going to be here any minute, with a 90 mm recoilless. I'll be shooting it myself, and it's going to be loaded with white phosphorus. So, I tell you what. I always liked you, and you don't have anything we need to know. You come out? I do you quick. You don't? I burn you alive."

Bolan nodded at the Australian. "You want to go? Go. No hard feelings."

"Naw, Chavo's full of shit. They're just trying to separate us. They want you alive, and bad. Me and you back to back is gonna make that a lot harder. I figure the chopper is bringing in gas. Ruzzo told me once about a mission in Mexico City where they lobbed in some kind of Russian sleep gas. Figure they'll do the same here."

Bolan knew that would probably be fentanyl, what the Russians called Blue Blitz. All they would have to do would be lob in one or two grenades' worth, and he and Dundee would go lights out. There were no gas masks or countermeasures within arm's reach.

Bolan shook his head. "You know, I really don't want to wake up with old Uncle Omega looking down at me."

"Naw, me neither." Dundee sighed. "Guess it's just about Gallipoli time, then."

"Yeah." Bolan nodded. "It's just about time. We'll wait until we hear the choppers."

The two men waited for a miracle. What they got was the thump of rotors in the distance. "Last chance!" Chavo bellowed.

"Well, Coop, or whatever the hell your bloody name is—" Dundee stuck out his hand "—it hasn't been nice knowing you, and thanks for getting me bloody killed."

Bolan shook the little Australian's hand. "Anytime."

Bullets began hitting the bungalow in swarms again. But Bolan knew it was to keep them down for the gas deployment.

Bolan filled each hand with a submachine gun. Dundee slung his Uzi and clicked his bayonet onto the end of his G-36. "On your mark, then, Hombre?"

Bolan squinted out a hole in the adobe. "Hold that thought."

Out beyond the golf course to the south, something gleamed on the road that led up to the compound. Bolan smiled. Something gleamed like chrome.

Dundee waggled a hopeful eyebrow. "Is it the cavalry, then?"

"Of a sort." Bolan pulled out Scott's phone and punched Redial. Static blasted back after the first ring.

"That you on the road?" Bolan coded.

Esteban came back. "It's me."

Bolan keyed quickly. "A helicopter is landing. It's the enemy. One ally with me. We are in bungalow surrounded by bad guys."

Bolan watched as the El Camino roared through the compound gate and smashed aside the gatepost.

"Acknowledged."

An olive-green Huey UH-12 had landed out of rifle range on the twelfth hole. The black-and-chrome El Camino tore through the compound. It took a few hits from small-arms fire and then thundered onto the fairway. The tactical radio web blew up.

Omega was shouting, "Chopper 2! Take off! Take off now!"

Six men had already deployed from the chopper, each carrying a heavy crate between them. They scattered as the El Camino thundered down upon them in 400-horsepower fury. The Huey's engine screamed into the redline as the pilot tried to take off under emergency war power.

The chopper got two feet off the ground when the El Camino's armored grill struck the landing skids at 50 mph.

The helicopter tilted violently, and its rotors struck the ground and snapped. The El Camino slewed out from under the helicopter and fishtailed over the twelfth hole. Bereft of lift, the chopper fell to its side with a crunch and rolled twice down the sloped green. The El Camino spun to a stop, and fresh turf spewed up beneath its wheels as the driver stomped on the accelerator.

Esteban snaked his torso out of the passenger window with a Ruger in each hand. The men from the chopper dropped their crates and tried to flee, but Esteban gunned them down without mercy. The El Camino's grille swung toward the bungalow and roared forward. Esteban slid back inside as Chavo and the boys opened fire on the oncoming automobile. The El Camino came on like doomsday.

A Raptor stepped out from behind a palm tree and into the car's path, AG36 grenade launcher loaded beneath his rifle. The weapon shot yellow fire and bucked against his shoulder. The grenade detonated straight on against the grille of the El Camino, and the front of the car was eclipsed in a burst of smoke and fire.

The vehicle roared on, streaming smoke. Vast swaths of black paint had been scorched and scored off the hood, but the engine was in an armored box, and shell fragments were exactly the kind of trauma the armor glass and body panels had been intended to resist. The Raptor screamed and held his rifle's trigger down on full-auto. He came apart across the El Camino's grille like a rag doll. Bits of him flew over the top as the car came on.

Bolan jerked his head at Dundee. "Now!"

Bolan kicked the bullet-riddled door open and emerged with guns blazing. Chavo had taken cover behind a huge stone BBQ, but he had turned to fire on the car barreling in.

Chavo spun. Bolan shoved the Uzi forward in his left hand and burned a 10-round burst into Chavo's chest. The giant staggered slightly as he took the hits on his armor and sparks flew from his rifle. Bolan shoved the Mendoza forward. He flicked the selector to semiauto and squeezed off a single shot. Chavo's temple cratered. He stared at Bolan glassily, and some still functioning part of his pysche made him raise his rifle.

Bolan's second shot bisected Chavo's brain from front to back. The giant toppled like a tree to the lawn. Dundee took a hit on his armor and shot the man in the face for his trouble.

The surviving six Raptors ran for the hacienda. Bolan snapped open the Mendoza stock and took to a knee. Three men fell to his snap-shooting before the rest got out of range.

The El Camino screamed to a stop, and Esteban popped out the passenger door. Griffin was behind the wheel. Bolan raised a disapproving eyebrow.

"The Bear sent us a map and directions." Esteban looked down sheepishly. "I…can't read."

Bolan peered inside. Griffin looked pale and shaky. "You okay?"

Griffin's lips made a hard line. "I'll be okay."

Bolan was tempted to tell her to go find cover, but the armored cockpit of the El Camino was probably the safest place for a hundred miles. "Drive us back to the helicopter."

Bolan dropped his submachine guns and stripped Chavo of his rifle and spare magazines. Dundee did the same and they jumped into the truck bed.

The Australian grinned as the El Camino lurched beneath them. "A bit too bloody familiar!"

They sped to the crumpled helicopter. Bolan leaped out and ripped the crates open with his tomahawk. Chavo hadn't been lying. One crate contained a 90 mm recoilless rifle. The second crate contained a number of shells, but they were high explosive rather than incendiary. The third crate was smaller and contained twelve soda-can-sized cylinders. Each had blue Cyrillic writing on it and the universal symbol for chemical hazard.

Blue Blitz gas.

"Let's load up."

Bolan, Dundee and Esteban piled the ordnance into the truck bed. Bolan tapped on the roof. "Griffin, take us to the front of the hacienda. About three hundred yards away!" The El Camino rumbled forward toward the black-and-white pyramid. Bolan knocked on the roof again when he had a good line on the giant black glass double doors. He didn't doubt they were armor glass, as well. "Here!"

Bolan hopped out. He swung open the breech of the 90 mm gun and slung the four-and-a-half foot launch tube over his shoulder. He put the crosshairs of the sight onto the middle of the double doors. "Stand away."

Esteban and Dundee prudently stepped away to either side.

The recoilless rifle belched orange fire from both ends. The six-kilogram high-explosive projectile hit the double doors and they disappeared in orange fire. The smoke cleared to reveal a jagged ten-foot hole, and the remaining window walls opaque with spiderwebs of cracking.

"Hey, Hombre." Dundee was looking north through the optical sight of his rifle. "Is that the cavalry, then?"

Bolan loaded a fresh HE into the M-67 and swept its sight out onto the desert. Ten horsemen were galloping forward a few miles out. They all wore cowboy hats. One of the horsemen was a horsewoman, and red hair streamed out behind her. "That's not the cavalry. That's the Texas Rangers."

"'Bout bloody time if you ask me."

Bolan lowered the recoilless and took out his phone. Ranger Hootkins answered immediately. "That you, Matt?"

"Yeah. We've got a bit of a situation here. Do all of your men have rifles?"

"M-16s. With scopes."

"Put a loose cordon around the main hacienda. Shoot at any window that opens."

"Forgive me for being obtuse, but…"

"But what?"

"It looks like you have a cannon. Why don't you blow that Omega son of a bitch to hell?"

"There'll be innocents in the hacienda. Hookers, servants. I took out the front door, but I don't want to start a general bombardment."

"So you and the Guitar Player are going to walk in by yourselves and take down Omega and the rest of his men between you."

Bolan reviewed his options before replying. "Just keep the place buttoned up tight." Bolan gazed at the hacienda and considered the towering modern art monstrosity. "I have an idea."

23

Bolan pulled down his gas-mask. "Hit it."

The radio crackled with Dundee's reply. "Beginning fumigation now, Coop."

Down in the basement, the Australian began popping Blue Blitz grenades and dropping them into the main air-circulation unit. Moments later, Bolan watched as gray gas began oozing out of the air vents on the first floor. Except for a few balconies and the windows in the penthouse, the hacienda was a sealed building with a central HVAC. There were thirty grenades in the case, and Dundee was lighting them off like the grand finale on the Fourth of July.

Gray, narcoleptic fog crawled down from the ceiling vents in every room of the hacienda.

"Esteban, put on your mask. Let's go."

Esteban put on one of the masks they'd taken from the crates and filled his hands with has .45-caliber Rugers. Bolan had acquired a G-36 with a grenade launcher, and both were loaded. He and Esteban began to sweep from room to room. They had to move rapidly to save innocents. Most of the women and servants had run screaming from the hacienda after the 90 mm projectile had hit the front door. However, there was every reason to believe that Untouchables and Raptors would use the ones who hadn't gotten out as hostages or shields.

The Blue Blitz was an effective countermeasure, but it was far from safe. The gas was expanding into enclosed spaces in high concentration, and there was no way to regulate the gas

levels from room to room, so there was no way to make sure
no one went under so deep their vital functions shut off. They
entered the restaurant-sized kitchen to find two Raptors behind
a light machine gun. One had slumped over his weapon, and
one was staggering drunkenly.

Bolan clubbed him down. "Two in the kitchen."

Hootkins came back. "Roger that."

Bolan checked his watch. Sixty seconds of exposure was the
maximum he would allow. "Dundee, vent the building."

"Copy that, Coop." Dundee hit the ventilation switches and
began venting the building on all floors.

Bolan and Esteban moved from room to room and went
up the stairs to the second floor. There was another machine-gun nest on the landing, but the two gunners were
drooling and gasping on either side of the weapon. They
swept on and found a room full of Omega's harem. Two men
with grenades and rifles lay on the floor among the collapsed female flesh. So far, the gas was doing its job, and no
one was dead.

Hootkins's voice came across the radio. "Someone's outside
on the penthouse. We don't have a shot. They're staying below
the level of the railing wall."

"You got a number?"

"Two at least, possibly more."

"Roger that."

Bolan and Esteban moved up to the penthouse suite.
Omega's main building was opulent in the extreme. Ten years
of ripping off, taking over and receiving tribute from the most
lucrative crime syndicates along the border had paid off well.
The hacienda's interior was all fur rugs, leather furniture and
golden Aztec treasures. Mexican mosaics in cool blues and
greens flowed from wall to wall.

Bolan took off his mask. The air had an odd tang, but several breaths told him that Omega's climate control system was
state-of-the-art efficient. Bolan turned to Esteban. He was the
wild card in the situation. "Esteban."

Esteban stripped of his mask. "Yes, Matt."

"Wait for me to make the first move. If I go down, do what you've got do."

Esteban nodded slowly. His Rugers were cocked in his hands. "I will wait for your move, Matt. You are the man."

Bolan shouted loud enough to shake the walls, "Raza!"

Moses Xavier Raza came back off the penthouse deck. Donato "The Butcher" Chapa was with him, looking terrified. Both men had pistols. Chapa's .44 Magnum looked three sizes too big for his tiny hands. Omega held a nickel-plated silver-eagle-gripped Colt .38 Super.

It was pointed at the back of Citlalli's head.

Omega locked his disturbing steel gaze with the arctic blue eyes of the Executioner.

Neither man flinched.

Omega's lips skinned back from his teeth. His eyebrows arched in amusement like the devil making a deal. "El Hombre and La Guitarista."

Bolan didn't bother to respond. His rifle was shouldered. He could take Chapa at will. Omega was behind Citlalli like a fencer, crouched, arm extended. If he couldn't make him move, the woman would die no matter who did what to whom afterward.

Omega's smile went from devilish to satanic, reading Bolan's mind. "You like her, Coop? She likes you, and her life is in your hands."

Bolan spoke, playing for time. "What do you suggest?"

"I'll make it real easy. You just drop your weapons and let me go."

Bolan's shook his head almost imperceptibly. "Not gonna happen."

"Why not?" Omega nodded sympathetically. "Oh, I know. You don't trust me. You think I'll kill you. No, I need you. Once I'm on my way down, I need you to radio your horsey friends down there so we can cut a deal. You tell them to let me get in your car and let me go.

"I live. You live. The girl lives. I disappear. Central America? South America? You don't need to know. You can always try to hunt me down later. If I get out of here, the girl lives. I have no reason to kill her once I'm gone. Hell, you can have Chapa."

The Butcher threw down his revolver and dropped to his knees with a shriek. "Jesus, God! Don't shoot me! You promised you wouldn't!"

Omega sighed. "It's not a bad deal." His voice went ugly. "You don't like it? I can shoot you, through her head, right now."

Citlalli let out a heart-rending whimper.

Bolan had already calculated the angle. Omega was good. The .38 Super would blow out Citlalli's brains and go on to rip through his throat. "Yeah, but you can't get us both. My friend here will burn you down."

Esteban stood with his twin pistols held loosely at his sides. His face was a blank slate. Bolan had called the tune, and he was waiting for Bolan's move.

"So, we have an, oh, I don't know…" Omega laughed aloud. "Mexican standoff? Fine, let's just stand here until my *federale* and army friends show up. How many horsemen you have out there, Hombre? You know? I could be wrong, but I counted around ten. I've got the Nuevo Laredo SWAT team and the last fifty Raptors on the way. They're coming in armor and in choppers. They'll reap your Ranger friends like wheat."

Bolan shrugged, never moving the muzzle of his weapon. "No one's reinforcements are going to show up in time, Omega. Not mine. Not yours. This is going to go down. This is going down now."

"Okay." Omega shrugged back. "You call it, tough guy, but you just remember the girl dies first." Citlalli moaned as he pressed the Colt's muzzle harder against her head. Omega's smile was sickening. "C'mon, El Hombre. Let's see how tough you really are."

Bolan had no shot, but Esteban did. But Esteban was waiting. Bolan grimaced and lowered his rifle. "Esteban?"

"Yes, Matt."

"Remember what I said about waiting for my move?"

"Yes, Matt."

Citlalli made a tiny noise of terror as her head was pushed forward.

"I'll blow her head clean off," Omega snarled.

Bolan arranged his face into a tightrope grimace. "Let me talk him down."

"Do it quick."

"You'll let the girl go?"

"I got no reason to kill her unless you give me one."

"Esteban." Bolan chose his words very carefully. "You remember the first movie? *El Mariachi?*"

"Yes, Matt."

"Remember what his brother did for him?"

His brother had shot El Mariachi in the hand.

"I need you to forget about what I said about taking Omega down."

"Good." Omega nodded. "Good."

Bolan tried to bore every ounce of meaning through his eyes into Esteban's damaged brain. "I need you to do the same thing now."

Esteban's shoulders relaxed. His pistols loosened in his hands. "Yes, Matt. I understand."

"Good." Omega nodded. "Now drop your guns. This is going to go real smooth."

Bolan dropped his rifle and raised his hands. For a heartbeat, Omega's eyes flicked toward the action. In that same instant, Esteban's left-hand pistol rose and the .45 barked off a single shot. The .38 Super flew from Omega's hand in a spray of blood. Citlalli screamed and fell to her knees. Omega staggered back. He ignored his ruptured right hand and reached for something at his waist with his left.

Bolan's Hi-Power was already drawn. The pistol barked three times, and a triangle of bloody holes appeared on Omega's forehead faster than thought.

Omega sagged to the carpet with the top of his head in ruptured ruin.

Chapa started screaming. "You said you wouldn't kill me! You promised! You swore!"

Citlalli ran screaming from the room.

Esteban leveled his pistols at Chapa.

Bolan grimaced. God only knew what executing a man on his knees would do to Esteban's fractured personality. "Esteban."

Esteban spoke without moving his eyes. "Yes, Matt."

Bolan slowly shook his head. "Not like this."

"You're right, Matt." To Bolan's surprise Esteban holstered his pistols. His hands dropped to his sides again. He spoke in a voice as casual as someone commenting on the weather. "Give him a gun."

"You promised!" Chapa screamed.

Bolan picked up Omega's bloodstained .38 automatic. He ejected the magazine, leaving it with a single round in the chamber and the pistol cocked. He tossed it to the carpet in front of Chapa. "I promised you, Chapa. But you raped this man's sister and had a hand in killing his family. You two settle it."

Chapa stared at the gleaming pistol inches from his fingers.

Bolan holstered his Hi-Power.

Esteban stretched out his open hands to either side like a man being crucified. "Draw."

"I'm not afraid of you!" Chapa's voice rose to a scream. "You're a retard!"

Esteban's face was a blank mask. "Draw."

"Your sister loved it!"

"Draw."

"You retarded mother." Chapa scooped up the pistol with surprising speed.

Esteban slapped leather like lightning. The twin Rugers roared in his hands like thunder.

Chapa jerked and shuddered as a hailstorm of .45-caliber rounds tore through him. He wasn't wearing armor, and the effect was horrendous. Esteban's pistols clacked open on empty. Chapa's body flopped to the carpet. He would never butcher anyone with his knives again.

Bolan holstered his Browning and put a hand on Esteban's shoulder. "Let's go downstairs. Your sister will be worried about you."

Epilogue

Bolan raised the detonator. "Fire in the hole."

They had found Omega's armory. Between the grenades, plastique and the remaining round for the recoilless rifle, they had an impressive amount of high explosives. Two hundred gallons of strategically placed aviation fuel from the airstrip would only help matters.

Bolan pressed the button, and the hacienda shuddered like an earthquake. Black armor glass windows blew out in front of plumes of orange fire like spewing dragons. The second floor collapsed, and the penthouse met the basement in a classic demolition-charge implosion.

Hootkins shook her head. "I have no idea how I'm going to write the report on this."

"Don't bother. The witnesses will all tell the same story. Omega and his men all began killing one another."

Hootkins looked over at the sullen group of Raptors under guard on the first hole. "What about them?"

"I'll pass their names along to all the right people. I know people with friends in the Mexican government and military. Their criminal careers are over."

The Ranger looked over at Esteban. He sat on the hood of the El Camino next to Griffin and Dundee. Esteban's empty pistols hung in his hands and his eyes stared at nothing. Bolan picked up two gym bags and walked over. "Dundee."

The Australian looked up from his reverie. "Yeah, Coop."

Bolan tossed the bag into his lap. "Here."

The Australian goggled as he opened the bag. Bolan had taken some C-4 and cracked Omega's safe. One million American dollars were in the bag.

"Bloody hell…"

"I told you that you had a free pass." Bolan leaned in and glared into the little man's eyes. "I'll be watching you, Dundee. Do some good."

Dundee snuffled, almost overcome with emotion. "Bloody…"

Bolan handed the other bag to Griffin. "I have friends in Ixtapa. Their number is in the bag. That's a fresh start right there."

Griffin opened the bag and trembled at the contents and what they meant to her and her brother. Esteban continued staring at nothing. Bolan put a hand on his shoulder. "Esteban."

Esteban shot to his feet. "Yes, Matt."

"What are you going to do?"

Esteban blinked in confusion. "What am I going to do?"

Bolan looked deeply into the young man's eyes. "Your enemies are dead."

Esteban repeated that slowly. "My enemies are dead."

"Your family is avenged."

Griffin nodded desperately. "The family is avenged, brother."

Esteban spoke like he was quoting scripture. "My family is avenged."

Bolan nodded very slowly. "So what are you going to do?"

Bolan could almost hear the gears grinding in Esteban's damaged mind. The young man looked at Bolan for long moments. His brows slowly bunched in concern as he turned to look at his sister. "Griffin?"

"Yes, Esteban?"

Esteban let out a long sigh. "Can we get a dog?"

"Yes!" Griffin burst into tears. "We can get a dog!"

Esteban cocked his head in thought. "Can we get two?"

"Yes!" Griffin flung her arms around her brother and wept. "We can get two!"

Hootkins stared at Bolan in awe. "We gotta mount up and

head out. We got to cross fifteen miles of desert and evade the Mexican police before we ford the river."

Bolan rolled his shoulders. He was very tired. "Let's do it."

As the Texas Rangers mounted up, Bolan turned to Esteban and tossed him the keys to his car. *"Vaya con dios, amigo."*

As they began the long ride north, Bolan could hear the powerful engine roar to life behind him. Esteban, Griffin and Dundee roared off in a cloud of dust to start their new lives. For Bolan, the perilous ride to the border lay ahead. Beyond that he didn't know, but the next mission was never too far over the horizon.

NEUTRON FORCE

The ultimate stealth weapon is in the hands of an unknown enemy…

A grim presidential directive comes down to
Stony Man: an unknown entity is in possession of
one of the deadliest weapons known to man, and the
death toll across the globe is mounting. It's a silent
murdering machine, killing with no heat, no noise,
no radiation—just silent, invisible slaughter from
ultrafast, subatomic particles. With no nation able
to defend against it, Stony Man's only option is to
destroy it. But first, they must find it….

STONY®
MAN

*Available
June 2007
wherever
you buy books.*

TAKE 'EM FREE

2 action-packed novels plus a mystery bonus

NO RISK

NO OBLIGATION TO BUY

GE07

ROGUE ANGEL™

AleX Archer
GOD OF THUNDER

When a former colleague is murdered, archaeologist Annja Creed continues her research on the Norse god of Thunder. When coded clues lead her on a treasure hunt in the forests of Latvia, she realizes that a ruthless corps of mercenaries are also on the hunt—and they're willing to do anything, including murder, to find it!

Available July wherever you buy books.

GOLD EAGLE®

GRA7